Praise for

Emma
A Latter-day Tale

"Emma has climbed to the top of my favorite-characters-of-all-time list. She's witty and flawed. It was so much fun to follow her in this story."

—JULIE N. FORD, author of *Replacing Gentry* and *Count Down to Love*

Praise for

Persuasion
A Latter-day Tale

"I adored this book. Utterly, posilutely, LOVED IT. Rebecca H. Jamison has crafted a great set of modern characters and circumstances to complement Jane Austen's classic story line. But truth be told, I really think this story was strong enough on its own to be marketed completely separate of the *Persuasion* title. Call me simple-minded, but if I hadn't known this was the *Persuasion* story line, I wouldn't have guessed it. I would've just gone with it being a really captivating love story—it was that good."

—CHRISTY, popular blogger at *The Sweet Bookshelf*

"Overall the book is filled with fun twists and turns and just lots of great romance; there is not one thing I did not love about this story!"

—MARJOLEIN, popular blogger at *Marjolein Book Blog*

"Fans of Jane Austen's *Persuasion* are going to enjoy Rebecca H. Jamison's novel *Persuasion: A Latter-day Tale*. Jamison places the familiar story line in a modern-day setting and gives many of her characters an affiliation with The Church of Jesus Christ of Latter-day Saints. Although the plot follows the original story very closely, Jamison weaves enough different elements through the novel that it doesn't feel completely the same as Austen's."

—LAUREN ZACHARY, *Deseret News*

"*Persuasion* is an inspirational, uplifting, sweet story of coming to terms with past mistakes and learning to start over and love again. This is an LDS fiction book. The main moral is the same even for people of other religions, and that is to put your faith in the Lord and hold firm in your beliefs. Rebecca H. Jamison has done a wonderful job portraying someone who is doing that."

—KRAZY BOOK LADY

"I couldn't settle down to go to sleep until I had read every single word. I went to sleep with a smile on my face."

—LISA, popular blogger at *Bookworm Lisa*

"I loved the book. It's a light read that kept me turning pages, and the characters and pacing make it one of my favorite reads in months. LDS content runs throughout the book, but it is not overly didactic, nor does it require the reader to be LDS to enjoy the cultural situations. I would highly recommend *Persuasion: A Latter-day Tale* to anyone, and Jane Austen loyalists will not be disappointed."

—LAURIE L. C. LEWIS at *A View from the Other Side of the Hill*

"It was the perfect blend of inspiration and fiction. I didn't feel preached to at all, just uplifted. It kept me reading long into the night."

—KAYLEE BALDWIN at KayleeBaldwin.com

"I absolutely give *Persuasion* five stars, and I can't wait to see what Rebecca Jamison comes up with next."

—HEATHER, popular blogger at *Six Mixed Reviews*

JANE AUSTEN'S **CLASSIC** MATCHMAKING TALE
WITH A **MODERN TWIST**

Emma
A Latter-day Tale

a novel

Rebecca H. Jamison

Bonneville Books
An Imprint of Cedar Fort, Inc.
Springville, Utah

ALSO BY REBECCA JAMISON

Persuasion: A Latter-day Tale

The views expressed within this work are the sole responsibility of the author and do not necessarily reflect the position of Cedar Fort, Inc., or any other entity. This is a work of fiction. The characters, names, incidents, places, and dialogue are products of the author's imagination, and are not to be construed as real.

ISBN 13: 978-1-4621-1260-9

Published by Bonneville Books, an imprint of Cedar Fort, Inc.
2373 W. 700 S., Springville, UT 84663
Distributed by Cedar Fort, Inc., www.cedarfort.com

LIBRARY OF CONGRESS CATALOGING-IN-PUBLICATION DATA
    Jamison, Rebecca H., 1970-
    Emma : a latter-day tale / By Rebecca H. Jamison.
        pages cm
    ISBN 978-1-4621-1260-9 (pbk. : alk. paper)
    1. Mormon women--Fiction. 2. Eating disorders--Fiction. 3. Friendship--Fiction. I. Title.
    PS3610.A56645E44 2013
    813'.6--dc23
                     2013017375

Cover design by Angela D. Olsen and Kelsey Webb
Cover design © 2013 by Lyle Mortimer
Typeset and edited by Melissa J. Caldwell

Printed in the United States of America

10 9 8 7 6 5 4 3 2 1

To Dad

who reminds me just a little of Mr. Woodhouse

Chapter 1

My best friend was on her honeymoon, and I deserved a vacation myself, which was sort of what I got. A blizzard blew in a few hours after we dropped the newlyweds off at the airport, leaving us with no electricity, an unplowed street, and a refrigerator full of reception leftovers. Chicken salad, anyone?

That was one good thing about living in northern Virginia—a foot of snow meant no work for a few days. Still, it was nothing like Hawaii. Instead of lying on the beach in the sun, I huddled over dying embers in the fireplace, wondering how I was ever going to find another friend like Tanya.

If there were so many websites to match me up with the perfect man, shouldn't there be a website to help me find a new best friend? A quick search on my phone confirmed that there was no friend-finding website in my area. The best I could do was a personal ad in the *Fairfax Gazette* classifieds. I imagined what I'd write:

> *NOT Looking for Love: Single woman (23) seeks best friend to chat on the phone, shop the clearance racks, watch chick flicks, and eat Dove dark chocolates.*

That wasn't asking too much, was it?

While I was on the newspaper's website, I looked around for

someone else in need of a best friend. I found no one—at least until I came to the twenty-five-year-old accountant who hadn't posted a real picture.

That's when someone knocked on the door. Dad got up from his recliner to answer it, and Justin Knightley walked in, carrying an armful of chopped wood. "I'll give you this wood if I can sit by the fire." Justin lived a block away. Since he didn't have a fireplace, his house was even colder than ours.

I whooped. "How'd you know we were out of wood? Come on in."

We stacked a couple logs on the fire and placed the others to the side of the hearth. I picked my phone back up. "Listen to what I found in the personal ads: 'Swoon-worthy accountant (25) likes editing videos, fixing up his fixer-upper, and rocking out to country music. Seeks non-smoking female age 20–25. Photograph required.' Remind you of anyone we know?"

Justin wore his ski gear and the casual grin of a guy who hadn't had to shave that morning. "Not really. Are you gonna send him a photo?"

I pushed an armchair closer to the fire for Justin, being careful not to snag the sisal rug. "There can't be all that many accountants in Fairfax County who like to edit videos and line dance," I said. "It has to be Phil Elton."

Justin examined the ad on my phone. "No way. Phil wouldn't put an ad in the *Fairfax Gazette*. He'd use one of those sites for LDS singles."

"You're right." I stoked the fire with a rolled up newspaper. "But what about the fixer-upper and the country music? It sure sounds like Phil. I think I've even heard him say *swoon-worthy*."

Justin handed me back the phone. "I'll bet there are hundreds of accountants around here who live in fixer-uppers and listen to country music."

"But did you see the picture? It's Rapunzel's boyfriend from *Tangled*."

Justin sat in the armchair and leaned over to look at my phone. "I guess that means Rapunzel's finally cut him loose. I always thought she was too good for him."

I laughed. "Phil once told me the guy from *Tangled* was his cartoon look-alike."

"Want some chicken salad, Justin?" Dad asked.

Justin propped his feet up on the hearth. "That'd be great."

I turned my phone off. "Even if Phil didn't write this ad, he seems lonely. Last week after family home evening, he stayed late to help me clean up, then he talked to Dad for an hour. We should find someone for him."

Justin's eyebrows popped up. "*We* should find someone for him? Leave me out of this, Scarlett."

Scarlett was the nickname Justin gave me back when I was in high school. As a teenager, I had a temper to match my red hair. "I wish you would just call me Emma," I said, "especially since my hair's gotten darker."

For a second, I thought we were going to have another debate about the color of my hair. His hair was in between blond and brown, so he couldn't relate to my worries about hair stereotyping. "I'll call you Emma when you're behaving yourself."

"I *am* behaving myself." I put a fist to my hip. "You can't tell me Phil wouldn't be better off with someone I picked than with anyone who'd answer an ad like that."

"I don't think you can make a better match than you did with Tanya and Randall," Justin said. "You should quit while you're ahead."

Dad walked in from the kitchen with a plate of chicken salad and handed it to Justin. My father was a semi-retired family practice doctor. A thin, bald man, he was the kind of guy most people underestimated. They didn't realize he'd graduated from Harvard and started a successful medical website. "Justin has a point," Dad said, grabbing his newspaper and returning to his olive green recliner, the only piece of furniture in the living room that didn't have a white slipcover over it. "If you keep up this matchmaking hobby, you'll marry off all your friends. Don't you think one was enough?"

What Dad and Justin didn't know was that I couldn't ignore someone in romantic distress. It was like telling the Good Samaritan to keep walking, never mind the guy dying on the side of the road. "I wouldn't mind marrying off all my friends if it meant they'd be as happy as Tanya."

My Aunt Tanya, who was also my best friend, spent a decade and a half of her life helping Dad raise me after my mom died. To pay her back, I'd found her the perfect husband. Getting them together was like living through the most romantic movie ever made—finding excuses for her to see him, hinting to Randall about her favorite bands, getting him to ask her to a concert, teaching her to flirt, and seeing the way they always looked at each other. "I like helping people get what they want," I told Dad and Justin. "It's my calling in life. That's why I'm going to be a life coach."

Dad popped up his footrest. "As long as you don't match yourself up with anyone. The last thing I need is for you to get married too."

"If I'm going to find someone as great as you, Dad, it's going to take me a few more years. I'm not good enough for that kind of guy yet."

My father smiled. "There's nothing as attractive as a woman who avoids commitment. Isn't that right, Justin?"

Justin stared at the floor and finished chewing his bite of chicken salad. "Sure."

My thoughts went back to Phil Elton, the swoon-worthy accountant. It wasn't like there were many options left for him. He'd already dated almost every single woman I knew. No wonder he'd resorted to the personal ads. Then I remembered. "What about that new girl at church? I think Phil would like her. What was her name again? It was something masculine. Harri, I think—short for Harriet."

Justin gave me a blank stare. "You don't mean the nanny."

I snapped my fingers. "That's exactly who I mean. I was looking at her the other day. Take away the dyed black hair and the baggy clothes, and she'd be beautiful."

"She seems young," Justin said. "How old is she? Eighteen?"

"She lives over on Plum Street. We should walk over and check on her—see if she has everything she needs." I'd struck Justin in his weak spot, the charitable side of him that always wanted to help people. He couldn't help but agree to my plan.

After filling backpacks with food, we headed out the door. Dad and I lived in a yellow split-level home, the only split-level left in our neighborhood. Land in Vienna sold fast because it was near Washington, DC. Developers bought the old houses only to scrape them off the lots and build what people called McMansions. In comparison

4

to those newer homes, our house looked small. But it was plenty big for Dad and me.

Harri lived in one of the newer houses—a huge two-story with a wrap-around porch. Walking up the front steps, Justin and I looked like powdered doughnuts from all the snow that had stuck to us along the way.

Harri answered the door, carrying a tow-headed little girl on her hip. I started to introduce myself, but there was no need. People always seemed to know who I was. Something about me being six feet tall with long, auburn hair left an impression. "We wanted to come by and see how you're doing," I said.

Harri's eyes glistened in a way that told me we'd done the right thing. She held a hand over her heart, struggling to respond without crying. "Thank you so much. My phone battery died, and I didn't think anyone would remember us." She looked at the little girl. "This is Avery. Her parents were away on business when the storm hit. Her mom's a congresswoman from Nebraska. You've probably heard of her: Karen Cole?" I hadn't heard of her. "Anyway," Harri went on, her voice shaking. "I'm from Utah, so I'm used to snow. But I didn't know everything would shut down."

Justin handed me his backpack and grabbed one of the snow shovels. "Mind if I shovel your walk?"

"That'd be great. Thanks," Harri said, wiping her eyes with her sleeve.

I handed Harri my phone. "You should probably check in with the Coles. I bet they're worried."

Harri thanked me and invited me inside. The interior was new and elegant with oriental rugs, shiny wood floors, and damask upholstery that didn't look at all appropriate for children. "I brought some stuff to make s'mores," I said. "But maybe that's not such a good idea, considering the furniture."

"I was totally craving s'mores!" Harri said as she punched in some numbers on my phone. I waited while she told Karen Cole that everything was fine and we were there to help. After a brief discussion, she said good-bye and handed me back the phone. "It's a good thing you let me call. Karen was starting to spaz."

Harri already had a little fire going in the fireplace. "There are a few problems with these s'mores," I said. "We only have chocolate graham crackers, chocolate marshmallows, and Hershey bars with almonds." The fact that Harri was excited about a triple dose of chocolate was a good indication that we were destined to be friends. After taping a few wooden skewers together, we roasted marshmallows with Avery at our side.

We made the first s'more for Avery, being careful to pick all the almonds out of the chocolate bar. Sitting in her high chair beside the fireplace, Avery peeled the top graham cracker off and smashed the marshmallow up to her face, giving herself a chocolate-marshmallow goatee. She ate the graham cracker, letting the crumbs drop into her marshmallow beard. When she finished, she held her hands out. "More, *pease*." I gave her two more s'mores and a little bit of chicken salad.

Harri read the side of the graham cracker box before deciding to have a second helping. "I never eat more than the serving size."

"No wonder you have such a great figure," I said, wondering why I never read the serving sizes.

After we ate, Harri knelt on the Coles' oriental rug and braided the fringe on the edges. Avery watched her, then played with the fringe as if it were a new toy. I sat beside them. "You're really good at this nanny thing, Harri."

Harri's eyes were a light blue. Her skin was clear and fair with a few freckles across the top of her nose, making her dyed black hair look a little more unnatural. "I don't feel like a good nanny," she admitted. "This morning I was all for going back home."

"Are you kidding me? You're an awesome nanny. I can see how you'd be homesick, but I'd be so bummed if you went home now. We're just getting to know each other."

Harri tugged at the edge of her gray sweatshirt. "I like being a nanny and living so close to Washington, DC, and all. But I've been here for two months and I've hardly met anyone, except for the Coles and the Martinezes—I guess you know them. Rob Martinez drives me to church sometimes, and his mom had me over a couple times for dinner. Rob is pretty much my only friend here."

I wanted to help Harri the same way everyone wants to help George Bailey and Tiny Tim. She needed a friend, someone to help her feel at home in our little town. And I knew I could be that friend. I had all the resources she needed, starting with a support group. "We have a family home evening group for singles that meets at my house every Monday night," I said. "You should come."

Harri bounced up and down. "That would be awesome. I'd love to meet your friends."

Her reaction was so enthusiastic, I wondered if she imagined a big group of college-age kids hanging out in a hot tub. How I wished our family home evening group was like that. The truth of the matter was that Vienna was a wasteland when it came to college-age church members. "It's not a huge group, but at least a few people come. Phil Elton usually comes. I think you'll like him."

Harri pointed to the front of the house. "Is Phil the one shoveling?"

"No, that's Justin. He comes to family home evening too." Justin was twenty-nine-and-a-half years old now, so he wouldn't count as a young single for much longer, though you couldn't tell by looking at him.

"He's cute. Are you two together?"

I shook my head. "No, just old friends. My sister married his brother, so he's sort of like my brother-in-law."

Harri kissed Avery on top of her head. I was betting Harri came from one of those families where the mother and father held hands in church and the children fought only in the privacy of their own home. I'd sometimes wished I came from a family like that.

While I watched her playing "This Little Piggy" and "Ring Around the Rosy" with Avery, I planned how I'd show Harri everything she needed to know about Vienna. I'd be the kind of friend to her that Tanya had been to me. I'd take her to my favorite hairdresser, show her where to shop for the best deals, teach her how to get around on the metro, invite her to Zumba class, and introduce her to Phil Elton. Something told me she was the right one for him.

Plus, Harri could be my first life-coaching client. I'd coach her for free while I completed my certification. I needed Harri as much as Harri needed me. That storm was the best thing that could have happened to both of us.

Chapter 2

Coach's Tip of the Day:
The best way to solve your own problems
is to help someone else.

Phil Elton had no idea he was going to meet his new girl-friend that day, and all it took was a little preparation to get Harri ready. I was dying to give her a makeover. With her skin tone, she needed something light and pastel, something with a gold tone to it. Plus she cried out for waist definition. We found a peach-colored, v-neck blouse in her closet, which I cinched in with a belt.

Then we fixed her hair in a messy bun. Other than some black kohl eyeliner and dark purple lipstick, Harri didn't own any makeup. Luckily, I'd stuck my purse into my backpack along with the food, so I had a few basics—peachy pink gloss, peach shadow, and light peach blush. We topped it all off with a blue, beaded necklace that brought out her eyes.

I led her to a big oval mirror in the entryway. "What do you think?"

She looked at her reflection, turning her face to check out her profile. "Wow! I look like a flight attendant."

"Is that bad?"

"No. I love it. It's so retro." She held up her arm as if carrying a tray of beverages. "Would you like peanuts or pretzels?"

I laughed. "You look fabulous."

Harri got permission for Avery to stay at our house with Dad and Justin so I could take her out to get to know the neighbors. Justin was good with kids. By the time we left, he was crawling on his hands and knees, pretending to be a horse, with Avery on his back. "If you're going to visit Phil," he said, "why don't you check on Barbara Bates while you're over there?"

I looked at my watch. If we hurried, we could get in two visits before it got dark, but that meant keeping both visits short, which could be a challenge with Barbara. She was a talker. Usually, I'd plan for a half hour to chat along with a good excuse for leaving after the half hour. My dad, who wasn't as good at planning his excuses, once dropped by to see how she was and ended up staying over three hours.

Barbara Bates's house was small enough to be a two-car garage on one of the McMansions, and it was constantly in need of repair. There was always a leak in either the roof or the basement. Still, Barbara managed to keep things neat and orderly, so, even though the thermostat was set a little too low in the winter and a little too high in the summer, it was a comfortable place to spend an hour.

Barbara, wearing a jean jumper with a snowman applique, was happy to see us. One thing about Barbara was that she was always cheerful, like a morning news anchorwoman with short salt-and-pepper hair. "Come on in," she called and motioned for us to sit on her light blue couch. Barbara had a thing for antiques, so her furniture had curvy wooden legs that sometimes creaked when I moved too much. She brought out a box of chocolates to offer us. I took a piece of the solid dark chocolate and bit off the corner.

Barbara pulled a piece of paper off the top of a stack beside her chair and put on her reading glasses. "We had some great news from Jena the other day."

Barbara's favorite topic of conversation was her only child, Jena Farley. For years, people had assumed Jena Farley and I were friends. We were the same age, came from the same neighborhood, and attended the same church. I'd always wanted to be her friend. It just never happened. Most of the time when Jena was around, instead of feeling the bond of sisterhood, I ended up wishing I hadn't quit taking piano lessons after only two years.

It's not that I hadn't tried to be her friend. I'd invited her to every birthday party, pool party, and girl's night out I could dream up. I'd tried talking about how my mother died when I was six, hoping she'd open up about her father leaving. It didn't help. We'd never been close. It was too bad. I could've used a friend like Jena, someone with high standards and ambition.

"I got the email before the power went out," Barbara went on. "It's lucky I printed it out, isn't it? People always say you shouldn't print out emails. I know it's bad for the environment, but my computer isn't as reliable as most. And what would I have done today with the power out? I couldn't have read you this email if I hadn't printed it out."

Even though I loved Barbara, it was sometimes hard to listen when she went on and on about ordinary things like emails. Turning my attention to the stack of articles about Jena, I had to admit that Barbara had every right to brag. Jena had, after all, made it to the top of the country music charts—not that I knew anything about the country music charts.

Barbara smoothed her jumper and went on. "Oh, Harri, I forgot you haven't met Jena yet. Of course not. You just got here, didn't you? I have to tell you about Jena. Or maybe you've heard of her. Have you ever heard of Jena Farley, the country singer? She sings 'Mulling It Over in My Mustang' and 'Purple Roses on My Pillow.'"

Harri tilted her head and considered. "No, I don't—"

"How about 'Lost-and-Found Love'?"

Harri shook her head.

"No. Oh, I know. 'Boomerang Boyfriend.' Lots of people know that one."

Harri shook her head again. "I like country music, but lately I'm into more hard-core stuff."

Barbara grabbed a magazine from her stack, opened up to an article in the middle, and handed it to Harri. "This is her, right here. 'Jena Farley, Country Music's Rising Star.' She's coming to visit for a few months. Poor thing—she's been sick with sinus problems. Her doctor says she has to take a break, so you'll get to know her soon enough. She's lived in Nashville for the past few years, and she's friends with Reggie Van Camp and his wife, Veronica Dixon. Have you heard of them? They're very famous, especially Reggie. Ever heard of Reggie Van Camp?"

Harri looked up from the magazine and squinted. "Maybe. It sounds kind of familiar."

"His wife, Veronica, is the one who gave Jena her first big break. She had Jena sing backup for her. Jena's recorded a few duets with Reggie too."

I'd heard this stuff about Reggie Van Camp and Veronica Dixon so many times, but this was the first time I'd heard about duets with Reggie. "Why doesn't Reggie sing duets with his wife?" I asked. "I thought she was a singer too."

"Yes, but Veronica's talents don't lie in duets. The country duet has a little more acting in it than a normal country song. Sometimes it's like you're arguing, and sometimes it's like you're in love. Jena's so good at it. A lot of the fans think she and Reggie really have something going on between the two of them. Of course, it's all an act. But the tabloids—they're terrible. You can't believe anything you read in those things. Those papperonis love to follow Jena around."

I wanted to say, "You mean the paparazzi?" But Barbara kept on talking.

"Then there's the blending. Jena's voice blends better with Reggie's than Veronica's does. Veronica has a great voice, but it's a smoky voice. Do you know what I mean?"

"I think so." I wasn't convinced that Reggie wouldn't be attracted to Jena. She was much prettier than his wife. Poor Jena! She probably had to come stay with Barbara to get away from him.

Barbara grabbed another article out of her stack to show Harri. "I'm sure you've heard how Jena saved Reggie's life?" She pointed to a picture of Jena with Reggie. "It was all over the news. They were at one of those fancy celebrity parties last summer when Reggie choked on his steak. Everyone was in a panic except for Jena. She grabbed him from behind and did the Heimlich. Oh, I keep forgetting—I was going to read you that email."

While Barbara read Jena's email and showed us a few more

magazine articles, I took another nibble of the chocolate. Letting the little piece roll across my tongue, I counted to thirty while it made its way to the other side of my mouth and melted. Then I swallowed, trying to stamp the taste on my memory.

I divided that little piece of chocolate up into ten more bites and counted to thirty with each bite. By the time I finished the chocolate, Barbara started showing Harri the pictures of Jena on the walls and in the albums. We didn't have a lot of pictures at our house. Dad kept what little we had in boxes. That's mostly how I remembered things about my mom—looking through boxes. As children, my sister Isabella and I had spent whole summer afternoons digging into boxes of Mom's pictures, her high school yearbooks, and her old report cards containing A after A after A. To us, she was perfect in every way.

I always knew there was life after death. That was how Heavenly Father compensated for taking my mom away when I was so young: He helped me know my family was forever. What I didn't know was whether Mom would approve of me. I'd watched my friends' parents enough to know that one parent was always the stickler—checking up on grades and credit scores. If one of my parents was strict, it had to be my mom. She probably wished I were a little more like Jena Farley.

As Barbara ushered Harri into the kitchen to look at Jena's wall of fame, I headed for the front door. "You know what, Barbara, while you're getting to know Harri, I'm gonna see if I can shovel a little snow off your driveway." Harri seemed comfortable enough, and I couldn't leave Barbara's house without doing something to help her out, not to mention that I'd already seen Jena's wall of fame.

Barbara glanced out the window at her snow-covered driveway. "Well, that's really sweet of you, Emma. Just promise me you won't overdo it. I see so many news shows about people injuring themselves while they're shoveling snow. Someone's always having a heart attack or pulling a muscle. I'd hate to have to face your father if anything happened to you."

That was why everyone loved Barbara. It was so obvious she cared about people. "I promise I won't hurt myself, Barbara. I'll only do a few minutes. We've got to be going soon anyway."

The snow shoveling gave me a chance to think. I'd planned on introducing Harri to Phil, but I hadn't planned how I'd do it. It wasn't like me to show up on Phil's doorstep. I had to come up with something clever to say, not just, "Hi, Phil, I met this girl, Harri. I thought you might like to date her."

Maybe if I asked to borrow something. It would have to be something unusual, something worth walking a mile through the snow to get from him. What would a single guy have that I would want to borrow?

I was so lost in thought, shoveling away the snow, I didn't notice when Phil Elton himself came up behind me. "Emma, what are you doing here?"

I jumped a little and turned to see Phil, stylish in a gray wool coat. He hadn't worn a hat, so his brown hair had the usual arranged disorder to it. I couldn't help smiling. "Hi, Phil." It was a lucky break, but I should have expected something like that to happen. Phil was always helping people.

Phil had his own snow shovel and was already at work on the driveway. "I can take care of this if you want to go inside and warm up. I guess I should have gotten here earlier."

"Oh, that's okay. I didn't really come here to shovel. I brought my new friend, Harri, over to meet Barbara. They started talking, and I decided I could help out a little bit while I'm here. Harri's more interested in country music than I am."

Phil nodded his head and chuckled. "Got it."

It was amazing how much more snow Phil could pick up with his shovel than I could with mine. He cleared three feet of the driveway before I was done with one.

"When we're done, if you have time, you should come in and meet Harri. I think you two will get along."

Phil stopped and looked at his watch. "I'm planning to do a couple more driveways before it gets dark."

"I'll go get Harri now if you're in a hurry. She wants to meet you."

Phil leaned on his shovel. "Harri is a she?"

"Her real name is Harriet. She moved here a couple months ago and she's hardly met anybody. I think you'll like her."

Phil threw his head back, laughed, and started shoveling again. "I thought you were trying to introduce me to your new boyfriend."

"You think I would be out here shoveling snow while my new boyfriend stays inside?" I grabbed a handful of snow and threw it at him. I didn't mean to hit him in the face, but that's where it landed.

Phil wiped the snow off his face and grinned. "I wondered why you were dating such a loser." I expected him to throw a snowball at me, but he just stood there. "So you don't have a boyfriend?"

I giggled a little at his awkwardness. "Nope. Harri doesn't either."

Phil threw another shovelful of snow away from the driveway. "So you . . . I mean, you and your friend are . . . available?" Phil didn't open his mouth enough when he talked. That was the one thing about him that always distracted me. I couldn't help staring at his mouth.

I had to force myself to look into his eyes. "Why is that a shock, Phil? Every woman in that house right now is available. You can take your pick—Harri, me, or Barbara. You're surrounded by single women." It was safe to assume Phil wouldn't pick me. I was at least three inches taller than he was, and it was a rare man who dated a taller woman.

While we finished the driveway and sidewalk, I gave Phil a little background information on Harri. I told him how I got to know her, where she was from, and where she worked. I finished it all up with a great big hook. "The guys at church are going to swarm all over Harri. She's beautiful, she knows how to cook, she's great with kids, and she has the sweetest personality." The conversation was going better than I'd thought it would. He was a fish ready to bite, and I happened to have the right lure.

Phil stayed quiet for a while, probably imagining how he could be married by June. After a minute, he stopped shoveling. "Didn't you just meet this girl?"

"Yeah."

"And you already have such a high opinion of her?"

"I'm a good judge of character. Wait 'til you meet her. You'll see what I mean."

So I wouldn't describe the introduction as love at first sight. In fact, when Phil and I came into the house, Harri had the back of her sweater pulled up to show Barbara a tattoo of something that looked like an octopus on her back. Luckily, she knew enough to cover up quickly once we came inside. Not quick enough, though. Phil came in right after me, so I'm pretty sure he saw it too. It was a good thing he wasn't the judgmental type. I imagined a lot of other accountants would have placed a big minus mark beside Harri's name because of this.

There was no time to waste, so I plunged ahead, hoping to coach them both into a better first impression. "Harri, this is my friend Phil Elton. Phil, this is Harri." Harri smiled. Phil smiled back. It was a balancing act trying to help those two get to know each other. At any second, Barbara was liable to reach for her stack of Jena paraphernalia. "Phil's our ward mission leader. You two should see him shovel snow. He could rival a snowplow." At this point, I allowed Barbara to jump in with her thanks. As she introduced the topic of Jena's frail health, I broke in again. "Well, Barbara, it was nice to see you. We'd better get going, though. Phil reminded me it's getting dark soon."

Phil reached for the door. "Yes, thanks for letting me warm up, Sister Bates. I've got a few more driveways to check on, so I'd better head out too."

We followed Phil to the road, where he turned and asked, "Where are you off to now?"

Should I have admitted it or not? I pulled on my gloves and looked at him. "Our plan was to go by your house, but seeing as how you're not home, I guess we'll head back—unless you could use our help with those driveways."

"How about I walk you home?"

This couldn't have gone better if I'd planned it. "Only if you stay for chicken salad and wedding cake."

As long as the street in front of our house wasn't plowed, we had the best sledding hill in all of Vienna—a straight slope heading down at a forty-five-degree angle. Justin was pulling Avery uphill on a sled when we arrived. Avery smiled from red cheek to red cheek. "I have the slope groomed if you want to try it out," Justin called. We watched him as he hopped onto the sled behind Avery. The two of them went whooping down the hill together.

"What if someone decides to drive down this road?" Phil asked. "They won't be able to see us sledding until they've crested the hill."

I shrugged. "No one ever drives down the road when it isn't plowed."

Dad opened the window and yelled that we ought to be wearing helmets. "See," I told Phil. "If it was a problem, my dad would have told us not to sled on the street."

Harri held her hand up to her mouth. "Oh, I should've thought of a helmet. Like Avery needs a head injury today."

I pointed to Avery walking up the hill with Justin. "I'll get her one of the helmets we use for my nieces." It was a good excuse to leave Harri and Phil alone.

I found some bike helmets and a big wooden sled—the kind built for two—in the garage and dragged everything out to the hill, where Phil and Harri stood. I wanted Phil and Harri to have as much time to themselves as possible, so I tried to put the helmet on Avery's head. She screamed. "Come on, sweetie," I coaxed. "It'll keep your head from getting owies."

Harri rushed to retrieve the little girl. "You don't want to wear the helmet? That's okay. You don't have to wear the helmet. We'll just look at it for a while. This is a cool helmet, a princess helmet. Princesses take their crowns off to wear it. Did you know that?" Harri went on talking like that, making up stories about princesses until Avery begged to put on the helmet.

This was the perfect scene for Phil to witness—it showed off Harri's kindhearted nature. "She's so good with children," I whispered to him.

He smiled. "You gonna take a turn?"

"Oh no, you and Harri go first. I'll stay with Avery."

After a little encouragement, Phil hopped onto the sled. Harri got on behind him. Justin gave them a push that sent them racing down the hill. Harri screamed, keeping her hands on Phil's shoulders instead of hugging his rib cage. She was smart to play it safe, to pretend she could take him or leave him.

After we'd gone down the hill a few times, I noticed a man

walking toward us. As he got closer, Harri waved and called out, "It's Rob." She jumped on the sled and motioned for me to join her, "Come on, let's go talk to him." But I wasn't going to let her go talk to Rob Martinez without Phil, so all three of us piled on.

Rob met us at the bottom of the hill. He was a small man with thick black hair and acne scars. The apartment where he lived with his parents was about a mile away. "I was on my way over to Harri's house to check on her. I guess I shouldn't have worried. Thanks for taking care of her."

"Oh, you're welcome. It's been fun. We'll keep an eye on her until the roads get plowed," I said. My conscience told me I should invite Rob inside for something to eat. That was exactly what Harri needed; a little competition might spur Phil along to action. "You should come inside and warm up before you go home. It's too bad you had to walk all the way over here. I could have called you if I'd known."

Rob drew his gaze away from Phil and Harri to answer me. "It was no trouble. With the electricity out, I didn't have much to do at home."

"Have you listened to those songs I told you about?" Harri asked.

"Not yet," Rob said. "I'll listen to them tonight if the electricity comes back on."

Justin slid past us with Avery on his lap, stopping a few feet away. "Hey, Rob. Come take a turn. This is the best hill for sledding I've ever found."

Rob stole another glance in Phil's direction. "No, I'd better go. It'll be dark soon."

Justin stood up and hefted Avery onto his shoulders. "You should at least come in for some food. Emma has a ton of chicken salad. You don't mind, do you, Emma? I'm getting hungry."

I rubbed my hands together to warm them up. "You'd be doing me a favor to come inside and eat. I'm sick of reception food."

Rob shook his head. "Thanks for the invite, but I've got to get going."

Phil grabbed the sled to follow Justin up the hill. "You're missing out, Rob. Emma's a great cook." He turned to smile at me. Later on, I'd tell him how we bought the salad at Costco.

Harri and I stood at the bottom of the hill while Rob went one way and Phil went the other. "What do you think of him?" she asked me.

"I think he's perfect for you. The real question is, what do you think of him?"

"He's hot, but he's way out of my league. There's no way I can get a guy like that."

I walked up the hill. "Sure you can. I'll help you."

Harri followed along behind me. "I almost freaked when he said he still hadn't listened to that music."

"What music?" I stopped and looked at Harri. "Did you think I meant Rob? I was talking about Phil."

Harri giggled. "Oh."

Chapter 3

Coach's Tip of the Day:
Sometimes all it takes to solve a problem is a little
money and a good hairdresser.

For Harri's birthday on Thursday, I gave her a gift certificate to my favorite salon. She called right away and got an appointment with my colorist for Saturday morning. I figured we could make a day of it—spending the morning in pursuit of beauty and the afternoon in pursuit of Phil. Since Harri didn't have a car, I drove to her house on Saturday morning and walked down the back stairs to her little bedroom in the basement.

Harri's room was about as desolate as a hospital hallway. The walls were a stark grayish white. Harri had brightened it up a bit with an orange comforter on her bed. As far as the furniture arrangement went, though, the place could've used some feng shui action. The twin bed, bedside table, and dresser stood against the wall in a straight line.

Harri's coral-pink sweater provided a little contrast to the color scheme. After a good five days of practice, the girl had definitely developed some style. She wore a belt over the sweater and had picked out dangling earrings with pink crystals. Her clothes were still way too baggy, but we'd work on that later. "Are you sure this belt doesn't make me look fat?" she asked. "It feels so tight."

"You look perfect."

"I do not."

I sat on the bed beside her. "Have you decided on a hair color?"

"I was thinking I'd keep it the same. What do you think?"

"I think it's best to go a little lighter than your natural shade, so your hair ends up being the same color as when you were in pre-school. What color was your hair when you were little?"

"Blonde. I have a picture. You want to see?" Harri looked around her room. From what I could tell, her possessions consisted of about ten hangers full of clothes, a duffel bag, her phone, a sock monkey, an iPod, and three pairs of shoes. She grabbed her phone, clicked a few buttons, and handed it to me. "Here's one." A little girl with curly blonde hair smiled up at me through the screen.

"Cute! You look like a baby Taylor Swift. How long has it been since your hair was that color?"

Harri stood up and stared into the little square mirror that hung crookedly above her dresser. "It got darker as I grew up. My natural color now is like a dishwater blond. My dad always says I should go blonde again."

"It'd be so pretty blonde, especially with highlights. You could take this picture to have her match the color."

Harri looked at the picture on the phone. "That's a good idea."

We were fifteen minutes early for the appointment. The salon was located in a nearby strip mall, but it had a spa-like atmosphere with accents of wood, orchids, and earth tones. "I've never had my hair done at a salon," Harri confessed. "My mom always cut my hair to save money." Before I could find out more, the colorist came to get Harri. Soon she was sitting in a salon chair, wearing a blue smock, and picking out shades of blonde while I sat in a wooden folding chair nearby.

As we waited for the color tests, Harri answered text messages. At first, they were from her little brother in Utah, then Rob Martinez started asking her opinion on food and movies. She read all his messages out loud to me. First question: Does she like Mexican food? "I don't know," she said. "I don't like anything hot. I like tacos sometimes, but not enchiladas or anything with beans. I wouldn't want to offend him, though. His parents are from Mexico."

I pulled my chair closer to her. "Be honest and tell him you don't like Mexican food."

She keyed in her response, waited for his response, then turned back to me. "How about Indian? He wants to know if I like Indian food."

"That's hotter."

"Are you serious? I guess that's a no too."

Had she seen any good movies lately? Were there any she wanted to see? It was obvious that Rob was going to ask her out. I had nothing against Rob, but it seemed to me that Phil needed Harri more. He was desperate enough to place an ad for a new girlfriend in the *Fairfax Gazette*—not to mention that he was completely worthy of Harri's affection. He was the ward mission leader, a college graduate, and a homeowner. I had to look out for Harri's interests. She deserved the best. Before she got her first round of color, I called out, "Don't forget we have plans for tonight."

She put a hand to her lips. "Oh, I must have forgotten. I better tell Rob. I hope he's not too bummed out."

I dialed Phil's number. He answered on the second ring. "Hi, Emma. What's up?"

I walked to the front of the salon, away from the sound of hair dryers, and stood by the display of products. "Harri and I are hanging out at the salon. What are you up to?"

"Nothing important."

"So . . . I've heard you're good with videos."

"I don't know if I'd say *good*. I'm an amateur."

"Don't be so modest, Phil. You like to do videos, don't you?"

"Yeah. I have an HD camcorder and video-editing software. I'm not a professional, but I can make a decent video."

"I want to surprise Harri's family with a video," I said, "so they can see what her life is like out here. Do you think you could help us?"

"Sure. That sounds like fun."

"Are you busy this afternoon? We could treat you to lunch and then spend a couple hours filming."

"Name the place," Phil said, "and I'll be there."

I looked at my watch and added two hours. "One o'clock at . . ." Harri didn't like spicy food. "Someplace American?"

"How about Mike's Place?" Phil suggested. Guys liked Mike's Place because there were TVs mounted on the walls tuned to the sports channels. It wasn't the best choice to impress Harri, but if we were late, at least Phil wouldn't be bored.

"Okay, see you at Mike's Place at one."

I spent the rest of our time at the salon reading articles in bimbo fashion magazines. They made life seem so superficial, as if a woman's self-worth had to do with the amount of skin she showed or the cost of her outfit or the makeup she wore. I hoped Harri knew this whole makeover thing was meant to enhance her natural beauty, not to substitute for it. She was so much more than a head of hair and a hanger for clothes. I closed the magazine and looked at Harri. She caught my smile and tossed one back at me. I shouldn't have worried. It was in her nature to want to be beautiful. That was the way it was with all women.

Harri may not have had money, but she was blessed with a beautiful face. In some ways, beauty was more powerful than money. When a woman looked good, people respected her as if she had money and power. That was all I wanted—for people to respect Harri enough to notice what was inside. And Phil Elton was first on my list to notice what was inside of Harri. All I had to do was bring Harri and Phil together, and then the forces of attraction could take over.

When we walked out of the salon, Harri's hair was a deep caramel with butter-colored highlights—so much brighter and happier than the dull black she'd had before. She looked even more stunning than I'd imagined. We had her hair cut to graze her shoulders with long layers; that way, if she wanted, she could still have a ponytail, the hairstyle of choice for nannies. For our lunch with Phil, it was styled in loose curls.

As we walked into Mike's Place, I had my eye out for Phil. He'd gone early to order our food, and I didn't want to miss his reaction when he saw Harri. Typical of Phil, he already sat at our table, having ordered our food with mathematical precision. He'd calculated the exact time when we'd arrive. Sure enough, as we walked to the table, the server brought in our tray. Phil's eyes traveled from me to Harri.

He drew in his lips as if he were about to whistle, rubbed his chin, nodded, and stood as we approached. "That hair's going to look great on camera. It really picks up the light." For the first time, Phil could see the real Harri, the one I'd seen all along.

I slung my purse down on the seat across from him. "Doesn't she look beautiful?"

Phil told the server I had the salad before he snuck another peek at Harri. "She looks . . . great—you both do." He was polite enough to think of me even though he was much more interested in Harri.

"You look pretty swoon-worthy yourself," I said, watching for his reaction. He drew his brows together, as if wondering whether I'd figured him out.

Harri sat between us. "Thanks, Phil. And thanks for ordering for us. I'm starved." From what I'd heard, gentlemen preferred women with hearty appetites, so I was glad to see Harri go after her kid-sized hamburger with gusto.

Phil brought a paper out of his pocket. "I've planned out locations for the different shots. Here's my list of options. You can look it over while we eat." He pushed the paper across the table toward me and took a bite of his California club sandwich.

I chewed a forkful of my salad and read the list: Mount Vernon, Smithsonian, White House Christmas tree, monuments, DC temple, and Church Street. If I had my choice, I'd go anywhere other than the Smithsonian. It was one of the places that reminded me of Mom. She'd taken me there so many times as a kid. I pushed the list to the center where Harri could read it too. "Those sound great, Phil," I said. "I think you're better at this than you want to admit. How many places do you think we should plan on?"

Phil leaned over to look at his list. "That depends. If you choose the Smithsonian, there's no problem walking over to see the White House Christmas tree and the monuments. But, say you choose the temple. It's out of the way, so if we went there, we'd only be able to do one other thing."

Harri'd just taken another bite of her hamburger. There was no chance she'd give her opinion anytime soon, so I gave mine. "Well, I usually avoid the temple for dates. It's too much pressure. But in this case, no one's dating, so I guess it'd be okay."

Phil glanced at Harri, then at me. "No one's dating . . . yet."

Harri smiled at Phil but said nothing. I couldn't resist encouraging him. "That's true. We could go to the temple if Harri thinks it's a good idea." I waited for Harri to respond. Nothing. How was Phil going to get to know Harri if she was so quiet? Sticking my fork into a chunk of lettuce, I vowed to be silent or, better yet, absent. "You know what? I think I forgot to lock the car. I'll be back in a minute." I grabbed my purse and, before either of them could object, bolted for the door.

It was a warm day for December, so I sat in my Civic for a while. There was a text from Justin asking when we would have our annual Christmas tree decorating marathon. After I texted him back, I called my sister, Isabella, who lived down in Richmond. She was in a hurry, so we only talked long enough for her to tell me my nieces had gotten over their ear infections. Once she hung up, I couldn't think of any reason to stay in the car longer.

Back inside the restaurant, Phil's gaze was locked on Harri. I should've gone back out to my car, but the curiosity was too much. As I approached the table, I heard Harri's reply. "We had a ginormous outbreak of food poisoning at the restaurant I used to work at. I got it too. The health department thinks it was from employees not washing their hands."

Maybe I'd come back too soon. If I'd stayed away longer, their conversation probably would have come around to a discussion of each other's hobbies or plans for the future. As it was, though, I wasn't at all sorry to interrupt. "So do we have a plan? Are we going to the temple?"

Harri giggled with a little snort. "Oh, that's what we were supposed to talk about."

I sat down and grabbed my fork. "I'm behind on this salad, so I'll let you two hash it out. Where do you want to go, Harri?"

Looking at the list, Harri reached for a french fry. "I don't know. They all sound good to me."

I munched on lettuce and stared at Phil until he spoke. "You don't have any places you like better than any others?"

Harri dipped her fry in ketchup. "Nope."

"So have you already seen any of these places?" Phil asked.

"No, not really."

It went on like this for a few minutes—Phil asking questions, Harri having no opinion, and me making a mental note to coach Harri on decision-making skills. Finally, I couldn't stand it any longer. "Why don't we go downtown? We can see the Christmas trees and the Smithsonian. Plus we can get the White House, the Capitol, and all the monuments in the background." There it was. I'd picked the only place I really didn't want to go.

Chapter 4

Coach's Tip of the Day:
The art of conversation isn't so much about being
interesting as it is about being interested.

We drove downtown in Phil's black Honda Accord. Phil and Harri both thought I should sit up front because of my height—I got that a lot. But there was no way I was taking Harri's place. I assured them I was happy to sit in the back, as if I were any girl of average height.

Phil's car felt like a rental. There was absolutely nothing inside. It made me wonder if he'd raked all the clutter into a box before vacuuming up every bit of dust, crumb, and nature. I inhaled and caught a whiff of Windex. He'd definitely cleaned—good sign. He was trying to impress her.

Sitting in the backseat with my lips pinched together between my thumb and forefinger, I wished I could cast a magic spell over Harri and Phil to get a conversation started. Sometimes that was the way it was when two people were attracted to each other. All the words left their brains and jumbled around somewhere near their kidneys.

After a few minutes, Harri broke the silence when she sneezed. Phil jumped at the opportunity to respond. "Bless you." He handed her a tissue from his glove compartment.

Harri took the tissue. "Thank you." She sneezed again. "My allergies are out of control here."

Phil groaned. "Tell me about it. Before I moved to DC, I hadn't used my inhaler for at least a year. Now, I use it once a week or more."

Harri wiped her nose. "Really? You have asthma?"

Phil's ears turned a little red. "Yep. Had it since I was a kid."

"Me too," Harri said. "I can't go anywhere without Albuterol."

It was the sort of small talk that could build the foundation of a great relationship. I could see Harri and Phil as an old couple sitting on the front porch, talking about their asthma and what they ate for dinner. Sure, it may have seemed a little boring to an outsider like me, but to them, it was the stuff of life.

Phil lucked out and found a parking space near the Washington Monument—the monument Harri thought looked like a big gray pencil sticking up in the air. We figured we'd start walking and work our way down to the Capitol Building, where Congress met. On the way, we'd zigzag over to see the Christmas trees on the Eclipse in front of the White House, then over to the Natural History Museum, and then to the carousel and to the Air and Space Museum. That gave me at least a half hour before I had to worry about memories of Mom.

As Phil fiddled with his camera, I played tour guide for Harri since she'd never been downtown before. "People who live around here call this place 'the mall.'"

Harri looked across the huge expanse of field between where we stood and the Capitol. "That's random. It doesn't look much like a mall to me."

"Yeah, this mall obviously has nothing to do with shopping."

Phil laughed, lifting the camera up in front of his face. "I should've gotten that on video. Why don't you do it over? Three, two, one, action." He pointed his finger at me.

I felt like someone on the movie *Groundhog Day* saying the same thing over again, but Harri acted along as if we'd never said those words before. This time I added a little more explanation, so I wouldn't seem like such an airhead. "The word *mall* used to mean a place where people walked around. That was before they had shopping malls."

Phil gave us both high fives. "Beautiful."

Phil ran ahead to film us walking across Constitution Avenue. Then he filmed us playing hide-and-seek around the fifty state Christmas trees. On the way to the Natural History Museum, he turned off the camera so I could finally make a suggestion. "You wouldn't mind if I used the camera at the Natural History Museum, would you?"

Phil frowned. "As long as you don't film me."

"But that's the whole point," I said. "I think it'd be nice if you were in the video too. Harri's family wants to see all her friends here, not just me."

Phil showed me how to use the camera while we stood in the rotunda at the Natural History Museum, the place where they had the stuffed elephants. I remembered standing there with Mom while she tried to explain that the elephants weren't exactly real. They were real elephant skins mounted on a kind of sculpture. I was five years old, and the idea of something dead looking so alive disturbed me. Considering that Mom died less than a year later, it still turned my stomach to look at those elephants.

I focused the camera on Harri, trying to forget about death. "I think I've got it figured out," I told Phil. "You can go now." The problem was he was so shy. He preferred to stand beside me, explaining details about his camera, instead of walking around with Harri, who weaved through the crowd, pretending to be an elephant. After what I figured was enough instruction about the camera from him, I used my best schoolteacher voice. "Phil, it won't be as much fun if you're not in any of the shots. Harri's family will want to see what you look like."

"Okay, but don't expect me to walk around like an elephant."

He went to the sign that said, "Welcome to the Elephant's World," folded his arms, and read the detailed paragraphs. Harri ambled up beside him with her hands clasped in front of her like an elephant trunk. The two of them were so different. Like yin and yang, they balanced each other.

We headed up to see the Hope diamond, something that didn't remind me at all of Mom. I suggested that Phil could pretend to propose to Harri in front of one of the gems. He was too shy to agree to that, so Harri ended up reading Phil's future in the big crystal ball. We draped her cardigan over her head like a scarf, and I coached her a little bit about what to say. She spoke in what was supposed to be an Italian accent but ended up sounding a little Caribbean. "I see happiness in your future. I see strength. You are eating fruits and vegetables. You are taking a multivitamin. You are dating a mysterious and beautiful woman. Your future is getting cloudy, too cloudy. I can't see any further."

Phil grinned and talked through his teeth. "A mysterious and beautiful woman, huh? Sounds good."

I looked at my watch. "We'd better hustle. The carousel closes in fifteen minutes." That was when Phil lifted the camera out of my hands, ending the brief romantic drama starring Harri and Phil. I can't say I was disappointed to leave those elephants behind for another few years.

When we got to the carousel, I showed Harri my favorite horse, which wasn't really a horse. It was an indigo dragon whose head and hooves looked like a horse but whose back contained the scales, wings, and tail of a dragon. "I wish I could bring my little brother here," Harri said. "He'd love this dragon."

Harri sat on the dragon while I took the white horse behind her. I remembered riding this carousel as a child with my mom standing beside me. Dad had stood outside the cast-iron fence, where Phil now stood with his camera up to his face. Unlike the elephants, the carousel held only happy memories for me. The first time we passed Phil, we waved. The next time, Harri pretended to throw a lasso. The third time, we threw kisses. Phil threw us a kiss back on the fourth go around.

I held my stomach as we exited the carousel. "I'm starving."

Phil pointed out a popcorn stand. "Want some popcorn? I'll treat."

Harri and Phil headed for the stand, but I hung back. If Phil was going to treat someone, it was going to be Harri, not me. When they got to the front of the line, Phil asked if I wanted some.

"No thanks," I answered from about five feet away.

Phil stepped in my direction. "You sure?"

I shoved my hands into my pockets. "I'm not into popcorn. Those little brown parts always get stuck in my teeth." I walked toward the Air and Space Museum. "I'll go grab a hot dog."

Phil bought two bags of popcorn and handed one to Harri before he caught up with me. "Most women I know hate hot dogs. They have too much fat."

I shrugged. "Hot dogs don't seem like real food to me. It's kind of like eating virtual fat and calories."

"So I'm supposed to meet a mysterious woman, huh?" Phil said, grinning.

We watched Harri throw popcorn up in the air and catch it in her mouth as I responded. "Maybe you've already met her."

After I ate my hot dog loaded with hot peppers and mustard, we had enough time to spend five minutes in the lobby of the Air and Space Museum. Phil showed Harri where to stand in line to touch the moon rock, which, to me, looked like any other flat, black triangular rock. Harri jumped up and down. "I've never touched a piece of the moon before. I've never touched anything from another planet."

Phil and I smiled at each other as Harri ran to the back of the line. I whispered to Phil. "Isn't she adorable?"

Phil nodded and looked across at Harri. "You're a good influence on her."

"I didn't have anything to do with it. She's a natural beauty."

Phil looked down at his camera. "And you're the treasure hunter, finding all the hidden treasure."

"It's not like I had to dig deep or anything. She has a great personality."

As Harri advanced in line, Phil put the camera up to his face. "Yeah, she's fun."

"It's nice having a friend close by. Since Tanya got engaged, I've been pretty much on my own. Of course, Harri will probably be engaged by summertime."

Phil took his face away from the camera to look at me. "She's very attractive, but I don't think you have to worry about losing her that soon."

I winked. "I just have a feeling."

Phil tilted his head to the side. "Hmm." I hoped he realized he'd have to make his move soon. His future happiness depended on it.

We got back to the car three minutes after the meter expired— three minutes, and the meter maid's car with flashing lights was just leaving. I wasn't going to let this ruin Phil and Harri's first date, so I grabbed the ticket from under Phil's windshield wiper and sprinted. It wasn't too hard to catch up with the meter maid, a thin African American woman with long braided hair. What was hard was convincing the woman to take back the ticket. "It's already in the system," she kept telling me. I explained that it was Harri's first time in DC *and* her first date with Phil. After that, I told the meter maid I liked her hair. She held her hand out. "Give me the ticket. I'll void it out when my shift ends."

We drove home to the sound of country music. First there was a song about someone's brother who died in the war. Then there was a song about a guy who dumped his wife for his secretary. The next one was about a woman who drank too much. To top it all off, we listened to a guy sing about his favorite disposable plastic cup. The only thing that helped me tolerate it was the way Phil and Harri bonded. They both sang along. Harri chair-danced.

I had Phil drop Harri off at her own place so he'd know how to get there. When he dropped me off at my Civic afterward, he acted like he wanted to sit there and talk—probably about Harri—but my phone buzzed. I thanked Phil and exited his cramped backseat to answer the call.

It was Harri. "Come see what I got. Someone left a package for me."

"What do you mean? What kind of package?"

"You'll have to come see."

I drove to the McMansion where Harri lived and parked at the curb. She was already headed out the front door with the box in her hands. It was wrapped in red wrapping paper and had a big purple bow on top. She showed me the card that said, "A secret message for Harri."

I fluttered my eyelashes. "Well, if it's so secret, maybe I shouldn't

31

help you read it. That reminds me—do you know what Phil said about you today? He said you're fun and very attractive."

Harri sat on the front step with the package on her lap. "Really?"

I held up three fingers on my right hand. "Scout's honor."

She pulled off the bow and wrapping paper. "I've never gotten a package like this before." She parted the tissue paper inside the box to reveal six round sugar cookies with transparent red candy centers. She unfolded a note that lay on top of the cookies. "It's a bunch of scribbles."

I sat beside Harri and looked at the paper. "Maybe you're supposed to read the message through the cookies."

Harri put a cookie on top of the paper and laughed. "Oh, you're right, but I have it upside down." She moved the paper around and read. "Harri, I think you're so sweet. This New Year's will be a treat, if you'll give me a chance, to take you to the dance. Your friend, Rob." Her jaw dropped. "Rob's asking me to the dance."

I took the cookie and the message to read it myself. "That's clever. They're like cookie decoders."

"I didn't know there was a New Year's Dance," Harri said. "Nobody's ever asked me to a dance before. I don't even know what to do."

"It's easy. You answer him."

Harri folded the paper over the top of the cookies and placed the top back on the box. "He went to a lot of trouble. He must really like me."

"You should answer him right away. It's best not to string a guy along if you're not interested. That only leads to more disappointment."

Harri twisted a lock of hair around her finger. "So you think I should say *no*."

"I didn't say that. You need to decide for yourself. If Rob's the man you have your heart set on, you should say yes. But if there's someone you like better, you might want to leave yourself open for another invitation. It's okay to be a little picky." I tried to read her expression. "I can see it in your eyes. There *is* someone else."

Harri giggled and covered her face with her hands. "Oh, I don't know. I'd hate to disappoint Rob."

She was right—he *would* be disappointed, but it was better to be up-front with men. I'd learned that the hard way from Kyle Perry, a guy I dated when I was nineteen. I should have broken up with him after three weeks. Instead, I'd waited three months. "He'll get over it," I said. "You don't have to go with the first guy who asks you, especially if that might disappoint someone else. Rob's a nice guy, though, if you want to go with him. Do what makes you happy."

Harri bit the edge of a cookie. "These are good," she mumbled with her mouth full. She held the box out to me, motioning for me to take one too.

I shook my head. "No, thanks."

She held two cookies up like glasses in front of her eyes. "But how should I answer him?"

"If you want to go with him, say *yes*. If not, thank him and tell him you have other plans."

Harri dropped the cookies back in the box. "But I don't have other plans."

"I think you do. I think you might go to the dance with Phil."

When I got home, I called Phil and asked him to give Harri a ride to church.

Chapter 5

Coach's Tip of the Day:
You are stronger than the force of your habits.

I wasn't a chocolate chip cookie–baking type of woman. That's why it was so surprising that every Monday night I hosted the family home evening group. Normally, I didn't stress about the program. I delegated and hoped for the best. Today was different, though. It was Harri's first time. I'd asked Phil to give the lesson. And I'd promised to serve something that included the deadly duo of fat and sugar.

Being a receptionist at a dentist's office, I usually got off work a little after 5:00. But the second-to-last patient had come in late, so I couldn't leave until 5:45. It was times like these when I had to remind myself I wouldn't be a receptionist forever. I'd already attended the Life Coach Summit and Coach Academy Bootcamp. Now all I needed to do was complete my online training to become a certified coach. As soon as I got some clients, I'd make a difference in people's lives instead of sitting behind a desk.

I'd promised myself when Tanya got married that I wouldn't ever call her in to solve my problems at home. This day was an exception, though, and, anyway, this was the longest Tanya and I had been apart for as long as I could remember. When I drove up to the house and saw her get out of her Toyota Prius with her pink baseball cap and jean jacket, it almost felt like nothing had changed. I ran up and gave her a hug. "How was Hawaii?"

She tucked a wisp of her light brown hair into her baseball cap. "Wonderful."

I sighed. "I was so jealous."

"Your dad told me about the snowstorm," she said.

"It was pretty bad having the electricity out for three days, but I still liked it better than work."

Tanya opened up her trunk. "Oh, Emma, I wish we could have brought you along."

I laughed. "You do not."

Tanya giggled and grabbed a plate of brownies and a bag of take-out from her car. "No, you're right. We had the most perfect honeymoon. I wouldn't have changed anything."

Most people felt sorry for me when I told them my mom had died in a car accident when I was six. My childhood was happy enough, though. I'm not saying it wasn't hard. It was, and I still missed Mom. But Tanya was always there to compensate for my loss. Before Mom's death, Tanya had been a student at BYU. She'd always said she didn't give up anything when she came to stay with us since she took classes at night and eventually became a physical therapist like she'd planned. Now that I was older, I knew better. She'd given up her social life when she came to live with us. Sure, she'd gone to the singles ward activities, but, speaking from my own experience, I'm pretty sure those activities hadn't compensated for *her* loss.

I hurried up the front steps and opened the door for her. "It's about time you focused your attention on someone other than me."

Tanya walked inside and deposited her things on the kitchen table as if she'd never been gone. The kitchen was the only room in the house that was still the same as when Mom decorated it, and it was going to stay that way, floral wallpaper border and all. Tanya dished up a plate of shrimp panang curry—my favorite. "I still think about you all the time. That reminds me—guess who called last night."

"Hank?" I asked. My heart rate spiked every time I said his name.

Tanya handed me the plate. "How did you know? He's going

35

to visit us after his finals are through. I'm so nervous to meet him. I have no idea how to be a stepmother to a grown man. Although, if it's like the last time he decided to come, he'll cancel at the last minute anyway, so I have nothing to worry about."

I'd heard it's important to think happy thoughts while you eat, and Hank Weston went perfectly with shrimp panang curry. I'd heard so much about Hank I felt like I actually knew him. The product of Randall Weston's first, short-lived marriage, Hank was my image of the perfect guy—tall, good-looking, smart, and spiritual. It didn't hurt that he was rich too. Since his family owned ten private schools, he'd be rich for his entire life. Unfortunately, the closest I'd ever come to meeting him was when he friended me on Facebook.

Tanya went to work wiping down our counters. No one had wiped them since the day before her wedding. "Oh, and I shouldn't tell you this. Justin called me this morning. Don't tell him I told you, okay? He's worried about you."

I picked through the take-out box, looking for one more shrimp. "Why would Justin be worried about me?"

"Because of your friendship with Harri."

I found another shrimp, popped it in my mouth, and chewed, trying my best to enjoy nature's original low-fat protein. But it was hard to focus on the joy of eating shellfish when Justin had nosed into my business. "Why does he think it's bad for me to be friends with Harri? It's not like she's a bad influence."

Tanya rinsed out the dishrag. "He thinks you have too much influence over Harri."

"Why is that a bad thing?" I asked, trying to keep my voice from raising.

"I'm not sure it is. From all your dad's told me, I think she's much happier for having you as a friend. And I think you're better off for having her as a friend too."

I stabbed a shrimp with my fork. "Justin finds fault with everything I do."

Tanya sat down at the table beside me. "He said some nice things about you too. He said you're beautiful and talented but you're not stuck up. I'd say that's a pretty big compliment."

I mulled that comment over while I picked at my curry-flavored rice. He thought I wasn't stuck up. It was nice to know Justin could see a tiny bit of good in me. But I wasn't ready to take a consolation prize in this conversation. I was still ticked. "I'm beginning to wonder if I should trust his judgment at all."

"Emma, you know Justin has good judgment—most of the time, at least."

As if on cue, the doorbell rang with Justin's telltale jiggle. He had this way of rocking the button a little to produce an extra ding after the ding-dong. Tanya placed a finger over her lips. "Don't you dare tell him what I said."

I ran down the stairs, flung open the door, and stared up into his face. "How are you, Justin?" If my eyes could've shot darts, he would've felt them right between the eyes.

"Great. How are you?" He smelled like laundry detergent and Irish Spring soap.

I folded my arms across my chest, trying not to inhale. "You look a little worried. Something I did?"

Justin looked at me and walked inside. His Adam's apple moved up and down. He put a hand on the doorknob. "Okay, Scarlett, maybe it'd be better if I came back later."

I leaned against the door until it shut. "So you're worried I've made a new friend?"

He folded his arms across the front of his *Ender's Game* T-shirt and looked down at me from his six-foot-two-inch height. "I'm glad you've made a friend. It's this whole makeover obsession you've got going." I could hear his Southern accent coming through. That's what happened when he got nervous.

I could always be myself around Justin in a way I couldn't with other people. I knew I couldn't offend him by getting angry. I was comfortable with him—he was like an old pair of jeans I couldn't bear to throw away or like a cushy pair of sneakers. "So you're worried about Harri?"

"A little."

I put a hand on my hip. "Harri's totally fine with the makeover. She's happy. You can ask her yourself. She'll be here tonight."

Justin dug his hands into his pockets. "Correct me if I'm wrong, but isn't a coach supposed to help people achieve goals they set for themselves?"

"That's right."

"It seems like you're the one setting the goals."

I shook my head. "Nope, they're all Harri's goals."

Justin chuckled. "I don't see it. Harri's not the type to have those kinds of goals."

"Maybe you've underestimated her."

Tanya came to the top of the stairs, her face red. "Emma, I thought we agreed you wouldn't mention—"

Justin held a hand up to stop Tanya. "It's okay, Tanya." He turned back to me. "I shouldn't have gone behind your back, Emma. I'm sorry."

"I don't see why you're so worried," I said. "Harri needs someone to help her. She's lonely and homesick. All I'm trying to do is get her social life going. Why is that so bad? I'm serving my fellowman—or woman."

He scratched his neck. "I know you want to help Harri. It's just that you have such a strong personality. Watching you with Harri makes me wonder whether she's become your friend or your follower. That's all."

I didn't know what to say. I'd never thought about my friendship with Harri that way. I just wanted her to be happy.

Justin twisted the doorknob. "It's only a hunch. I could be wrong. Tanya thinks I'm wrong . . . Listen, I'll be back later. You two have a lot of catching up to do."

Tanya leaned over the banister. "Want some curry shrimp panang, Justin?"

He patted his flat stomach. "I don't know. I'm watching my weight." He was kidding, of course. The guy had the appetite of a thirteen-year-old.

Tanya laughed. "Thai food is good for the metabolism. All those spicy peppers rev it up."

Justin took the stairs two at a time. "In that case, I'll have a glass of Tabasco on the side and a box of ice cream."

Phil was next to show up. He found me arranging Tanya's brownies on our long dining table. I was still trying to calm myself after hearing what Justin thought. I looked up when Phil placed his offering, a cylinder of Pringles, beside the brownies. "Oh, hi, Phil."

Phil took a step toward me. "Hi. I've worked a lot on the video. It looks great. Has anyone ever told you you're really photogenic?"

I took a step back. "I don't think so. How does Harri look?"

He leaned toward me. "Fantastic. That hair really looks professional. It'll impress her family. I wanted to ask you—would it be okay if I saved a copy of the video for myself? For my portfolio."

"For your portfolio? Sure you don't have any ulterior motives?" I teased.

I detected a hint of red on his neck and cheeks. "Well, maybe."

"Why don't you ask Harri? I don't think she'll mind. I wouldn't." The doorbell rang. "That's probably her now. Could you get it for me?"

"Sure."

Phil answered the door to find a neighborhood kid hawking cookie dough for a school fund-raiser. Harri didn't come until halfway through Phil's lesson on bad habits. He told a story from the scriptures about some people who buried their weapons to show they'd repented for their past violence. The point of the lesson was that anyone could get over a bad habit as long as they decided they were going to give it up forever.

We were supposed to write down our bad habits on pieces of paper, but instead of burying them, Phil thought it would be easier to burn them in the fireplace. He built a fire while the rest of us sat on the couch and decided what to write. I whispered to Justin, who sat beside me, "You ought to know a few things I could give up. What do you think I should start with?" I was testing him, trying to see if he still considered himself an expert on my flaws.

He whispered back, "I think it's supposed to be your own personal decision. Got any ideas for me?"

"We could both give up meddling in other people's business, but that wouldn't be any fun."

He raised an eyebrow. "I'm sure you and I have plenty of other bad habits to choose from." He scrawled something on his paper.

I snuck a look at what he'd written, but it was in Japanese—at least I thought it was Japanese. That was his mission language. "Are you going to tell me what that says?" I asked.

He folded his paper. "Nope."

I made a mental list of my bad habits: calling the dentist Dr. Mezzodork behind his back instead of his real name, Dr. Metzdorf; rolling through stop signs; waking up late; forgetting to say my morning prayers; not finishing things . . .

Phil stood back to admire a few flames dancing in the fireplace. "Time's up."

I was forced to come to a decision. I wrote down "lying about my hair color." I could call it auburn all I wanted, but it was still red.

Justin stifled a chuckle.

I squinted. "If reading other people's personal stuff is your bad habit, you're already in trouble."

He nodded. "Good thing that's not the one I picked."

Justin wadded his bad habit up and threw it to the middle of the fire, where the flames quickly consumed it. I tried the same, but my paper landed off to the side. It slowly smoldered, leaving the words *lying about* darkened and emphasized. Phil leaned much closer to the fireplace than I thought was necessary, tossed his folded paper into the flames, and then turned to tease me with a "tsk, tsk, tsk." I was sure he'd read the word *lying* on my piece of paper.

Should I have clarified that my habit wasn't as bad as it looked? Before I could decide, Justin grabbed my paper with the fireplace tongs and put it on top of the flames. Phew!

"Thanks for the save," I whispered, allowing some of my anger to melt away.

"No problem."

Phil looked at Harri, waiting for her to throw in her paper. "I still haven't thought of a bad habit," she said.

Phil drummed his fingers on the mantelpiece while Justin chuckled. "It's not a big deal," Justin told her. "Don't stress about it."

Harri looked at the piece of paper in her hand. "So it's okay if I don't write anything? Because I lost fifty pounds before I came out here, and it's really hard, now that I've lost the weight, to stick to my eating plan." No wonder all of Harri's clothes were so baggy and she paid so much attention to serving sizes. It was more and more obvious she didn't have the ideal background I thought she did.

Harri fiddled with her phone. "I didn't say anything about it before because I was always a fat girl growing up and I didn't want you guys to think of me that way."

Stealing a tip from *Introduction to Life Coaching*, I said, "You shouldn't call yourself fat. Even if you were still overweight, I'd hate to hear you talk about yourself that way."

Justin put his hand out to give Harri a fist bump. "That's great, Harri. It takes a lot of willpower to lose weight. I'm proud of you."

"Me too," I said.

"Yeah," Phil said, replacing the screen on the fireplace, "that must have been a lot of work."

We moved to the kitchen table for Justin's activity. He'd brought the card game Pit again. What was it with guys and card games? Justin and Phil had kept score since they'd started playing Pit together the year before. Now Phil had around 8500 points while Justin only had around 8000 points. Justin was trying his best to even the score. "Do you know how to play Pit, Harri?" I asked, making sure she got the seat next to Phil.

Harri looked up from texting on her phone. "Yeah, I love Pit." It was a good thing since we played Pit every time it was Justin's turn to pick the activity.

I shuffled the cards—nine cards each of Barley, Corn, Sugar, and Wheat. Then I dealt the cards evenly among the four of us. Phil rang the bell and started out, calling, "Three!"

We each called out the number of cards we wanted to trade, swapping cards when we found someone else willing to trade the same number. Before long, I noticed Harri had her cards face down on the table. She was still texting. I leaned over to her. "Are you going to play?" I whispered.

She whispered back. "I told Rob I couldn't go to the dance, but he asked me out again for this Friday. What should I do?"

I shrugged my shoulders. "You already decided you don't want to go out with him, right?"

"Right," Harri said, looking down at her phone. "So you think I should tell him I have other plans?" I took a quick peek at the other side of the table, where Phil happened to have his eyes on us. Did he hear? I hoped so.

"I think Phil wants you to have other plans," I whispered. "Why don't you finish texting later? We're all waiting for you to play."

Harri giggled and picked up her cards. "Oh, sorry."

How Harri managed to win the game after barely participating, I'll never know. We played five more rounds. She won three of them, and I won the other two, throwing off the whole balance of Justin and Phil's struggle for Pit domination. Justin and Phil wore fake smiles as Phil tallied up the results of the day. The male ego was a fragile thing. Luckily, it could usually be repaired with a generous serving of homemade brownies.

Phil put down his pencil. "Can I get you ladies something to eat?"

Harri giggled—no doubt because he called us *ladies*. "Sure, Phil. That'd be sweet."

"No, thanks," I said.

Phil returned with a brownie and a stack of Pringles for Harri along with a plate of brownies for himself. "You sure you don't want anything, Emma? Pringles are the fakest food I know. It'd make a great virtual snack." What he didn't know was that, for most women, chocolate always trumps fake.

Justin came back with five brownies. Tanya's brownies were his favorite. When he found Phil in his place, he scooted the remaining chair over to sit beside Harri. "Virtual snack?"

Phil leaned back. "You'll have to ask Emma."

I looked at Justin and shrugged as if I had no idea what Phil meant. "Don't you guys think Phil did a great job on the lesson?" I nudged Harri under the table.

Harri swallowed the food in her mouth. "It *was* a great lesson."

Phil slid a plateful of Pringles toward us. "I have an idea for our next activity," he said. "You know how Jena's coming to visit for a few weeks? She wants to teach us some line dancing while she's here. I was thinking we could ask Tanya and Randall if we could use their basement."

Harri's eyes widened. "Line dancing? That'd be so much fun."

Justin grinned. "That *would* be fun."

I stared Justin down. "Does that mean you're going to dance?" I'd never seen Justin dance, except when he was swinging our nieces around.

Justin laughed. "No. I thought it would be fun to watch everyone else."

I grabbed a brownie off his plate and imagined him teasing me about my line-dancing technique. "You would."

"I know a few line dances," Phil said.

Harri counted through the Pringles on her plate. "For real? You can line dance? Sweet! I love line dancing."

Phil circled his pointer finger in the air. "We should make a date of it—the four of us line dancing. What do you think, Emma?"

I faked a smile. "I'd love to." If I had to go line dancing to get Phil and Harri together, I was all for it. I'd be the facilitator. It would only be a matter of time before Cupid shuffled into their hearts and they realized how much they liked their privacy.

Chapter 6

Coach's Tip of the Day:
A gingerbread man is no substitute for a real man.

We didn't plan the Christmas party because Hank Weston was coming to town. Yes, I admit, it was an incentive, a kind of welcome party. But we probably would have planned a Christmas party anyway—a simple get-together at Tanya's house with hot cider and caroling. Then Hank cancelled—again. He had to visit his mother, so he wasn't coming after all. It seemed like it was always about his mother.

Hearing Hank wasn't coming made me feel like my Christmas was over and done with. What else was there to hope for? If I knew anything about myself, I knew I needed to have something to look forward to. The only thing on the horizon was a welcome party for Jena Farley. I shifted my focus to baking cookies, finding decorations, and planning out how to get Harri and Phil together at the party.

Justin and I spent the afternoon in my tiny 1990s-style kitchen. As I stood at the round kitchen table, rolling out gingerbread dough with all my strength, I vented. "Poor Hank Weston! Can you imagine having a mother who controls your life like that? She never lets him visit Randall. I think it's better not to have a mother at all than to have one like her, even if she is rich."

The kitchen timer rang, and Justin opened the oven to retrieve a pan of golden-brown gingerbread men. They smelled so good, and I'd promised myself I could eat a couple at the party. Justin set the pan down on top of the stove and grabbed a spatula, which he pointed at me. "Come on, Emma. He's twenty-four. Do you really think a twenty-four-year-old man would let his mother control his life that much? It's an excuse. If he wanted to come out here, he'd come."

I flopped my little uncooked man onto a cool cookie sheet. "I can't imagine how hard it must be to have an abusive parent."

Justin scraped a baked gingerbread man off onto a cooling rack. "You, of all people, would have trouble relating to that, Miss Scarlett."

It was hard not to point out that Justin couldn't relate either. His mom was one of those sweet Southern ladies who barely spoke above a whisper. While she was alive, she bragged about Justin to friends, family, and grocery store clerks. I grabbed the cookie sheet full of uncooked gingerbread men and stuck it in the oven. "You probably think *I'm* a control freak."

Justin took a deep breath. "Not exactly. I think I was wrong about you and Harri. Whatever you're doing is working. I have a friend who wants to ask her out."

"I think I know who you're talking about." I leaned against the counter, next to the cooling rack. I was not going to eat any of those cookies. They were for later.

"I had to convince him she isn't too young for him. He's twenty-five."

That was no surprise. Thanks to the personal ad, I already knew Phil was twenty-five. I had no idea Phil and Justin ever worked together, but that was another tidbit I could use in Harri's favor. "I don't think that matters," I replied. "Harri's mature."

Justin rinsed off the cookie sheet. "That's what I told Rob."

I froze. "Rob?" He wasn't talking about Phil Elton. He was talking about Rob Martinez, the same guy Harri turned down for the New Year's dance and two dates. Last night, she'd told him she just wanted to be friends. I grabbed a gingerbread man and bit off its head.

Justin found a kitchen towel to dry the cookie sheet. "Yeah, Rob Martinez. He's the one you were thinking of, right? He's studying mechanical engineering over at George Mason, so he doesn't have a lot of time to date. I think he has one more semester before he graduates."

I broke an arm off the gingerbread man. "I didn't know Rob was in school."

"Yeah," Justin said, "I wouldn't have brought it up except the last few times he's called her, she said she was busy. I told him to keep trying, that she's a little shy and not to worry about it. Maybe you could talk to her—tell her to make room in her schedule."

This was not good. Before I knew it, I'd eaten the whole gingerbread man and grabbed another. "I wish you'd asked me about this before you talked to Rob. It might have spared his feelings."

Justin stared at me while I bit off the gingerbread man's head, chewed it, and swallowed. He closed one eye as if he were about to look at me through a pirate's telescope.

"Harri isn't all that interested in Rob," I said, and then I ate another arm and leg while he continued to stare at me.

"Are you sure that's how *Harri* feels?" he asked.

I couldn't talk until I'd swallowed the rest of the gingerbread man. It was a good excuse to explore my thoughts. Of course it was how Harri felt. It was her decision. I'd barely even shared my opinion. I looked at the gingerbread men on the cooling rack. "How many of these things have I eaten?"

Justin rubbed the side of his cheek with his hand. "Three."

"Are you sure it wasn't two? I thought it was two."

"Emma, my friend's feelings are at stake here."

I counted the cookies on the cooling rack—there were nine out of twelve left. "Have you eaten any of these?"

"No."

"So, I guess I did eat three."

Justin groaned and covered his face with both hands. "You can be so infuriating sometimes." There was no teasing in his voice at all.

I took another cookie—I figured I might as well since I'd already messed up. "I'm really sorry, but I can't help it if Harri's not attracted to Rob."

He grabbed a ball of dough to roll out on the table. "She seemed to like him enough before she met you. Rob's a great guy. He's considerate and honest. He's good with people. I haven't found a job he can't handle. He can read a blueprint, operate heavy machinery, install trim, and work with electricity."

I finished chewing the last of gingerbread man number four. "If I wanted to hire him, that'd be great, but we're talking about romance—there has to be chemistry. Harri's very attractive. I'm not surprised that Rob likes her. But it can't be all one-sided. She has to like him back."

Justin pushed the rolling pin over the dough a few times. "There's nothing worse than a woman who's conceited about her looks."

"Are you saying Harri's conceited?"

He went back to rolling out the dough. "No, but she will be if she keeps listening to you." His circle of dough had grown so thin, it was transparent along the edges. He was mad all right.

I rearranged the gingerbread men in two rows of four each. "Harri never meant to hurt his feelings."

A muscle in Justin's jaw twitched. "Harri never meant to, but *you* did—you and your matchmaking or coaching or whatever you call it. Are you still trying to set Harri up with Phil because you think he wrote that personal ad?" I didn't answer, so Justin kept talking. "I might as well tell you he's not interested." He stopped and cradled the rolling pin in his hands while he stared at the circle of dough on the table.

Now probably wasn't the right time to mention that Phil dropped off something that looked like a dance invitation for Harri that morning—a cellophane bag of fortune cookies. I sighed. "If you want, I can find someone else for Rob. I know a couple of girls that would be perfect for him."

He clenched his teeth. "Emma, I know you mean well, but I think you've done enough damage for now." He set down the rolling pin. "I'm sure you can finish these on your own." Without washing the flour off his hands, he grabbed his coat and left. He didn't slam the door, but something told me it was hard for him not to.

When I reached for the rolling pin, I realized there was another cookie in my hand—my fifth—and it was half eaten. My stomach felt heavy, as if I'd swallowed a five-pound bag of flour. How could I have eaten so many cookies without thinking? There was nothing I hated more than being too full, yet I still wanted to eat the other half of my fifth cookie.

I wished I were more like Justin—so self-assured and confident in his decisions. For me, things weren't always so black and white. Life had a lot of gray areas and so many different options. As I gathered up the dough into a ball and rolled it out again, I remembered Harri was supposed to come over a half hour ago. Where was she?

Dad wandered into the kitchen to grab a plate of cookies. He usually avoided anything that contained refined sugar or hydrogenated oils, but he was all for eating gingerbread men. It was my mom's recipe. "Are you sure you don't want to come to the party tonight?" I asked. "It's going to be a lot of fun."

Dad shook his head. "I'd rather not risk it. We've seen too many cases of the flu lately. I wish you wouldn't go either. The weather channel's predicting freezing rain."

My phone buzzed. It was Harri. "You'll never guess who I called this morning," she squealed.

"Phil?"

"How did you know? I talked to him for a long time—at least a half hour. He asked if we're going to the New Year's dance. He wanted to know if we already had dates. That's good, isn't it?"

"It's about time!" Phil was so shy about talking to Harri that he'd called me up twice in the last week to talk about another video he wanted to shoot of her.

"I'm so into him," Harri said. "I think about him all the time. And I think he's into me too. I told him I couldn't come tonight, and you know what he said? He said he's going to miss me."

"That's good. I mean, it's good he'll miss you, but why aren't you coming?"

She groaned. "Didn't you get my text? I got strep throat from Avery. I feel fine, but the doctor says I have to stay home for twenty-four hours. So I can't go to the party."

"That's terrible!" I exclaimed. "It won't be the same without you." Three strikes and I was out. Hank had cancelled, Justin was mad, and Harri couldn't come.

Harri sighed. "Yeah. I was looking forward to the party. Phil says he's still coming to pick you up."

Now my choices were either to go to the party or sit at home with a bunch of gingerbread men staring at me. "Speaking of Phil," I said, "he brought something by for you—it's fortune cookies. Get it?" I waited, but Harri didn't answer. "Remember how you were the fortune teller in our video?"

"How could I forget? But why would he bring them to your house? He knows where I live."

"I don't know. Maybe because you're over here a lot." I reached for the cellophane bag of cookies. "The label says, 'To a mysterious woman.' I'll bet he put a message inside the cookies. Should I bring them to you?"

"No way. I can't wait that long. Open them up and read what it says."

I pulled open the bag and broke a cookie in half. "What is it about you that guys want to send you cookies? Okay, this one says, 'Every Man Must Adore you. And I adore you too.'"

"Every man must adore you?" Harri repeated. "That doesn't sound like me."

"Of course it does. I wish you could see yourself the way I see you. You're beautiful, healthy, and full of energy." I cracked open the second cookie and read, "'You phill men's hearts with Cupid's darts. Give me relief. Be my date on New Year's Eve.'"

Harri squealed. "Oh, that's so epic. I can't wait to go to the dance with him."

I cracked open number three. "There's one more. This one says, 'If you agree to be my date, I'll have something to celibate.' I think he meant celebrate."

"Aww, that's sweet."

It was sweet. I couldn't wait to see the two of them all dressed up for the dance. "We'll have to think up a way to answer him. He's expecting a reply that's as exciting as you are. I'll help you think of something tomorrow."

Chapter 7

Coach's Tip of the Day:
Never line dance with a partner.

After I finished baking the gingerbread men, I had fifteen minutes to dress for the party. Back when I'd thought Hank Weston would be there, I'd picked out a gold sweater, a chocolate-brown pencil skirt, and my favorite gold flats. Since Hank wasn't coming any more, I swapped the pencil skirt for straight-leg pants. I also swapped the long, curly hairstyle for a chignon with a few wispy curls on top. No need for me to get too fancy when it was the same old crowd.

I slapped on a pair of chandelier earrings as I answered the door to see Phil, wearing cowboy boots that raised his height by at least two inches. His cologne was overpowering—some musky scent I was used to smelling on middle-aged men. I handed him a box of snowman decorations. "Thanks for picking me up. I'm sorry Harri couldn't come." I grabbed the plate of cookies and shut the door behind us.

Phil opened his trunk to put in my decorations. "That's too bad she got strep. I hear it's going around. She was smart to go to the doctor and get tested."

In the car, I tried another angle. "Maybe we could drop by after the party to take Harri a plate of treats."

Phil grimaced. "As long as we don't stay too long. Strep throat is pretty contagious."

This germaphobic side of Phil was something I'd never noticed before. "I can go by myself if you want. You could write Harri a note."

The first person we saw when we arrived at the Westons' was a guy who stood across the street, holding a big camera. He wore a baggy parka and stared at us. "Barbara told me about him," Phil said. "He sells pictures of Jena to the tabloids."

Tanya and Randall lived in a big brick two-story that sat kitty-corner to the street with the garage door facing us. The long, asphalt driveway was murder when there was ice because it went downhill. Dad's prediction about the ice storm was wrong, though, so there wasn't any ice. But Phil held onto my elbow anyway as we walked down the driveway, each of us holding a plate of cookies. "I'm fine, Phil," I protested. "It's only sprinkling a little. There's no way I'll fall." But he kept holding on—the perfect gentleman. It was too bad Harri wasn't there to be the lady. He finally let go when we stepped onto level ground.

Out of habit, I walked around past the garage toward the back door. That was the way Tanya and I had always come in before she and Randall got married. It had been a good strategy to give Tanya a look at that kitchen—Randall's kitchen was the envy of every woman who saw it. It was big and sunny—twice the size of ours—with cream-colored cabinets and a big island in the center with an extra sink. Today, it was empty except for Jena Farley, who was sitting at the breakfast nook. She waved her phone at us. "Oh, hey, Emma. How's it going?"

I deposited my plate of gingerbread men on the kitchen island and walked toward her to give her a hug. "Hi, Jena. You look great." No one could deny Jena Farley was beautiful with her dark coloring. She wasn't simply dark. She was shiny dark with glowing skin, sleek chestnut hair, and gleaming dark-brown eyes. She was at least seven inches shorter than I was and looked great in her jeans and T-shirt. Wouldn't it have been nice to be that small? "Congratulations on your album," I said. "I hear it's doing well."

Jena shook her hair out of her face. "Thanks." She held a hand out to Phil. "And it's Phil, isn't it? Nice to see you again. Y'all ready for some line dancing?"

I folded my arms. "If you mean the Cupid Shuffle or the Cha Cha Slide, I'm ready. If you mean something else, there might be trouble."

Jena waved her hand like she was swatting a fly. "Don't worry. I tested the dances out on Mom to make sure they're all beginner level. You won't have any trouble."

Phil went back out to the car to bring in the snowman decorations, forcing me to think of something else to say to Jena. I was all for having a conversation, but most of these conversations ended with me feeling even more distant from her. Talking with her was like trying to open a tightly screwed jar. Sometimes it was impossible to get to what was inside. "How's the weather in Nashville?" I asked. "It must be warmer down there."

Jena typed into her phone. "A little."

Was it rude to walk away and find the others? Or maybe it was rude to stand there talking while she texted. I had to wait for Phil to bring in the decorations anyway, so I stayed. When Jena looked at me, I tried again. "So they don't get much snow in Tennessee, do they?"

"No, just a little." She paused to type something else into her phone. "Sorry. I had a little business to take care of. I'm done now." She slid her phone into her pocket.

"You don't happen to know Randall's son, Hank Weston, do you? I think he goes to school in Nashville."

"Yeah," Jena said. "I know Hank. We're in the same ward."

"Really? I'm all hyped up to meet him. What's he like?"

Jena examined her manicure. "He's . . . well . . . hmm . . . I guess most people would say he's a genuine person."

A genuine person? What kind of description was that? I dug a little deeper. "So he's outgoing?"

Jena watched as Phil came through the door with the decorations. "Sure. He has a reputation for being friendly."

Phil set the decorations on the kitchen island. "Who has a reputation for being friendly?"

"Hank Weston," I answered.

Randall walked into the kitchen, carrying a speaker from his stereo. "Where's your friend Harri?" Randall was the kind of guy who'd been popular and good-looking in high school. Since then, he'd put on a little weight and grown a mustache, so he had kind of a middle-aged cop vibe about him. He was perfect for Tanya—the sort of dependable husband a thirty-nine-year-old woman would want.

I opened the basement door for Randall. "Harri's sick. She's sorry she couldn't make it."

"That's too bad. We'll miss her." Randall stepped through the door. "I've been meaning to talk to her about getting her church records moved to the ward, but I don't have her number." Randall had just become a brand-new member of the bishopric and was anxious to magnify his calling.

"I'll have her call you," I said.

He descended the stairs. "Thanks, Emma."

Jena looked at her watch. "We should get going with line dancing. Once Randall has that speaker hooked up, we'll be good to go."

An hour later, I stood in the unfinished basement, having learned the Booty Dance and the Cleveland Shuffle. The upside was I was burning calories. (Think five gingerbread men.) The downside was I'd been upstaged by Barbara, Jena, Randall, Tanya, and Phil. Justin still hadn't shown his face.

The booty dance didn't seem hard at first. It was a few steps to the right, a few steps to the left, a few steps back, a jump and four stomps. Of course, that's what it looked like when Jena showed it to me the first time. Then she threw in some turns and I was all mixed up like a blindfolded child trying to hit a piñata. Even after they put me in the middle so someone was always in front of me, I either messed up the feet or faced the wrong direction.

In the break between songs, Phil informed us that he'd been on the BYU folk dance team and would help me out. During the next run through, Phil held my hand to help me through the steps. When that didn't work, he stood behind me with his hands at my waist so he could tell me the cues. I could feel his chest brush against my shoulder blades. I'd always thought the whole point of line dancing was not having a partner.

Of course, this was when Justin showed up. He grabbed a folding chair and sat on it backward with his legs spread and his folded arms resting on the back of the chair. I could tell he was trying hard to keep a serious expression on his face. Watching him struggle not to laugh made me crack a smile for the first time since we'd started the whole line-dancing ordeal. I started to laugh, which made me mess up so much that all I could do was stand there laughing. Justin excused himself and headed up the stairs.

"What's so funny?" Phil asked. The cologne he wore was starting to give me a headache.

I pried Phil's hands off my waist and followed Justin up the stairs. "Nothing. I have to get a drink of water."

Justin leaned against the counter in the kitchen. "I guess I should apologize to you for earlier. I was wrong about you and Phil. I had no idea."

Catching a whiff of Irish Spring, I poured water into my glass and raised it to my lips before I realized what Justin meant. He thought I was after Phil. I lowered the glass. "What do you mean? You think I have a thing for Phil?"

He put his hands in his pockets. "It sure looks that way to me. He definitely has a thing for you."

I took a drink and shook my head. "No, you've got it all wrong."

Justin squinted at me. "Does this have something to do with your anti-marriage vow?"

"I don't have an anti-marriage vow," I said. "Phil wouldn't be interested in me. I'm too—"

Phil came into the room before I could say *tall*. "You've almost got it, Emma. Don't give up now. You're so close." The way he talked without opening his mouth was so distracting.

I took another swig of my water. "Thanks for your help, but I'm all booty danced out for today."

Phil found himself a glass and filled it up. "Okay, well, I'll do whatever you want."

Justin suppressed a smile as Phil put his free arm around my shoulders and squeezed. All the endorphins from line dancing must have impaired his judgment. I took a step away from him. "Don't stop dancing for my sake, Phil. I'm happy to watch from the sidelines for a while."

Phil closed the space between us. "No, Emma, that's okay. If you don't want to dance, I'd rather do something else too." My eyes lingered on his lips. How could he talk so well without opening his mouth wider?

I clasped my hands around my water glass and raised it to my forehead. What if Justin was right about Phil being attracted to me? He couldn't be right.

Justin cleared his throat. Sometimes he did that when he was trying not to laugh. "Well, I'll let you two hash this out. I'm gonna go see what's going on downstairs."

This could not be happening. I couldn't be left alone in the room with Phil. "I'll come with you." I gulped down the rest of my water and followed Justin to the top of the basement stairs, only to find that everyone else was on their way up.

Randall called out instructions for everyone to head into the living room, then he grabbed my arm. "Emma, can you help me get everyone water? It'll give us a chance to talk. I just got some big news." I pivoted toward the kitchen with much more enthusiasm than I'd shown while line dancing.

"Great." Big news was what I needed to derail my negative thoughts about Phil.

I followed Randall to the sink and so did Phil. As Randall arranged a cheese platter, he started in on his big news. "Hank just found out he has an internship with a software company in DC."

Phil wasn't at all fazed by the news. "Where do you keep the water glasses?" he asked. Randall opened a cabinet for Phil.

"Does that mean he's coming after all?" I asked, filling glasses with ice.

Randall returned to the cheese platter. "That's what it means. He'll stay here with us for the semester. It's a sure thing now. Even if he doesn't like the internship, I told him he could work for me."

"Selling sports equipment?" I asked. Randall owned three sporting goods stores.

"I thought he could help with our computers," Randall said.

I had so many questions to ask, but Phil pushed two glasses of water into my hands. "We better hand these out. The troops are thirsty."

In the living room, which was still decorated in Randall's bachelor style—complete with black leather sofas and recliners—Jena talked about Danny, the guy we'd seen outside who followed her around to take pictures. "You all will get to know him, I'm sure. He tries to interview all my friends—even people who've only met me once. He's friendly, so he seems innocent enough. But he wants to get some dirt on me. That's how he earns his living."

Phil leaned toward me. "You have a seat. I'll get the rest of the water."

The good part about obeying Phil was I could choose my own seat—I plopped down on the black leather sofa between Jena and Justin, leaving no room for Phil. "So," I said. "It must be annoying to have that guy follow you around everywhere."

Jena sighed. "It's one of the trade-offs. It's good for publicity, but I have to keep my private life very private."

"Like your dating life?" I asked.

Jena rubbed her finger around the edge of her water glass. "Exactly. It can be stressful on a relationship." I waited for her to elaborate, but she didn't.

Justin leaned forward so he could see past me. "If you ever need a bouncer, let me know." Had Justin really said that? He had. And he was serious. An image of him in a muscle shirt—which he would never actually wear—popped into my head.

Jena swirled the ice cubes around in her glass. "Thanks, Justin, but I don't think it'll come to that."

My phone buzzed with a text from Dad. "Freezing rain." He wanted me to come home. If I'd been anyone else's daughter, it wouldn't have been an issue, but my mom had died in a car accident on a snowy night.

I texted back, "OK. Love you." I'd go home . . . right after I heard the whole story about Hank and maybe a little more about the paparazzi.

"If he ever bothers me," Barbara said, "I'm not sure I'll handle him as well as Jena does. I might have to call you to help me, Justin.

I don't think I would make a good celebrity at all. I feel obligated to answer questions. I was raised to be very open."

Jena smiled at Barbara. "Mom, there's nothing to worry about. You don't have anything to hide."

Barbara put a hand to her chest. "Oh, but I would hate to say the wrong thing or to be misquoted. I can see that happening. You know I get too chatty sometimes."

"I'll be happy to deal with him," said Justin. "Not that you couldn't handle him yourself, Sister Bates. You're better at answering questions than you think you are."

Randall came in with his cheese platter. "That was your dad on the phone, Emma. He wants you to know there's a thin layer of ice on the roads."

Looking out the window, I couldn't see any shine on the sidewalk or driveway. It was raining a little, but nothing looked icy.

Tanya wrung her hands. "Do you remember the ice storm we had when you were little, Emma? Everything was coated with ice: every branch, every blade of grass, the cars, and the power lines. It was impossible to drive."

Phil shrugged. "I'm not worried. I lived in Utah for five years. A thin layer of ice is nothing. I could drive on a glacier if I needed to."

Tanya looked out the window. "Maybe you'd better go, Emma. I wouldn't want Barry to worry."

I leaned back in the sofa. "I can go home in Justin's truck if it gets really bad."

When Jena got up to take a phone call, Phil rushed to fill her seat, scooting up next to me.

Randall offered us the cheese platter. "The worst that could happen is you'd all have to spend the night here. That wouldn't be so bad."

Phil pulled the classic dating trick of pretending to stretch so he could put his arm across the back of my shoulders. "That sounds fun."

Tanya blinked a few times. "Of course, we would separate the men and women."

I stood up from the sofa. "Dad's probably already standing at the front window waiting for me. I'd better go." My decision wasn't so much about avoiding the ice storm as it was about avoiding Phil.

I couldn't sit there, encouraging him to keep his arm around me. I couldn't betray Harri like that. "Do you mind driving me home, Justin?"

Justin stood up. "Sure."

Phil stood too, jingling his keys. "She and I came together. I'll take her."

I thanked Randall and Tanya for having us, then I turned to Phil. "It's all right, Phil. I can go home with Justin. You should stay and enjoy the party."

Phil latched onto my arm. "Hey, I'm not about to let you go home with another guy."

My mouth hung open as he escorted me past the others and into the kitchen, where we retrieved my plates and decorations. It was almost as if he thought of me as his date. What would I say to Harri? What would I say to Phil?

Before we headed out the door, I gave it one more shot. "Phil, I'd really rather go home with Justin. I know how much you've looked forward to this party. If you leave now, you'll never learn that other line dance. What was it called again?"

Phil opened the door. "Don't be ridiculous. I came because I wanted to be with you."

I stepped out into the dark. "Not Harri?"

Phil followed me, his arms full of snowman decorations. "Didn't you read the message in those fortune cookies?"

I hugged the plates to my chest as we headed up the hill. "I thought they were for Harri." My dad was right about the freezing rain. There was enough ice on the driveway that we had to walk on the grass instead of the pavement.

"Why would I bring them to your house if they were for Harri? I put your name inside one of the cookies. Every Man Must Adore? It spells Emma."

At the top of the hill, I caught sight of Jena's tabloid photographer sitting in his old Ford Taurus with the window down. I decided it was best not to say anything until we were both inside Phil's car. Phil, on the other hand, didn't seem to mind having an audience. He plunged ahead with his confession. "I can't believe you thought I liked Harri."

"Careful, Phil," I whispered. "You don't want us to wind up on that guy's website, do you?"

Sure enough, the bald guy flashed a few pictures of us standing together as Phil scraped off his windshield. Once we were both inside with the engine running, I decided I'd better say something. "Phil." I let out my breath. "You're everything I look for in a man, but I care about you too much to let our relationship go any further. I'm not good enough for you. I have all sorts of problems. My mother died when I was six. I've got a lot of hang-ups from that. Plus, I have an overprotective father, and I'm a control freak."

I paused long enough for Phil to insert, "We can work through that."

"I never finish anything. I quit three-quarters of the way into dental hygienist training, one semester before I could become a paralegal, and a day into my course on phlebotomy. I've never read a book all the way through without skipping to the end. I have absolutely no patience."

Phil shifted the car into drive and headed up the hill toward home. "But, Emma, that's what I like about you. You're so spontaneous."

"Harri would be much better for you. Are you sure you're not at all attracted to her?"

Phil put his hand on mine. "Is this your way of playing hard to get?"

I pulled my hand away and scooted toward my door. "I don't think you'd be happy with me."

"Then why do you call me all the time? And why do you keep looking at my mouth like you want to kiss me?"

It was best not to answer either one of those questions, so I changed the subject. "You and Harri have so much in common. I really think you'd be great together."

He slammed on the brakes, which made the back tires fishtail on the icy road. "Are you telling me the whole reason we've spent so much time together is because you're trying to set me up with Harri?"

If I said no, I'd be lying. If I said yes, I might betray Harri's feelings. We sat in silence for a while. This would be a much longer car ride than I was banking on, considering he had the car in park. I cleared my throat. "I'm really sorry, Phil. I think you're a great guy. You're smart, good-looking, a great dancer—"

"But not good enough for you."

"It's not that. I just don't think I'm the right one for you." I tried to think of something, anything that would disqualify me as Phil's latest infatuation. "I haven't told you this, but I don't really like country music."

Phil jolted the car into drive again. "I can't believe this is happening after all I've done for you. That parking ticket alone was one hundred dollars."

His driving was starting to scare me. I had to say something to calm him down. "But I got that ticket voided."

"Nope. They sent a notice in the mail yesterday."

I dug my wallet out of my purse and placed three twenty-dollar bills on the dashboard. "Here's sixty. It's all I have right now. I'll get you the other forty later. Unless you take credit cards."

He didn't laugh. "I don't want your money, Emma." That was what he said, but he didn't object when I left the money on the dash. The bills were easy enough to see in the glow of the street lamps.

I looked through my wallet for some more cash, but all I could find was a coupon from the dentist's office. "I have a coupon for a complimentary tooth whitening if you want it. It's worth at least three hundred dollars."

Phil clenched his jaw. "First you try to set me up with a nanny who used to be obese, and now you tell me I need my teeth bleached."

"That's not what I meant. I just thought if you were going to do it anyway, I could save you three hundred dollars. Lots of people bleach their teeth. And how dare you call Harri obese!"

"What were you thinking?" He slipped into a high-pitched imitation of my voice. "A girl with a tattoo who just lost fifty pounds—sounds like a perfect match for Phil."

There was no use telling him how much Harri regretted the tattoo. We rode in silence the rest of the way. Every second was painful, like having a tooth drilled without novocaine. I could not wait for it to be over. As soon as he stopped in front of my house, I pulled the door handle. "I'm sorry I misjudged the situation. I hope we can still be friends." I'd barely hopped out and shut the door when he drove off, ignoring the fact that my Christmas plates and decorations were in his trunk.

Knowing Phil, it wouldn't be long before he recovered. Within a few weeks, he'd find someone else and forget all about me. I didn't feel as confident that Harri would recover so well. However I broke this to her, it wasn't going to be good.

Chapter 8

Coach's Tip of the Day:
You don't need a degree to be a friend.

*H*arri unraveled before my eyes—in a way that made me wonder if I'd ever be able to repair the damage I'd caused. Mascara ran down her cheeks, and her nose dripped. Red splotches broke out around her eyes. "I knew it couldn't be true," she wailed. "I'm way too lame to date a guy like Phil. He's too perfect." She sat on the bed in her little basement bedroom while Avery slept in a portable crib outside the door. Usually, on Sunday, Avery would be upstairs with her parents, but the Coles were attending some sort of White House holiday luncheon.

Thanks to the ice storm, church was cancelled. It was a lucky break, considering we wouldn't have to see Phil. And if Phil skipped family home evening group, which was highly likely, Harri would have another week to get over him.

I wrapped my arms around her. "Nobody's perfect, Harri, especially not Phil."

"But he dresses so cool, and he has a real job. He's too good for me. I'm just a fat girl."

I handed her another tissue. "You're not a fat girl. You've lost fifty pounds, Harri. Your mind needs to catch up to that fact. Even if you hadn't lost the weight, you'd be beautiful. The more I get to know Phil, the more I think he's not right for you. You haven't seen this side of him yet, but he has a bad temper."

She blew her nose. "You're just trying to make me feel better."

"What you need is a real man—someone like Randall or Justin. Justin's always considerate. He may not always agree with everything I say, but he's always considerate of my feelings. That's the kind of man you should be looking for."

Harri threw her tissue into the wastebasket. "But Phil is considerate. Remember how he came to shovel Barbara's driveway the day I met him? That wasn't an act, Emma, and you know it. He's a hard-core nice guy."

I was so done with matchmaking. Of course, that new returned missionary I'd met the week before could've helped her get her mind off Phil. What was his name again? Oh, never mind. It was better not to do anything than to create another disaster like this one. If Harri was going to fall in love again, it was going to be her own idea, not mine.

Harri sobbed out, "I'll understand if you decide you want to go out with Phil. Don't let me stop you."

I patted her back. "That's sweet of you, Harri, but I'm on an extended vacation from relationships."

Harri rolled her eyes. "I don't understand you sometimes, Emma. Aren't you afraid you'll become an old maid?"

"Here's how I see it, Harri: it's better to be single than trapped in a bad marriage. I'm not saying I don't ever want to get married, but so far, I haven't met anyone I want to marry. I'm happy to be single for now."

Harri flopped backward on her bed. "You'll probably get married before I do—like everyone else in the world."

Since nothing I'd said seemed to be helping, I reached for the bag of Dove chocolates I'd put in my purse to take to the office. "What you need is chocolate." I opened the bag and held it out to Harri.

She scooted away. "No way. If I have one, I'll eat the whole bag. I have no self-control when I'm upset."

I let Harri cry it out for a few more minutes before I decided it was time to get our minds off this problem. After all, Christmas was a week away. It was bad enough she couldn't afford to go home for Christmas; I couldn't let her be depressed about Phil too. "Your hair looks beautiful," I told her.

She twisted a lock around her finger and brought it around in front of her face to check for split ends. "A lot of good it does to have great hair. The only people who're gonna see me today are you and Avery."

I stood up from the bed. "You need to get out of this house."

"I started the antibiotic twenty-four hours ago," Harri said, "so I can be around other people now. If I had a car and I didn't have to watch Avery, I'd drive over to the Martinezes' and return their dishes. They brought me dinner Friday night."

I dug around in my purse for my phone. "Do you think Karen will let us take Avery in my car?"

"I'll check." Harri said, grabbing her phone to ask permission.

I took Harri by the Martinezes' apartment. Avery and I stayed in my Civic with the engine running while Harri climbed the stairs to the second-floor balcony. Sister Martinez answered the door. She was a short woman, shorter than Harri, and she had to stand on tiptoes to give her a hug. When she gestured for Harri to come in, Harri showed her I was waiting in the car. Sister Martinez put her hand on Harri's forehead, and I guessed she was advising her to stay home out of the cold. Harri fiddled with the zipper on her coat as she responded. Then she twisted her hair around her finger, which made her look nervous.

Someone knocked on the passenger door window beside me. I turned to see Rob smiling at me through the glass. I opened the window, and he bent over to speak to me. "What are you doing over here, Emma? You're not having car trouble, are you?"

I pointed up at his apartment. "I brought Harri to return your dishes."

Rob looked up to where Harri stood. "Oh."

"It was sweet of you to bring her dinner," I said.

Rob smiled. "That was my mom's idea."

"Well, it was sweet of her. Harri really needed it."

Rob looked from me to the hood of my car. "So you don't need any help?"

"No, but thanks for offering."

We both watched as Harri descended the stairs. Rob gave her a quick nod as he held the passenger side door open for her. "I hope you feel better," he said.

Harri sat down. "You too." Obviously, she needed a little more coaching on conversational skills.

Rob shut the door. As I backed out of the parking spot, I told Harri how well she'd maintained her composure around Rob, but I had to admit to myself that Rob was really the one who'd maintained composure. Maybe I had underestimated him.

From there, we drove straight to Justin's house. Justin lived in a white rambler set on a woody hill so the main floor was level with the front yard and the basement was level with the back. It was the kind of house families have in sitcoms. I could hear Justin's two-year-old golden retriever, Buttercup, barking as we rang the doorbell. Justin answered, holding onto Buttercup's collar. "Come on in."

"How are you, Princess Buttercup?" I asked, bending down to rub the loose folds of fur on the dog's neck. I petted her head and velvety ears. Behind me, Avery panicked, crying for Harri to pick her up. "I'll take Buttercup to Justin's room," I said. Grabbing the dog's collar, I escorted her down the hall. She followed with her tail wagging, making me regret having to shut her up in the master bedroom. I could hear her whining as I walked back out to the living room.

From the looks of things inside Justin's house, you'd think his business was on the brink. His living room stood empty except for an old desk with a computer. There were no decorations, unless you counted the life-size cardboard model of R2-D2 leaning against the wall. The kitchen was the same way. The only furniture was a card table with four folding chairs. Before Justin's dad passed away, he'd handed over the family business—Knightley Remodeling—to his two sons. Justin ran the Northern Virginia branch while John and Isabella ran the original branch down in Richmond. From what Isabella told me, business was doing well. Justin stayed so busy fixing up other people's houses that he didn't have much time to fix his own.

"Did you just move in here?" Harri asked as she sat at the card table and looked through the cardboard box of toys Justin kept for our nieces. I wouldn't have known Avery was sick except she was still dressed in her pink footie pajamas. She ran in circles on the slippery floor.

"Nope," Justin answered as he pulled defrosted steaks out of the microwave. "I moved here five or six years ago." By my count, it was seven, but I didn't say anything.

Harri tilted her head with confusion. "And you've never bought a sofa?"

Justin opened a cabinet and pulled out vinegar and steak sauce to put in his marinade. "If I feel like sitting on a sofa, I go to Emma's house. That's the way I like it. I decided when I moved in that I might as well wait on the furniture. When I get married, I'll have to start all over with the decorating anyway."

This was the first I'd heard about Justin's decorating plan, but it jived with everything else I knew about him. I laughed. "It's much easier to furnish a house than it is to find a wife. You should let Harri and me help you with the living room at least. Who knows? Maybe having a nice living room will help you attract a wife . . . Not that you need any help with that."

Harri bounced in her chair. "That would be so fun. I'd love to help you decorate."

Justin wobbled his head from side to side. "Maybe. If you think you have time, which I kind of doubt since you haven't had time to help me decorate the Christmas tree I got two weeks ago. Now that Phil is going out of town, do you think you could squeeze me into your schedule?"

"Phil is going out of town?" Hallelujah! That was exactly what we needed. I tried not to look pleased.

Justin scratched his head. "You didn't know? He called me about it this morning. Wants me to watch his house while he's gone. He's going to the Big Apple for a couple weeks, a combination of business and pleasure. He leaves tomorrow. I can't believe he didn't tell you."

Harri squished her face up. "The Big Apple?"

Justin and I both answered, "New York City."

Harri sniffed and looked down at Avery. "Oh."

Before the tears spilled out onto Harri's cheeks again, I hopped out of my chair. "Why don't you bring the tree in, Justin? We can decorate it tonight. I'll finish up with the steaks." I was even willing to touch raw meat in order to distract Harri from any more thoughts of Phil. It was what I deserved.

As I washed my hands with Justin's bar of Irish Spring, he grabbed his coat off one of the folding chairs and headed outside to the back porch. "Is he for real about the decorating plan?" Harri asked. "He's waiting until he gets married?"

I dropped the steaks into a glass bowl. "If there's one thing about Justin you should know, it's this—he never says anything that isn't the truth." I thought of how he'd tried to warn me about Harri and Phil. "Sometimes it's hard to take, but at least you can trust him." We could hear Justin sawing off the bottom of the tree trunk on the back porch outside the kitchen door.

Harri lowered her voice a little. "That's so sweet he wants his wife to decorate the house. Kind of sad too. He's lived here a long time not to have furniture."

I opened a cabinet, searching for ingredients. "I can't imagine Justin ever getting married."

"Why not?" Harri asked. "He'd make a good husband and an even better dad. Avery loves him."

I poured some cooking oil over the steaks. "All kids love him. You should see him with our nieces. But I can't see him getting married. And I don't think he's trying either. Look at the way he dresses. He has plenty of money, but he wears old clothes and drives that stinky old truck. It's like he doesn't want women to be attracted to him."

Harri took a doll out of the box and handed it to Avery. "What about him and Jena Farley? They'd be cute together."

Justin swung open the door and dragged in the tree. "Where do you think I should put it this year?" As if it would be any different from the place we'd put it every year.

I sprinkled some spices into the marinade. "In front of the bay window. I was thinking we should use the Swedish ornaments."

Justin carried the huge Douglas fir across the kitchen, leaving a trail of needles in his wake. "Sounds good. How 'bout we go half-and-half? We'll put the Swedish ornaments up high so Buttercup can't eat them. The kids' ornaments can go down on the bottom half."

I followed Justin into the living room. "You're the one who has to look at it."

Harri helped Justin position the tree in the stand while I dug out the lights from the bottom of the ornament box. Avery stood with a thumb in her mouth, watching Justin turn the tree until it was right.

"Here, Avery," I called. "Help me check the lights."

Avery squealed as I plugged in the lights. She grabbed hold of the string and twirled until she was all wrapped up in them. "I a Kissmas tree."

Justin stopped fussing with the tree to look at Avery. "A pink Christmas tree. How about that?" He walked into the other room and came back with a bag of indestructible ornaments he kept for our nieces. He hung a fabric angel on one of Avery's ears, then a sequined star on her other ear.

Harri and I strung the lights around the tree while Justin started his playlist of country Christmas tunes. When he swung Avery around to the tune of "Grandma Got Run Over by a Reindeer," Harri warned, "Remember she's still getting over being sick." So Justin switched to "Blue Christmas" and rocked Avery in his arms while Harri and I fixed the lights. Though Justin wasn't much for dancing with adult women, he was pretty good with toddlers. When the Elvis song ended, he played Johnny Cash's "The Christmas Guest" and Faith Hill's "Silent Night." Maybe it was because of Avery that I didn't find the songs as annoying as I had last year.

Once we were done with the lights, Justin sat on the floor in front of the tree with Avery on his lap and let her pick ornaments out of his bag of indestructibles. I grabbed the shoebox full of Swedish ornaments and started on the top of the tree. They were made from straw and tied together with red thread to make different shapes. Harri helped me hang them. "I can tell this one's a star and this one's an angel," she said. "But what's this supposed to be? A reindeer?"

Justin answered, "It's a goat. The Swedes are big on straw goats at Christmas. Don't ask me why. My grandmother came from Sweden, and I guess that's why Mom loved these ornaments. I never liked them much when I was a kid, but now that Mom's gone, they've grown on me a little."

Harri hung a straw snowflake. "I think they're pretty. You must miss your mom."

Justin helped Avery hang a little mouse holding a wreath. A typical man, he didn't want to talk about his feelings. His mom and dad had been gone for four years—his dad died from a brain tumor; his mom died a few months later from something the doctors called Broken Heart Syndrome. Before they died, starting when his dad was sick, Justin spent every weekend in Richmond. During the times I'd visited, I'd seen him doing jigsaw puzzles with his mom, mowing the lawn, shaving his dad's face, and figuring out the medical bills.

I grabbed a chair out of the kitchen so I could put the star on top of the tree. "At least Justin knew his mom enough to miss her. That's one thing about losing my mom when I was six. I can't remember a lot. All I know about her is what I can find in old boxes. Everything about her was perfect. She got good grades, won a bunch of tennis matches, earned her Young Womanhood medallion, and played Clair de Lune on the piano. It makes me feel like I'll never measure up. I know she loved me when I was six, but I'm not sure she'd be happy with me now."

While I put the star on top, Harri and Justin were way too focused on hanging ornaments to reply to my little rant about my mother. It was just as well. I shouldn't have said anything. What with Harri all sad about Phil and Justin sad about his mom, the last thing they needed was for me to feel sorry for myself. I picked up a little straw person. "This one's cute. I like his little red hat."

"Emma," Justin said, "don't you think if you put all the things you've accomplished in a box, you'd look as intimidating as your mom? Every woman's pretty intimidating when you only look at her accomplishments. I'm sure your mom's up in the spirit world smiling about all the good things you've done. She's proud of you. You just don't know it."

I hung the little straw man and knelt next to the box while I picked up a braided straw heart. "That's the thing. I'm not sure Mom would be proud of me. By the time she was my age, she'd finished her master's degree in art history. I haven't finished anything except high school."

Justin, still sitting with Avery in his lap, swiveled to face me.

"You've probably taken enough credits at the community college for an associate's degree. Haven't you finished most of your generals?" He was so close to me, I could smell his laundry detergent, an undertone to the fresh pine scent from the tree.

I twirled the heart ornament around in my hand. "I have a lot of my generals done, but what good does that do?" I stood and hung the heart on a branch.

Justin watched Avery take the mouse ornament off the tree. "It makes a difference to show you've gone to college, even if you haven't finished. Employers like to see you're smart and that you can follow through."

"But I don't follow through," I said. "If I did, I would have a degree by now. That's where my mom and I are totally different. She finished things. I don't."

Justin put his hand on my foot. "What I meant is you can follow through to finish a class and get a good grade in it. I wasn't talking about degrees."

While Avery took another few ornaments off the tree, Harri wrapped her arms around me. "You don't need a degree to be the most awesome friend in the world. You already know how to do that." Sure, I could be a good friend, but when it came to life coaching, I hadn't helped Harri at all.

I watched Avery strip ornaments off the tree while I thought of how I'd spent the last four years bouncing around between careers and attending the community college instead of a university. The year I graduated from high school, Isabella got married and moved to Richmond. Dad took it hard. So I stayed with him instead of going off to school. Not being a full-time student, though, I'd taken too many detours. I'd procrastinated choosing a major or a career because I didn't want to commit the rest of my life to something I didn't love. But if I kept procrastinating, I would always be a receptionist, which wasn't anything close to the career I wanted. "I wish it were easier to figure out what I want to do with my life," I said.

Justin put a couple ornaments back on the tree. "I thought you were going to be a life coach."

I pulled a fir branch through my fingers. "I don't know if I'm as good at life coaching as I thought I'd be." All he had to do was look at Harri to know that was true. Her eyes were swollen and red from crying over Phil.

Justin sat still as Avery hung an ornament on his ear. "Nobody starts out knowing exactly what they want to do. When I was in high school, I wanted to be an orthodontist. I only ended up in construction because my dad needed me. When I first started out, I made a lot of mistakes, and I can't say I loved all the work, but I kept at it. Learning a career is like learning to play a musical instrument. People aren't born knowing how to play the guitar or how to be a life coach. There's no such thing as a perfect career. There's always something you don't like or something you don't do as well as you should."

Harri took a straw star out of the box. "I think your mom would say you're too hard on yourself, and she would say she's proud of you."

Justin laughed. "I think your mom would also say Tanya spoiled you, but you turned out okay anyway." I studied Justin's face to make sure he wasn't teasing. He wasn't. He meant it when he said I turned out okay.

I sat down and hugged my knees to my chest. "What if I keep going with life coaching and I'm so horrible at it that I mess people up? I might wish I'd stayed a receptionist."

Justin lifted Avery off his lap and handed her to Harri. "If you don't try, though, Emma, you'll always wonder who you could've helped. You've had a lot of experiences that qualify you to help people."

He was right about that. I was qualified to help someone who'd lost a mother, the one person whose love matters more than any other. Even though Dad and Tanya made sure I had everything I needed, I'd gone to grief counseling for years. I'd lived through sixteen Mother's Days, every time leaving a gift on Mom's grave. When my homemade coil pots and recipe card holders disappeared from her plot, I was smart enough to know they probably ended up in that dumpster behind the mortuary instead of in a drawer like other kids' presents.

Justin stood to get his laptop off his desk. "You're kind of a perfectionist. Maybe the reason you hate to finish things is because you're afraid everything won't turn out perfect."

I fingered the fir branch again. "But I never do anything perfectly."

Justin sat beside me, typing into his laptop. "No one does. But some people think if they try hard enough, they'll be able to do things perfectly. In your case, you think if you tried harder, you could be as perfect as your mother—or as perfect as you think your mother was."

I swallowed. "I guess you could be right."

"And, if it's so important for you to get a degree, there are plenty of options around here. You could get into George Mason or George Washington if you wanted to. Come look at this."

I stared at Justin's laptop screen while he brought up information about George Mason University. He pointed to a list of statistics from previous years. "You always get good grades, so you'd get in without any problem. Deadlines are coming up, though, if you want to get in for next fall."

I swallowed again. "I don't—"

Justin interrupted. "It's okay, Emma. That was a lot to spring on you—not that I planned to convince you to apply to colleges or anything." He'd slipped into his Southern accent again. "Why don't I put those steaks on the grill?"

I tried hard not to think of applying to colleges. But it was like trying not to scratch a bug bite. The more I told myself not to scratch, the itchier I felt. By the time I got home from our little barbecue-slash-tree-decorating party, the only thing that would soothe my itch was a good fifteen minutes sitting in front of my computer screen.

I logged onto the computer, thinking nothing could stop me from filling out an application. But I was wrong. There was one thing that trumped it all—a message from Tanya. Hank was coming to Vienna sooner than we'd thought. He planned to leave next Saturday.

Chapter 9

Coach's Tip of the Day:
If you want to meet the man of your dreams,
wear a sweatshirt in public.

This was it! I was finally going to meet Hank Weston. I'd already worked it all out. It was 653 miles from Nashville to Vienna, so—as long as he was a safe driver, which I was sure he was—it'd take him about fourteen and a half hours to arrive. He could come as early as that night, but I probably wouldn't see him until our Christmas Eve dinner the next day.

Still, you could never be too careful. I stepped up my hair and makeup routine. And I had to figure out what to wear for the dinner. Should I go formal or casual, high heels or flats?

What I needed was a guy—someone to give me honest advice—so when Justin knocked on the door early Saturday morning, I was happier than normal to see him. Besides his jacket, he wore his usual ensemble of T-shirt and jeans. Today's T-shirt featured a picture from *Dr. Who*. So he was a little fashion challenged? At least he was a man with opinions. I gave him a cheery, "Merry Christmas!"

He looked at me for a while, the corners of his mouth lifting a little. "Merry Christmas. What's with the big grin?"

"I'm happy to see you."

His smile faded as if he suspected a prank. "Well, I'm glad you're happy. What's up?"

I took the stairs two at a time. "Come sit down. I need your help."

I ran to my room and grabbed a selection of tops from my closet—a jean jacket, a soft green sweater, a gold wrap top, a teal tunic, and a ruffled rusty-orange cardigan. I brought them all out and draped them on the couch beside Justin. "I'm trying to decide what to wear for Christmas Eve. What do you think?"

Justin looked at the clothes. "Do you have any more of those gingerbread men?"

"I hid a few at the back of the freezer so I wouldn't eat more. But you've got to help me decide on some clothes. Hank Weston's going to be here, and I want to make a good first impression."

Justin went to the kitchen and opened the freezer. "Let me get a few cookies first." He brought the entire container of frozen gingerbread men out to the sofa and set them on his lap. "So you're after Hank Weston."

I shrugged. "I wouldn't say I'm after him, just . . . interested."

"You want my advice? Stay away."

I picked up the gold wrap top and held it in front of myself. "How about we pretend it has nothing to do with Hank? What do you think of this top?"

He stared at the window. "It's great. I like all your clothes."

"But which do you like best?"

Justin took a bite of his cookie and chewed. He motioned toward the Southern Virginia University sweatshirt I wore. "For Hank Weston, I think your best bet is a baggy sweatshirt. Listen, if he's a decent guy, he'll be more concerned with your personality than your clothes. He probably wants you to be attractive and modest, but guys don't care much about fashion."

Having dated my share of guys, I suspected Justin wasn't entirely correct. James Johnson had always liked it when I wore sandals and capris. Tyler Cox preferred fuzzy sweaters. Then again, maybe Justin wouldn't have considered them *decent* guys. They were the types that honked instead of coming to the door.

Justin held the container of cookies out to me. "Guys also aren't impressed if you refuse to eat cookies."

I shook my head. "I'll have an apple instead."

"As long as you eat it with abandon."

I grabbed an apple from the fruit basket, held it in both hands, and sunk my teeth into it as if I were a fruit-sucking vampire. I had to slurp up a little juice that leaked out. Justin laughed. "Try a little less Food Network and a little more Cookie Monster, but that's me talking. I'm sure you'll impress Hank. Where's the doctor?"

"Moderating a hypochondriac support group online."

Justin reached for another cookie. "I have something to talk to you about, but I don't think you'll want to hear it . . . It's about Harri."

"What about Harri?" I hoped this wasn't another conversation about Rob Martinez.

He put the container of cookies on the coffee table. "Last night, I stayed out late to take in a movie with Rob. On the way home—it was around midnight—I saw Harri running by herself near the Elks' Lodge."

I drew in my breath. The Elks' Lodge was the worst place to be alone at night. At least two people had been killed there. "That couldn't have been Harri. We went to Zumba together at eight. She was exhausted afterward."

Justin stared at his gingerbread man. "I stopped and talked to her. She said she was under a lot of stress, and running was better than eating. I guess she's gained weight lately. I told her she could call me if she ever needed to talk."

"Oh," I said, but I should have said it was all my fault for getting her stuck on Phil Elton. And why couldn't she have called me when she felt stressed? I thought we were friends.

He headed for the refrigerator. "Mind if I help myself to your milk?"

"Go ahead."

He poured himself what little was left in the milk carton. "Looks like I used the last of your milk." He bent down to stare into the open refrigerator. "You *are* planning on going shopping this morning, aren't you?"

"I wasn't planning on it." I'd spent so much mental energy on Harri, I hadn't thought of shopping for over a week, and now that Hank was coming, I didn't want to think about food. "I'll go later."

He closed the refrigerator. "You remember Tanya doesn't live here anymore? And John and Isabella will be here tonight? And tomorrow's Christmas Eve? And you volunteered to host the Christmas Eve dinner?" He picked up a pen and notepad near the phone. "We better get started on a list."

That's how I ended up wearing my big baggy sweatshirt at Giant Grocery store with Justin. We were standing in the meat aisle, trying to decide whether to have beef roast or chicken cordon bleu for the Christmas Eve dinner when along came Tanya, Randall, and—gasp—Hank Weston.

All the pictures of Hank Weston were nothing compared to seeing him in person. I didn't know what to call it—charisma, charm, or swagger. Whatever it was, he had it. The way he smiled—it was as if he'd anticipated our first meeting as much as I had. He was at least three inches taller than me and had the build of a quarterback. In the pictures I hadn't noticed the denim blue color of his eyes or the curls in his brown hair. "It's great to finally meet you," he said, giving me a hug.

With Justin standing behind me, I felt like I was on display. "It's great to meet you too." Why did I have to wear a sweatshirt? "I didn't expect you until later."

He winked. "I like surprises."

Randall put a hand on his shoulder. "It's good to have him home."

Hank kept eye contact with me. "It's good to be home. I've looked forward to seeing Dad's house and meeting my new mom for so long. It's all better than I expected." He flashed a smile at Tanya. "I love it here." The guy knew how to impress, that was for sure.

Randall puffed out his chest. "I'm going to take Hank around to meet all our friends. I've talked about them all so much that he wants to meet them in person." If he wanted to get to know all of Randall's friends, he couldn't be as inconsiderate as Justin thought.

I shook my finger at Randall. "If you're going to visit Sister Bates, I hope you planned for at least an hour."

Randall chuckled. "We're going to drop by there first thing. Barbara always loves a visit."

I smiled at Hank. "You already know Barbara's daughter, Jena Farley—at least she said she knew you."

Hank put a hand to his chin, trying to remember. "Jena Farley. I've met her a few times." He must not have been a country music fan.

I pushed my cart closer to the butcher station to allow an older man to look at the beef roasts beside us. "We're trying to decide on the meat for the big Christmas Eve dinner. What are you in the mood for?"

Tanya gave me a parting hug. "Whatever you decide on will be fine, Emma."

"If you want my advice," Hank said, "I like to have two choices at a big dinner—ham and turkey or pork and salmon, something like that. Personally, I'm a fan of ham and turkey."

I flipped my hair back behind my shoulders before I remembered it's bad to fidget in front of a guy. "Ham and turkey it is."

As Hank, Tanya, and Randall moved on toward the dairy cases, I glanced at the big turkeys. It looked like all the fresh ones were gone. Justin stepped into my line of vision. "I was here to catch you if you fainted, but you didn't even wobble."

I put my hands on either side of my face to conceal any sign of blushing. "Hank seems like a lot of fun. What did you think? Give me the male perspective."

Justin glanced around to make sure we were alone. "I thought he was cocky."

I looked at my watch to see it was almost noon. "How long do you think it'll take to defrost a turkey?"

"Are you kidding? Forget the turkey, Emma."

"Can you go find a ham for me?" I begged. "I'm gonna chat with the butcher." I walked to the butcher's station and asked the guy in the white coat if it was possible to defrost a turkey in less than twenty-four hours. He told me I could submerge the turkey in a sink full of cold water for half a day, or I could get a frozen, stuffed turkey that didn't have to be thawed before I cooked it. Since I was sure Dad wouldn't want salmonella germs swimming in our sink for half a day, I chose the turkey I could cook without thawing.

It was only after I had the turkey in my hands and I was reading the label that I remembered the giblets, those little jiggly inside parts that came in a sack with the bird. I pointed out the instructions to Justin. "You'd think that a stuffed turkey wouldn't have room for any giblets, but sure enough—it has giblets. The instructions say you have to remove the giblets, neck, and gravy packet before cooking the turkey. It must be some sort of marketing ploy to increase the poundage. And why would anyone want a turkey neck?"

Justin placed a ham in the cart. "The poundage?" He laughed. "I think people use the giblets and neck to make gravy."

I rested the turkey on the edge of the frozen food case. "I guess I have a decision to make."

"What's that?"

"Whether I'm willing to touch turkey giblets for Hank Weston. If it was some other guy, I'd say no, but I guess he's worth the sacrifice."

Justin shoved his hands in his pockets. "I'd say he's worth a ham sandwich. Look, if you're worried about the giblets, I can take care of them."

I threw my arms around Justin. "You would do that?" Standing there in the frozen food aisle with my arms around my sister's brother-in-law, I had to admit that now Tanya was married, Justin was my best friend. And my best friend had highly developed pecs, which could have been a problem if other women noticed. The last thing I needed was for him to get married too. It was a good thing he wore those geeky T-shirts.

Justin backed away and put his hands in his pockets again. "Maybe I like the idea of having a turkey. It doesn't all have to be about Hank, does it?"

I hefted a frozen turkey into the cart. "No. I want everyone to be happy." Especially Hank. This was my chance to make a great first impression on him, so, in a way, it *was* all about him.

Chapter 10

Coach's Tip of the Day:
If at first you don't succeed, pretend you did.

Once Justin removed the giblets, getting the turkey in the oven was easy enough. The problem was getting the turkey out of the oven. I should have asked for help, and maybe that disposable roasting pan wasn't the best idea ever. (We didn't have a pan for both a turkey *and* a ham.) The turkey was so heavy that as I took it out of the oven, the pan started to bend. When the pan bent, hot grease seeped onto my hot pads, which is why I screamed and flung the whole thing—pan, turkey, and grease—on the floor. It landed with a thud, spitting out bits of stuffing.

Dad and Harri, who were watching a football game with Isabella and John, rushed up the stairs. Dad sized up the situation fast. "Get your fingers under cold water, Emma. Be careful not to slip on all the turkey juice."

I turned on the faucet and plunged my hands into the cold stream of water. "Do you think we can save the stuffing?" I asked. I knew how Dad was about germs.

"We can still use it," Harri said. She grabbed the oven mitts and bent to pick up the turkey. At first, she grabbed it by its drumsticks, almost tearing them off. Then she grabbed it around the middle, but she had to push it along for about a foot before she got the hot pads underneath. There was no way Dad would let us serve a turkey that had slid across our kitchen floor like one of those magic dirt mops they advertised on TV.

"Watch out for the grease," Dad called out.

As Harri took a step toward the kitchen counter, her feet slipped out from under her, leaving her sitting on the floor, supporting the turkey on her forearms. "Hot, hot," she called, as Dad grabbed another set of hot pads and lifted the turkey from Harri's hands.

Dad placed the turkey on its platter. "Good thing you were wearing that hoodie, Harri. Otherwise, you might have gotten a second degree—"

Before Dad finished his sentence, Harri ran for the bathroom, unzipping her pants. That's when we realized she'd sat on the edge of the roasting pan—right in the hot grease. Dad followed her down the hallway and stood outside the bathroom door. "Hurry and get under some cold water. Use the shower. Don't bother to take off the rest of your clothes."

Justin came in the front door after a walk with our two nieces, three-year-old Kyra and eighteen-month-old Zoey. He must have heard the part about Harri's clothes. "Is it safe to come upstairs?" he asked.

Wondering why Harri always had to suffer for my mistakes, I opened the bathroom door and popped my head in. Harri was behind the shower curtain. "Can I get you anything?" I asked.

"I'll be okay," she said, "but I might be in here awhile. Can you lock the door for me?"

I locked the door and turned back to Justin. "Come on up. I dropped the turkey and Harri got burned in the grease. I hope she's okay. Don't let the girls come in the kitchen until I get it all cleaned up." Of course it had to be Harri who'd gotten hurt. As if I hadn't caused her enough pain already.

"She'll be fine," Dad said. "But she might have trouble sitting for a while. How are your hands, Emma?" He took both my hands in his to look them over. "It's a good thing you dropped the turkey. I've seen much worse from grease burns."

I went back to look at the turkey sitting on the kitchen counter.

"Everyone's going to be here in a half hour. What am I going to do? I can't serve the turkey after it fell on the floor, but I don't think there's enough meat on the ham for everyone." I'd wanted everything to be perfect, but I hadn't realized how hard it was to pull together a Christmas Eve dinner by myself.

Justin peeked into the kitchen while holding onto our nieces. "Why don't we take the skin off the turkey? That's the part that's really dirty, and it'll be healthier that way."

Dad put his glasses back on. "Try not to contaminate the meat while you're removing the skin." I kissed him on the cheek for being so flexible.

Thirty minutes later, the table was set with a pale, skinless turkey for the centerpiece. Harri wore my heather-gray skirt because she was too sore to wear pants. Justin had finished cleaning up the grease spill on the kitchen floor and was all decked out in a polo shirt and khakis—that was about as formal as he got outside of church. Dad wore a blazer. And I, for lack of preparation time, reverted to the gold sweater I'd planned to wear for Hank Weston's welcome home party. I'd just started with the curling iron when the doorbell rang.

Dad said we were eating at 6:00, and he meant it. "If we wait around, we're putting everyone at risk for food poisoning." His policy tended to cause a few awkward moments, like when I arrived at the table in the middle of the blessing. That was okay, though, because everyone's eyes were closed.

We managed to fit nine people at the dining room table. The other four—Justin, Harri, my brother-in-law, John, and Zoey—ate at the card table. We would have had one more, except that Phil went on his extended vacation.

After the amen, I slipped into my chair between Tanya and Barbara. Tanya looked at the turkey. "What happened?" she whispered.

I tipped my head toward Dad sharpening his long knife at the head of the table. "It's the way Dad wanted it."

Tanya looked like she understood. "Oh."

I stole a glance at Hank, who sat across from me. He greeted me with yet another wink, as if he and I were meant to be in one of those kissing mouthwash commercials. He wore a red plaid shirt, the perfect choice for a Christmas Eve dinner.

Barbara gave me a sideways hug. "Don't you look pretty, Emma? We should get a picture of you and Jena together after dinner. You're both growing up so fast. We have to preserve these memories while we can. Before long, you'll both be married and having children."

Hank leaned toward us. "Do any of you have something exciting under the tree?"

I scooped a spoonful of Barbara's green Jell-O salad onto my plate. It'd been a while since I'd been excited about Christmas gifts. I had great memories of American Girl dolls, makeup sets, and a Game Boy. Now that I was grown up, I was more interested in giving. I wanted to give the way people in Christmas movies gave. This year, I had Harri to help, but it hadn't been as easy as I'd planned. In some ways, it would've been better if I'd dropped a gift card off at her door.

Kyra piped up from the other end of the table. "I'm gonna get a red-haired doll that looks like Aunt Emma."

Hank chuckled. "Someone has a fan."

Isabella, my blonde sister, grimaced. "Do you know how hard it is to find a red-haired doll? Correction: a cute red-haired doll."

Barbara passed me the mashed potatoes. "Jena got an enormous Christmas package this afternoon. It was a special delivery from a courier. I don't think we've ever had a courier come to our house before. Jena has so many fans. I shouldn't be surprised that one knows her address here. I think I'm more excited to see what's inside than Jena is."

Hank lifted an eyebrow at Jena. "That's disturbing one of your fans knows your address when you're on vacation. I don't know if you should open it."

Dad paused in the midst of his turkey carving. "These days, you can never be too careful. I'll get you the police number for non-emergencies when I'm through carving. You should call right away."

Jena twisted her lips around as if trying not to laugh. "Oh, I'm not worried." I couldn't help suspecting she knew who sent the package.

My suspicions about Jena only occupied my mind for a minute. Once the plate of turkey made its way to my place, it was time for the final verdict as to whether my cooking proved me worthy of Hank

Weston. Tasting the turkey, I knew it was too dry. I couldn't let Hank think I was a bad cook. Standing up from my place, I grabbed the plate of turkey before it got to Hank. "I think this turkey's gotten cold." I snagged the gravy boat from the card table on my way to the kitchen.

"Where are you going with our gravy?" Justin called as I made my way to the kitchen.

"It's cold too. I'll heat it up and bring it back."

Once inside the kitchen, I poured what was left in the gravy boat all over the tray of turkey, stuck it in the microwave, then went looking for a gravy mix. By the time the microwave stopped, I still hadn't found a mix, so I took the tray of hot, juicy turkey out to Hank and headed back to the kitchen. What would I do for gravy?

After another look through the pantry, I found the best substitute I could manage—condensed cream of chicken soup. I whisked the soup with milk and a drop of Worcestershire sauce for color and heated it up in the microwave. There was no time for tasting. It'd have to do. I hustled out to the card table, where I handed it to Justin, who looked like he was waiting for the punch line to my latest joke.

It was best not to evaluate Justin's facial expression after he ate the gravy, so I turned my attention back to Hank. "What is it you're studying, Hank?"

Hank cut into his super-succulent turkey. "Computer programming, but don't be too intimidated. I like hanging out as much as the next guy. I don't sit around on weekends trying to memorize pi to the millionth place. What about you? Are you going to school?" I caught Randall giving me a subtle thumbs-up. I was not about to look in the other direction to see what Justin thought.

I set down my fork and gazed straight into Hank's denim blues. "I've gone to school off and on for years, but I think I've found my calling. I'm going to be a life coach."

Hank raised both eyebrows. "Wow! Considering how many misled people I know, that ought to keep you busy. So what are your other interests?"

"A lot of things: fashion, decorating, entertaining, nutrition."

"Tanya says you like music."

"I love music."

"I think it'd be fun to sing Christmas carols after dinner. What do you think?"

Barbara interrupted. "Oh, Jena and I were hoping you'd want to sing Christmas carols. She brought her guitar, just in case. I told her she ought to bring it. It doesn't feel like Christmas without music."

And so the conversation turned to Jena Farley. Though Hank had met Jena before, Barbara had to make sure he was thoroughly informed about her country music successes. "I'm sure you've heard about Jena's new album. It's been nominated for a Grammy."

Jena shook her head. "Mom, it hasn't been nominated for a Grammy. My album was submitted. They choose the nominees from the submissions and choose the winners from the nominees. There are hundreds of submissions, but only a few nominees."

Barbara wiped her mouth with her napkin. "Oh, I keep forgetting. I get all mixed up between submissions and nominations. Then there's that other award. What was it called?"

It seemed like a good time for me to refill the water pitcher, so I grabbed it and headed for the kitchen. Tanya followed me with the butter dish. "I think Hank likes you," she whispered.

I tried not to look pleased as I filled the pitcher. "Why do you say that?"

"I asked him."

I didn't have to fake any more. I really wasn't pleased. "You what?"

"He told me you're pretty and he wanted to make sure he got to sit across from you at dinner. So I did a little maneuvering for him." Before I could reply, she was across the kitchen, getting a stick of butter out of the fridge. When she came back, she whispered. "I think Harri's cold. She sat on her hands all through dinner. Do you mind if I turn up the heat?"

"Oh, I'll get it," I said.

By the time I got back to the table, the conversation had turned to Phil Elton and his incredible line-dancing skills. I motioned for Harri to follow me into the kitchen. "How's your bum?"

"Pretty bad." She sniffed. I couldn't tell whether the sniffles were for Phil or her bum—maybe both.

I wrapped my arms around her. "I'm so sorry." The pain killer she'd taken obviously wasn't working that well. "You don't have to sit down if it's uncomfortable. We can eat in the kitchen if you want."

"Maybe if I sat on something cold."

I rummaged around in the freezer. "Peas make good ice packs." I pulled out two packages and handed them to Harri. I also pulled out two boxes of vanilla ice cream to thaw on the counter. We'd need them later for the pie.

Harri held the peas behind her back as she walked out to the card table. She sat down with her hands still there as if smoothing her skirt. Justin leaned toward her to share some private joke that made Harri giggle. If I knew Justin, it was something about the princess and the pea. He was goofy that way.

Hank watched me sit down. "So, Emma, I hear you like to ski."

Did I like to ski? Sort of. At least I liked the new ski outfit I'd bought last winter. "Sure, I love skiing."

"What do you say a bunch of us plan a ski trip?" Hank said. "I'd like to check out the slopes in Pennsylvania while I'm here."

Hank was really smart about asking me out without actually asking me out. I had to admit he was in an awkward position, being my aunt's stepson. It was best to proceed with caution; we were liable to keep meeting each other for the rest of our lives.

Before I could give my opinion about the slopes in Pennsylvania, Barbara was off and running with the conversation. "You ought to go to Blaze Mountain. That's where Jena always goes."

Dad furrowed his brows. "You'll have to count me out. I had a patient who went skiing last year and ended up with a broken tailbone. I had another patient who lost his sight when he ran into a tree. I'm too old for that sort of thing."

"I'd love to go," Harri called from the card table. "I've always wanted to learn to ski."

Hank smiled at Harri. "You should come. So, we've got Emma, Harri, Jena, and me. We still have room for one more in my car. Anyone else want to come?"

Everyone was silent—or chewing—so I said, "Justin got a new snowboard last month."

Hank leaned forward to see Justin at the card table. "So are you in, Justin?"

Justin smashed his mashed potatoes with his fork. "That's hard to say. Work's busy this month. When are you planning on going?" I'd never, ever heard Justin talk about his schedule with anyone who wasn't his client, especially not in December. The winter holidays weren't exactly a busy time of year for construction contractors.

Hank took another helping of turkey. "As soon as possible—next week if that's okay with everyone else. What do you say, Emma?"

"Sounds great to me. I'm free until the day after New Year's. That's one good thing about working for a dentist. I get great holidays."

Harri scooted around on her peas. "I have Monday and Tuesday off."

Jena crossed her fork and knife on top of her plate. "I'm free the whole week. I might have to call in for a radio interview, but I think I can do that from the lodge." For a moment, I wondered if anyone at the lodge would want Jena's autograph. She wasn't that famous, was she?

Hank clapped his hands together. "It's a date. We'll go first thing Monday morning. How about it, Justin? Are you gonna let me take all these women to the slopes by myself? Come on. You ever heard of sharpening the saw?"

From the look on Justin's face, I could tell he'd heard of "sharpening the saw," and it wasn't something he wanted to discuss with Hank. Randall patted his son on the back. "Hank could teach you a thing or two about sharpening the saw, Justin. He gets excellent grades, but he still knows how to have fun. What was it you said you were doing this morning, Hank?"

Hank sliced his meat. "Oh, that—I got together with some old friends downtown for a little gaming."

"Like video games?" I asked. Out of the corner of my eye, I could see Justin turn away from us to hide his smile. He knew my opinion on guys who spent too much time playing video games.

"Exactly," Hank said with a little wink in my direction. "I hope you approve."

Hank had so many good qualities that it wasn't worth dwelling on a little video game habit. Besides, if he liked video games so much, he'd get along great with Justin. All I needed to do was convince Justin to come on the ski trip with us. "Justin, if you come, you can help me teach Harri how to ski. You know I need your help." I didn't have to remind him of my remedial skiing skills.

The corners of Justin's mouth twitched. "I'll try and make it."

Barbara put a hand to her chest. "It would put my mind at ease if you go, Justin. I worry about Jena being out in public. Most of her fans are good people, but you never know what might happen."

Hank crossed his eyes in my direction. I struggled to keep from laughing as Justin replied, "Well, if it's that important to you, Sister Bates, I'll rearrange my schedule."

After dinner, everyone was too full for pie, so we gathered in the living room to sing carols. Jena's repertoire included a lot of songs I hadn't ever heard before. By the time she got to "Christmas Shoes"— that song about the little boy who bought shoes for his dying mom— Hank and Jena were the only ones singing. It shouldn't have shocked me that Hank was a good singer. I mean, he seemed to be good at most everything. And it was natural he knew a lot of country songs since he'd lived in Nashville a few years.

When that song was over, Jena sang a song she'd composed herself:

"You're sick of shopping at the store
And Christmas is just one more chore
Don't give your credit card another swipe
Go home; get on with the fun part of life
Sled down a hill of snow,
Watch the Christmas lights glow,
Teach a kid to make fudge,
Let go of that old grudge.
Sing a carol or two,
Help a friend who feels blue,
Because Christmas is more,
Than shopping at the store."

Listening to the song, I started to feel guilty. I liked shopping at the store. Before she began the second verse, Justin crept up to ask if he could help me serve the pie. It was the perfect time, with everyone relaxing on the sofa and easy chairs. According to the etiquette website I'd looked up, I was totally prepped to do this the right way. I took everyone's order: whether they wanted pumpkin or pecan pie, then if they wanted ice cream or whipped cream. I wrote the orders down on a couple of sticky notes while Justin set out the plates and forks.

Even after the turkey disaster, I wasn't worried about the pie. I had it all under control—one, because Tanya made the pecan pie, and two, because The Pie Place made the pumpkin pie. What was there to worry about?

In the kitchen, Justin had his head in the freezer. "Where's the ice cream?"

I laid the sticky notes out on the kitchen table beside the pies. "I set it out on the counter to soften a bit."

Justin laughed behind me. "How long ago was that?" I turned to see the ice cream boxes surrounded by puddles of white goop. When Justin picked up a box, more goop squeezed out the top and onto his hand.

I winced. Not another mistake. "Is it completely melted or just partly?"

Justin pried the cardboard lid off a container. "There's a couple scoops' worth floating in the middle. How about I slice the pie? You can figure out the ice cream."

"Maybe we should give everyone whipped cream instead."

Justin pulled a knife out of the drawer. "When did you buy whipped cream?"

So I'd forgotten to buy whipped cream? As Justin dished up slices of pie, I slopped a spoonful of what-used-to-be ice cream on top. That's when I discovered that melted ice cream looked elegant drizzled across a slice of pie.

Justin took the plate from me. "This could be the type of cooking disaster that makes history—kind of like chocolate chip cookies and ice cream cones. Next year, we should melt the ice cream on purpose and maybe take the skin off the turkey too."

I laughed. "Thanks."

Justin put down the plate. He leaned toward me until I could see my reflection in his light blue eyes. "You've done great today, Emma, and I'm sure next year will be even better." I couldn't help it that tingles ran up and down my spine. Justin and I were just friends, but he was definitely better looking than my sister's husband.

I went back to scooping ice cream. "Do you think Hank noticed how much I messed up?" I asked.

Justin picked up a couple of plates to deliver. "No, but if he did, tomorrow is another day."

No sooner did we get all the pie delivered than Isabella announced it was time for her kids to go to sleep. Having a sister with children could be a letdown. She had signaled the exodus for everyone. Justin had to leave because Isabella's family was staying at his house. Then Barbara said something about how Jena needed her rest too. Next Harri decided she'd better get a ride home from Barbara. It wasn't eight o'clock, and the party of fourteen was reduced to five.

But here was that lesson again: sometimes a bad situation could have its advantages. Hank was helping me with the dishes. I had him all to myself in our tiny kitchen.

He rolled up his sleeves and sunk his well-toned forearms into the suds. "So what do you think of Jena? You're a better judge than I am. Do you think she's celebrity material?"

I fumbled around in the drawer for a dish towel. "Of course she's celebrity material. She's already a celebrity. She has a beautiful voice."

He handed me a soapy plate. "She looks a little sick to me, and she's too skinny. I like meat on a woman."

I slapped him on the arm with the kitchen towel. "Come on. That's how celebrities are supposed to look. I think she's gorgeous . . . How long have you known Jena anyway?"

He lifted a dark, well-groomed brow at me. "Did you see those people who followed her over here? Five teenage girls ran up to get her autograph. There were more waiting on the curb. One of them wanted a hug."

"That doesn't sound too terrible. What can five teenage girls do?"

Hank's mouth was a little open, showing a glimpse of his tongue. "I could tell you stories about what teenage girls can do."

I bet he could. "Sounds like someone has a troubled past."

Hank sighed. "If you only knew. Seriously, though, I do have to watch my reputation. Dad's probably told you how my family runs a group of private schools. Someday, I'll be the CEO. I can't take Jena on our ski trip if it means my picture might be all over the Internet or in a tabloid. All I want is a quiet ski trip with you and a few of your friends."

I dragged my attention away from the cleft in his chin. "We can't leave Jena out because she's famous. What if I find a way to bring her without her fans knowing?"

Hank's hand brushed mine as he handed me a washed glass. "Do you think you could do that?"

"I was a teenage girl once."

Hank stepped closer to me. "If you can sneak her out, I'll be very impressed."

Chapter 11

Coach's Tip of the Day:
Love your enemies to death.

Black wasn't my color, so I was going with an eggplant sweater and dark-wash jeans. And, no, I couldn't believe I was up at 5:45 a.m. on the day after Christmas. More to the point, I couldn't believe I was doing this for Jena Farley, someone who didn't like me at all. I figured this could be a sort of rescue mission for our friendship. Didn't people say that if you need to love someone, you should serve them? Maybe it would also work in reverse, and Jena would love me back. I could always hope.

According to Barbara, Jena's fans could have shown up at any time of day or night. The only way to make sure they didn't see us was to sneak Jena out the back in the dark. I'd gotten permission from Barbara's back-door neighbor to go through his yard. (He'd promised to keep his Siberian Husky inside.) I'd also agreed to have Justin come along. Dad said it was for my protection. At six feet tall, I was still Dad's little girl.

So, there we were, rattling along in Justin's old truck, which squealed out its need for a new serpentine belt, at 5:50 a.m. in Barbara's quiet, little neighborhood. My Civic would've been quieter—too bad it wasn't equipped for Jena's skis. The houses along the street were all like Barbara's—they reminded me of boxes, evenly spaced along the narrow roads.

I showed Justin where to park, then we both hopped out, shutting the doors with gentle thuds. Thanks to the half-moon and some streetlights, we could see well enough to sneak around to the neighbor's gate. I swung it open to be greeted by a dog—the dog Jena's neighbor said he would keep inside. Only, this dog wasn't a husky; it was a chocolate lab, and it barked a lot more than I thought was necessary. Justin held out his hand for the dog to sniff. "It's okay, girl." He grabbed the dog by the collar and dragged her back inside the fence while I closed the gate. "I should have brought some of Buttercup's treats," Justin said as the dog continued to follow us, barking, while we crossed the yard. She wasn't the only dog barking, either. Five or six neighborhood dogs joined in. "Are you sure this is the right yard?" Justin asked before he took the chain-link fence with a single vault.

I crammed my foot into a link and swung my other leg up to perch on the top rail. "I don't know. All these houses look the same to me." Justin held my elbow to steady me as I pulled my foot out of the chain link and brought it up to crouch with both feet on the top rail. He gave me a little tug, and I jumped down to stand beside him.

Justin put a finger to his lips and pointed to the yard next to us. Two people stood outside the sliding glass door. It looked like they were trying to see inside. "That's Jena's house over there," he whispered. "We came through the wrong backyard."

I stared across the yard at the two would-be voyeurs peeking into Jena's window. "Great! The whole point of coming in the back way was to avoid people seeing us. It's 5:45 in the morning. What is wrong with these people?" I reached for my phone. "I think we should call the police."

Justin put a hand on top of mine. "They're just kids, Emma. We're not gonna call the police on them."

"They're peeking in the windows."

"I have a better idea." Before I could ask about his idea, he whipped out his flashlight, ran over to the edge of Jena's yard, shined the light straight into the two trespassers' faces, and yelled, "Police!"

That sent the two kids scrambling across Barbara's patio and tripping over the bushes on the other side of the house. We could hear their sneakers clapping down the street as we hopped one more chain-link fence and made our way to the sliding glass door. It wasn't sneaky of me, but I couldn't help laughing as we stood there waiting for Jena to answer the door. "You could get in big trouble for that," I told Justin. "It's illegal to impersonate an officer."

"I wasn't impersonating an officer. I was calling the police, like you said we should."

It was Barbara who opened the door and invited us into her little kitchen. She was wearing a dark-blue zip-up robe. "Make yourselves at home. I'll go wake up Jena."

Justin and I sat across from each other at Barbara's glass-top kitchen table. "Now that Jena's making so much money," I whispered, "why doesn't she get herself a place in one of those gated communities?"

Justin looked at the cross-stitched sampler on the kitchen wall. "I guess having money doesn't change the way she feels about the place where she grew up. This is still her home."

"I'll bet she could get herself a really nice house."

Justin stretched his arms above his head. "Take it from me, home ownership isn't all it's cracked up to be."

"Speaking of which, when are you going to let me help you pick out furniture for your living room?"

Justin unzipped his jacket, grinning. "Is that a proposal?"

I swung my foot out to give him a light kick in the shin, but he moved just in time. I stared at his black T-shirt, which bore the image of Spider-man. "What makes you think your future wife is going to be at all interested in decorating?"

He still grinned. "Can you think of a woman who wouldn't be more interested in decorating than I am?"

Barbara came back, this time toting a bright red electric guitar, which looked completely out of place next to her robe and slippers. "I have to show you what Jena got from her secret admirer." Her secret admirer? I thought that was a junior high thing.

Justin swiveled in his seat. "Is that a Gibson?"

"It's a Gibson Les Paul, and it's custom," Barbara said. She bent closer to Justin and lowered her voice. "I looked it up on the Internet.

You would not believe how much it costs. I think it's worth more than my Corolla."

Someday it'd be nice to get something romantic for Christmas, but, for now, I was happy I'd gotten practical gifts: a set of organic cookbooks from Dad, a half a cord of split wood from Justin, a sweater from Isabella, and a gift certificate for five free pizzas from Tanya. I wasn't jealous that Jena had a secret admirer, just curious. "Are you sure you have no idea who sent it?"

Barbara shook her head. "No idea at all. The note said, 'With love, from your secret admirer.' I was speechless when she opened it. Can you imagine me, speechless?"

While Justin and Barbara discussed the guitar, I stared at the kitchen wall—the wall where Barbara kept all of Jena's awards, the one Barbara called Jena's wall of fame. There were pictures of Jena standing with celebrities, Jena with a steel-string guitar, Jena with an electric guitar, Jena holding a trophy, and Jena holding some sort of plaque. In the middle of it all was a diploma from Belmont University. Could it be that with all her concerts and albums, Jena had managed to graduate from college?

I walked to the wall. "Is this diploma an honorary degree or did Jena actually earn it?"

Justin drew his eyebrows together, signaling I'd said the wrong thing. Barbara didn't seem to mind, though. She laid the guitar on the table. "Oh, she earned it—a BA in musical performance. It took her longer than most because her concert schedule kept her busy toward the end."

Justin ran his finger along the guitar strings. "Emma's thinking about finishing her degree." To tell the truth, I hadn't thought much about it since Justin and I'd discussed it that one time.

Barbara punched her hand into the air. "Jena's a finisher. She finishes everything she starts."

I yawned. "That's very inspiring."

"You should see her list of goals. Why, if I weren't a Mormon, I'd think she was the reincarnation of Ben Franklin himself. It's like the experts tell you to do with the long-range and short-range goals." Barbara stood up from her chair. "You know what—I'm going to show them to you."

I straightened a picture on the wall. "Do you think Jena would mind?" It would be good research for life coaching.

Barbara headed out of the kitchen. "Oh, no. She says the more you share your goals, the more likely you are to achieve them."

"Don't get all intimidated," Justin whispered as he stood to help Jena with the ski equipment she'd dragged into the kitchen. Jena was dressed in black like we'd planned.

As Justin slid open the door, Barbara came back waving three pieces of paper, which she placed in my hand. I scanned through Jena's long list of goals, noticing categories like Physical, Social, Performance, Marketing, and Spiritual. Each category had three or four sub-categories with short-term goals like "Read two chapters in the Book of Mormon every day" or "Do sixty crunches five times a week" or "Get six interviews a week." It was like Jena had reinvented the Young Women's Personal Progress program for country music stars. I raised my eyebrows to Barbara. "Wow." I knew I wasn't supposed to compare myself to Jena, but how could I help it? She had so much more persistence than I did. That was the reason she'd achieved so much more.

The cold air rushed into the kitchen from the open sliding glass door, so I thanked Barbara and headed out onto the patio. Justin and Jena were already beside the fence—this time they chose the right one. Justin stood on the other side while Jena handed him all her equipment. When she started to climb, I ran and took the fence at the same time, which would have worked well except my sweater caught on the top of the chain link. The husky, which should have been inside, came to greet me. While I tried to unhook my sweater with one hand, I pushed the dog off me with the other. He was one persistent dog, though, and pretty soon his claws were caught in my sweater. I tried not to remember the story I'd once heard about a husky disfiguring a boy's face. "Nice doggy," I said as I lost balance and fell back toward Jena's side of the fence. The only thing keeping me from falling to the ground was my sweater, which was still attached to the dog and the fence.

Justin pulled me back up as Jena fed the dog a cookie from her bag. "Hey, Snowball," Jena reassured him, laughing. "Emma won't hurt you." She grabbed Snowball's collar to keep him still so Justin could unhook his claws.

"Are you okay?" Justin asked as he detached my sweater and lifted me down from the fence.

I couldn't help shaking. "Yeah. Just a little freaked out."

When we got to the car, Jena thanked Justin for coming to get her. "It was Emma's idea," Justin said. "I just came along for fun."

"Thanks, Emma," Jena said. It wasn't much, but it was progress. Maybe, if I tried a little harder, I could heal my relationship with Jena after all.

Harri, Justin, Jena, Hank, and I met at the Westons' house for a pancake breakfast with no paparazzi or fans to be seen. Justin loaded up the equipment in Hank's Lexus SUV while Harri gave Jena a Goth makeover or make-under—whatever we called it, no one would recognize Jena when Harri was through. That left Hank and me in the kitchen, flipping pancakes.

"Did you hear about Jena's secret admirer?" I asked, waiting for bubbles to form in the batter.

Hank wore a blue fleece pullover that brought out his eyes. "No. Tell me."

"Someone sent Jena a really expensive electric guitar. Barbara says it's worth as much as her car."

Hank looked like he was trying not to laugh. "You can't be serious. What kind of fan would have that much money?"

"The note on it said, 'With love, from your secret admirer.' Barbara says they have no idea who sent it, but I'll bet Jena knows exactly who it is."

Hank picked up a spatula and flipped pancakes. "Have you asked her?"

"Like Jena would tell me anything! She's so tight-lipped. I have to come up with my own theories about her."

Hank laughed his deliciously deep laugh. "So what's your theory on the secret admirer?"

My heart beat faster as I considered sharing my suspicions about Jena. It wasn't wrong to gossip about Jena, was it? Everyone gossips about celebrities. "Promise you won't tell?"

Hank made an *x* across his chest. "Promise."

I lowered my voice and leaned close enough to catch a whiff of some spicy scent—probably his deodorant. "I think it's from Reggie Van Camp."

Hank shook his head. "Reggie Van Camp? No way." He paused to remove a few pancakes from the griddle. He still looked like he was trying not to laugh. "Well, I guess it could be from him. Anything's possible. And you're better at figuring things out than I am. Why do you think it's from Reggie?"

"Because he'd rather sing duets with her than with his wife. Tell me that isn't suspicious." There, I'd said it, and now I was all jittery—like I'd snuck and opened a present two weeks before Christmas.

Hank laughed. "Well, maybe you have something there. I'll bet Jena's paparazzi would love to hear about that. Has anyone interviewed you yet?"

I took forks from the drawer to set the table. "Do you know how much trouble I'd be in with Barbara if I told the paparazzi something like that? It's not like I think Jena actually likes Reggie back or anything. She's not the type to consider a married man, but it makes sense if you think about it. She came out here to get away from him. Otherwise, she'd be on tour."

Hank cracked up. He had to wipe a few tears from his eyes before he could reply. "That makes total sense, Emma. The tabloids would love to hear about it."

I dropped the forks on the counter and poked my finger against Hank's sternum. "You promised not to tell anyone."

He held both hands up, shaking his head. "So I think it's funny that Reggie Van Camp has fallen for Jena. He's what? Forty-six? You've gotta admit, it'd make for great reading in the tabloids."

Why did I feel torn about this conversation? Gossiping with Hank was a good way to get to know him. But at the same time, I had this nagging bit of conscience that told me I'd betrayed Jena's trust. "Another thing that makes me suspicious is the way Jena saved Reggie's life. Did you hear about that?"

"Yeah. I was at the same party. It wasn't that big of a deal. He choked, and she did the Heimlich."

"I thought maybe it showed a certain intimacy between the two of them. Out of all the people there, Jena was the first to come to his rescue. Maybe Reggie liked the way it felt to be wrapped in her arms."

Hank laughed again. "Intimacy?" Then he composed himself. "Maybe you're right. I wouldn't want to give the Heimlich to just anyone, and she didn't hesitate at all. You've got me convinced that Reggie sent the guitar."

I put a finger to my lips. "It's just speculation, so don't go spreading it around."

As if I didn't feel guilty enough for gossiping, I felt worse when I saw Jena walk into the kitchen. She looked like one of those harlequin clowns—powdered white face, purple lips, thick black eyeliner around her eyes, and little teardrops painted across her cheekbones. She held up her black fingernails for us to admire. "What do you guys think? Will anyone recognize me?"

Hank was the first to speak. "Absolutely hideous. Even Reggie Van Camp wouldn't know you." I elbowed Hank. He grabbed my arm. "Emma and I were just talking about you."

We sat down to eat, but all I could think about was how I shouldn't have gossiped about Jena and how I should be applying to colleges. Then I thought of Harri, whose life had been spiraling downward since I'd met her. There were dark circles under her eyes all the time now. Was she still running in the middle of the night? Or was it because she'd quit doing her hair and makeup like I'd taught her? Everything was slipping out of my control.

While the others ate, I snuck away to calm myself. What I needed was Tanya. I found her down in the laundry room, sorting Hank's laundry. I sat myself on the dryer like I'd done when I was a kid. "How did I end up this way?"

Tanya looked up as she placed a pair of jeans in the washer. "What way?"

"A twenty-three-year-old receptionist."

Tanya dumped detergent into the washer and turned it on. "There's nothing wrong with being a receptionist."

I hugged my knees to my chest. "But it's wrong for me."

Tanya climbed up beside me on the dryer and put her arm around me. "I think you're being too hard on yourself."

"The problem isn't that I'm being too hard on myself. It's that I'm too easy on myself. I'm an underachiever at everything."

Tanya squeezed a little harder. "I wouldn't say that. You've done well in school. Everyone loves you at the dentist's office. You're a good daughter and a wonderful aunt."

"Did you know Jena has a bachelor's degree?"

Tanya sighed. "Is that what this is about? Jena?"

"I've dabbled around at the community college while everyone else achieved their dreams. I'm tired of being on the sidelines. I want to be in the game. I need to set some goals."

Tanya hopped down off the dryer. "Well, it's the perfect time of year to work on resolutions."

I straightened my legs. "These won't be resolutions. I never keep my resolutions. These are going to be goals, and I'm going to achieve every single one of them."

Tanya dumped out another bag of Hank's laundry to sort into piles. "Did you get to see Jena's new guitar while you were at Barbara's?"

I laughed. "What do you think?"

"It was the first thing Barbara told us when we dropped by last night," Tanya said. "We got to see the secret admirer note." She paused while checking Hank's pocket. "You know what I think?"

"About the secret admirer?"

She grinned. "What would you say if I told you it was Justin?"

"I would say you're wrong."

She tossed the pair of jeans into the washer and put her hands on her hips. "Hear me out, okay? First of all, he's always admired Jena. Second, he has enough money. And third—this is what made me think of him—last month, he told me Jena ought to get herself a Gibson guitar."

I shook my head. "I'm still not convinced."

"He's been over there a lot lately. Last week, he painted Jena's room. The week before, he remodeled the bathroom. This secret admirer gift is the sort of thing he would do. You know how shy he can be around women. It's about time he found someone. He's been alone for a long time."

I hopped down off the dryer. "He's not alone. He has Dad and me."

Tanya threw a pair of jeans into the washer. "His parents are gone. His only brother is married and lives far away. I think it's about time he got married."

Feeling the adrenaline surge through me, I grabbed a bag of clothes to sort. I had to be doing something. "I don't think Jena's his type."

"She's exactly his type. Haven't you noticed he always goes for the intimidating ones? Remember Erica Nash?"

I pulled a couple coins and a guitar pick from Hank's pocket. "I didn't know Hank played guitar."

Tanya took the coins and the guitar pick. "I didn't either, but it doesn't surprise me. He's very talented. But we were talking about Justin and Erica Nash."

"He broke up with Erica," I said.

"And Mercedes Jimenez?"

"He broke up with her too."

Tanya closed the lid on the washer. "My point is they were both alpha-female types—like Jena."

How had I missed that Justin was spending so much time at Jena's house? He'd never told me he was painting Jena's room or remodeling her bathroom. If Tanya was right, Jena Farley could become my best friend's wife and my sister's sister-in-law. No wonder Justin wanted me to apply to colleges. He needed more space.

I was capable of giving Justin more space. I made sure he got the front passenger seat in Hank's car. And I didn't say much at all on the trip through Maryland and Pennsylvania. I sat in the back, beside Harri, writing out a long list of goals that were going to transform me into a successful person. I wrote them on paper—not because that's what Jena did, but because writing things out by hand made me feel like I was doing something serious and permanent.

We passed long stretches of woods, old wooden barns, little towns with white-steepled churches, houses surrounded by hedges, and graveyards. But my main focus was the piece of paper. I wrote down every goal I could think of: pray every morning, help Harri have better self-esteem, practice cooking meat, pay off my credit card, reduce my carbon footprint, exercise, write 100 thank-you notes, and read *Gone with the Wind*.

The longer I worked, the more complicated the list became. For my long-term goal of getting a degree, I had the short-term goal of applying to universities, but that meant finding out all sorts of information about requirements, deadlines, and applications. Even my short-term goals ended up having shorter-term goals, which had shorter-term goals. It was a lot to do, but I could do it all. I wasn't going to quit this time. I was in complete control.

Chapter 12

Coach's Tip of the Day:
Enjoy the view.

*I*s that your stomach growling or is it mine?" Jena asked me as we rode the express ski lift to the top of Blaze Mountain. I sat in between her and Hank.

Pushing a fist against the front of my turquoise blue ski pants, I faked ignorance. "I didn't hear anything." The people skiing below us were really, really far below us. When I was four, I'd gotten stuck in my friend's tree fort, terrified to descend the long ladder. Mom had to climb up and get me. Ever since, I'd been scared of heights. "Doesn't it freak you out to see how high up we are?" I asked.

Jena's expression was as blank as it could be considering her Goth teardrops. "No." Was Justin really her admirer? Except for the fact that their names sounded good together and they both liked country music, I couldn't think of much they had in common.

Hank reached above us to pull down the restraining bar. "As long as the wind isn't very strong, the angle of the lift prevents you from falling out. You don't have to hold onto the back of the chair."

He must have noticed I had one arm clamped to the back of the seat—as if I were a giant paper clip. I laughed. "Oh, I didn't even realize I was doing that."

Hank reached across the back of my seat to squeeze my hand. "I'm heading for the black diamond trails. Are you in?"

I shook my head. "I think you can tell by now I'm a blue square sort of girl. You and Jena can go risk your lives over there. Don't worry about me. Just remember we're meeting for lunch in an hour."

He lifted the restraining bar, preparing to get off the lift. "That's funny. I had you pegged as a risk-taker, Emma."

"I know my limits," I replied. It was time to get off, so I put my skis down on the snow. As I stood up, it was like someone pulled a shade down on my eyes. I was about to faint. In front of Hank. Why couldn't I keep just a little bit of dignity? Thanks to my low blood pressure, this had happened to me enough times that I knew exactly what to do. Hoping Hank wouldn't notice, I gave a little push on my ski poles, so I was out of everyone's way and crouched down. I heard Hank's voice. "You okay, Emma?"

With my head between my knees, the world came back into view. Jena had disappeared and all I could see were Hank's red skis on the snow. "Yeah, I stood too fast. I'm better now."

"I'll bet you're dehydrated. I'll give you a sip out of my hydration pack when you feel like standing up." He reached a hand out in front of me.

I took his hand and let him pull me up to stand. This was the closest I'd ever been to anyone while I was on skis (not counting that guy who fell on top of me). He held out the tube from his hydration pack. "Take all you want. It's easy enough to refill."

I rested my hand on his shoulder and sipped through the tube while looking into his dark-lashed eyes. If you ever saw one of those vintage soft-drink ads with a guy and girl both drinking the same soda with two different straws, that was the way it felt. I traced his features with a sculptor's eye—not that I'd ever sculpted. His jaw was a definite square near his ear and then angled down into a rounded point at his chin. His lips were balanced on top and bottom—not too thin or too full. His nose had a slight curve. His teeth were straight and white. Believe me, working at a dentist's office, I hardly ever saw such great teeth. I wished I could stand there with him for a little longer, but I could only drink so much. I handed him back his tube. "Thanks. That helped a lot."

His hand was at my waist as if we were dancing. "You think you'll be okay now? I don't want to leave unless you're sure."

"I'll be fine. This happens to me all the time—low blood pressure, you know. I don't want to take you away from the slopes."

Hank pulled his ski goggles over his eyes. "Well, I had a pretty good view here."

Was he talking about me or the mountain? "My view wasn't so bad either," I said. As he skied away, I looked down the hill at the leafless trees surrounded by snow, the shiny white ski slope, various colored skiers, and the lodge in the distance. It wasn't that great of a view, unless he meant the little gray bump of a mountain set in the distance against a pale blue sky.

I pushed off from the top of the hill with my skis pointed inward. Snowplowing was about as good as it got for me—I leaned toward the left and pushed with my poles, then I leaned toward my right and pushed. According to Justin, I could've improved if I'd taken more lessons, and maybe I should have. But after waking up so early and skipping breakfast, I was beat. So I wove my way down the hill, then I did a little cross-country imitation over to the bunny hill, where I was supposed to meet Harri and Justin.

I stood there in front of a group of kids lining up for a lesson. Even with my goggles on, the sun was so bright against the snow, I had to shade my eyes to look for Justin and Harri. I could see one couple wearing black like Justin and pink like Harri on the green circle hill, but the woman skied much too well. Harri was a beginner, so she'd probably be flat on her back most of the time. This woman flew down the hill with her skis parallel, jumping to change directions every few seconds. I turned to look for Justin and Harri at the lodge, but before I could get far, I heard Harri yelling, "How do I stop?" That was when I saw that the woman who skied so well was headed straight toward me. It was Harri after all.

"Turn," Justin yelled.

I scooted to the side as Harri raced past. Then I remembered—there were kids in back of me.

"Fall down," Justin yelled again. Right as he said it, Harri crash-landed as the kids scrambled to get away. Her skis came to rest inches away from them.

I pushed myself over to help Harri to her feet. "You looked awesome before you had to stop."

Justin was behind me. "You're catching on fast, Harri."

Harri dusted the snow off her ski pants. "That was epic. Let's go again."

Justin took his goggles off. "Sure, but we're going to practice stopping a few times before we get to the bottom of the hill." He turned to me. "I better take one more run with her."

I folded my arms and decided I'd test out Tanya's theory on Justin. "Are you anxious to catch up with Jena?"

He rubbed his hands together. "I can't wait. The snow's great today. It's almost like powder."

I probed a little more. "Hank's somewhere up there too. He's a pretty good skier from what I can tell."

Justin put his goggles back on. "Better than I am?"

I shrugged. "Maybe."

Harri headed back for the lift. "Are you coming with us, Emma?"

"No," I said. "I'm a little whipped after my last run. I'll sit this one out."

Ten minutes later, I caught sight of Harri and Justin approaching. This time, Harri ended with a sideways slide—not exactly the hockey stop I'd seen Justin do so many times, but much better than her last stop. I waved to Justin as he headed to the express ski lift. It would've been nice to know whether his excitement about the black diamond trails had more to do with Jena or with the killer moguls.

Harri and I took another run down the green circle hill, but that was all I had the energy for. There was no way I was heading back to the lift with Harri. I hoped Jena appreciated me getting up so early for her. Plus, my nose stung from the cold.

Before Harri had a chance to get away from me, I asked her, "How about a break?"

She took off her goggles. "Sounds awesome."

After I washed my face in the bathroom, I clunked around the lodge in my ski boots, looking for Harri. I found her at the other end of the lodge, relaxing beside a round fire pit that was placed in the center of the room. A huge metal hood covered the pit, funneling the smoke up into a chimney that rose to the ceiling. Benches circled the fire pit, allowing front row seats for lots of cold bodies. Harri's face and hair glowed in the light from the fire. She looked almost like an angel. Except for her lips. They were dry and crinkled. But I could fix that. Pulling some tinted lip gloss out of my pocket, I sat beside her. "Looks like you could use some of this."

Harri sent her eyes for a roll when she saw the lip gloss. "Emma, did you ever think maybe you should focus a little more on your own problems instead of obsessing about mine?"

Chapter 13

Coach's Tip of the Day:
Fear can be a sign of progress.

*I*f Harri thought I wasn't focused on my own problems, she must not have paid attention in the car that morning. "I *have* been focusing on my own problems," I said. "You should see my new list of goals."

She blew out her breath. "Emma, you're a total stress case today. You need to relax."

I sat on the hearth with my back to the fire, facing Harri. "You really think I'm a stress case?" Whoever heard of a stressed-out life coach?

"I could be wrong, but I didn't see you eat any breakfast. And why were you so quiet in the car?"

I looked around to make sure no one else could hear our conversation. "I've got a lot on my mind."

Harri scooted closer to me, lowering her voice. "Want to talk about it?"

I took my list of goals out of my pocket. "I feel like I've drifted the past few years. I haven't accomplished anything, and I don't want to keep spinning my wheels. I want to have a career with a purpose. Remember how we talked about me getting a degree?" I unfolded the list—both pages of it. "This morning Barbara showed me Jena's list of goals, and something clicked inside me. I think what I need is clear goals—something that'll keep me on track."

Harri took the papers from my hand and looked them over. "Emma, there's like twenty things on your list."

"Twenty-seven," I corrected, hoping she wouldn't notice the one about her self-esteem. I held my hand out.

Harri folded the list up and handed it back to me. "So you think if you do these twenty-seven things, you'll what? Be a famous country singer?"

"No." I stared at the fire. "Jena wouldn't like me even if I were a famous country singer."

"And why should you care if Jena doesn't like you?" Harri asked. "Hank is totally into you."

It was true—Hank *was* totally into me. "But Hank is so perfect."

"And you are too."

I shook my head, unfolding my list to look at all twenty-seven things I needed to improve. "Except for my cooking skills and the way I never finish anything. The longer he knows me, the more he's going to find what's wrong with me."

Harri got up off the bench to sit beside me on the hearth. She rubbed her hand across my back. "If Hank cares about you, it won't matter to him that you're not a great cook. He doesn't expect you to be perfect."

I rested my elbows on my knees and looked at the first page of goals. "Some guys do expect women to be perfect. Justin likes perfect women. Tanya thinks he's Jena's secret admirer. Did you hear about the guitar she got?"

Harri nodded. "I heard. Did you ask Justin about it?"

"No," I said. "Tanya says he's been spending a lot of time at Jena's house. He never mentioned it to me. Maybe I need another goal—something about gaining Justin's trust."

Harri bent over to look at the list. "Why is my name on your list of goals?"

Great! Now she sounded angry. I folded up the list. "I was worried about you, okay? Justin said you've been going out alone at night."

Harri held out her hand. "Am I your friend or your project, Emma? It feels like you're trying to remodel me."

Figuring it was best to be honest, I offered her the list. "I'm not trying to remodel you. I'm helping you remodel yourself. You design your own destiny."

She grabbed the paper. "Now you're gonna start with the coaching again? Don't you think if I can lose fifty pounds and move all the way across the country by myself, I can handle my own problems?"

I hadn't written anything I didn't want Harri to read. "I never said you couldn't handle your own problems."

She scanned through my list again until she got to the line that read: *Help Harri have better self-esteem.* "You know what I want to do with this list?" she asked. Before I could answer, she wadded up my twenty-seven goals and threw them into the fire.

I reached for the burning piece of paper, but the fire was too hot. "Harri!" I yelled. "How am I going to remember everything I wrote down?"

"You're never going to be able to do twenty-seven goals at once. Focus on what's really important. You're on a ski trip with two fabulous guys." She got up and walked away.

Harri had a point. Every time I'd tried to help her, I'd ended up hurting her. I stood by the fire, watching my paper burn until it wasn't there anymore. It'd taken me two hours to write that list. How could she throw all my effort into the fire? It reminded me of the time Isabella threw out the centerpieces I'd made for her wedding reception. I still thought the peach-colored roses would've looked just as nice as the pink ones she chose.

I stayed by the fire until noon when I was supposed to meet the others for lunch. Justin and Jena were already eating at an extra-large booth in the cafeteria. Hank and Harri waited in line to buy food. After adding my coat to the growing pile of outerwear beside Justin, I walked over to stand behind Hank and Harri. Harri glanced at me and then looked away. I wondered if she was going to give me the silent treatment.

"The snow was great today, wasn't it?" I said.

"Yeah," Hank said. His hair was all ruffled along the side of his head—in an attractive way. Everything about him was attractive. He rubbed the side of his face where the goggles left a mark. "So you got over feeling light-headed?"

I nodded while I thought of what to say next. "Did you ski much with Jena? I hear she's good."

"Passable," he admitted. "I think you're right about the secret admirer. She gets embarrassed every time I bring it up." Hank tilted his head toward the people in front of us in line and put a finger to his lips. "But we better not mention it here."

I lowered my voice. "You know what Tanya thinks? She thinks Justin is the admirer."

We turned to look at where Justin and Jena sat at the booth. They were on opposite ends, Justin with one leg stretched out across his bench, Jena leaning on the table with her elbows. I wished I knew what she was saying. Maybe she did have a thing for Justin. She never talked to me that way.

"They *are* cute together," Harri said as Hank stepped up to place his order.

I sighed. "I don't see it."

Hank's order took longer than ours, so Harri and I ended up walking back to the table together with our food. "Thanks for listening to me vent," I said. "It helped." I didn't want to admit it, but I also felt better without that list in my pocket.

Harri raked her teeth over her bottom lip. "Sorry I freaked out on you. I was supposed to be helping you feel better." She avoided eye contact as we grabbed straws, napkins, and ketchup. "I shouldn't have burned your list. That was lame."

"I shouldn't have made you feel like a project," I said. "I only want to be your friend. Promise you'll talk to me when you feel stressed?"

Harri stared down at the food on her tray for a long time before answering, "Okay." It was almost as if she'd wanted to say no.

We squeezed into the booth with the others and dug into our food. Hank came after us, carrying a pile of something that looked like chili-cheese fries—only there was more than chili and cheese. "What is that?" I asked.

Hank sat down by Harri and popped a fry in his mouth. "It's

my own original recipe. Chili-cheese-gravy onion-ring fries. They're delicious." He held a fry up for me to eat from his hand. "Here."

I bit. It did taste pretty good—too salty, but good. Hank held out another for me. "I've always wondered what it's like to have a girl eating out of my hand."

Justin groaned. "You're reminding me of the only scene I hate in *Star Wars*."

"What's that?" Hank asked.

Justin crumpled up the paper wrapper from his hamburger in his fist. "The part where Darth Vader feeds the pear to Queen Amidala—total sap."

"That wasn't Darth Vader. That was Anakin," I said, biting into my grilled chicken sandwich.

Justin threw the crumpled up wrapper into the garbage can behind me. "Anakin *is* Darth Vader, Emma."

I could tell Jena thought she was above this conversation by the way she excused herself in a sort of huff. "I have to make a phone call." She grabbed her water bottle off the table. Hank had to get off the bench to let her out.

As she walked away, Hank raised an eyebrow at me. Then he dug into his fries with a fork, eating faster than I'd thought anyone could eat. When he was halfway through, he said, "I'm gonna head to the ski shop. I'll catch up with you guys later."

As soon as Hank was out of sight, I shook my head at Justin. "I know you don't like him, but comparing him to Darth Vader? I think you offended him."

"She's right," Harri said. "Did you see how fast he ate? He totally wanted to get out of here. He didn't even finish his fries."

Justin put his feet on the opposite bench. "Can I help it if he reminds me of Darth Vader?"

While we ate, I remembered what Harri had said—that I should ask Justin about Jena. I looked him straight in the eye. "What do you think of Jena's secret admirer?"

He shrugged. "I think he's a wimp. A real man wouldn't keep it a secret."

Somehow, that was exactly the answer I needed.

After lunch, I found Hank heading out of the ski shop. "They've found us," he said, looking as if he'd witnessed an alien abduction.

"What?"

"Jena's fans. There are at least twenty of them, texting and tweeting and who knows what else in there. We've gotta get out of here before the rest of them come."

I looked through the glass door to the ski shop. There were so many stickers advertising ski supplies on the glass that I couldn't get much of a view of the shop. "I thought she went to make a phone call. Why is she in the ski shop?"

Hank zipped his jacket. "She used her credit card to buy something, and the clerk recognized her. Now everybody knows."

A teenage girl flung open the door of the gift shop to snap a photo of us. "I got her boyfriend!" she shouted.

Hank put an arm around me and pulled me toward the girl. "What are you trying to do? I'm not with Jena—I'm with Emma." A thrill ran through me. We were already together. Capturing his heart was easier than I'd thought.

The girl covered her mouth and giggled. "Sorry."

Hank kept his arm around me. "Come on, let's hit the slopes. It's gonna get ugly here at the lodge. Or maybe you'd rather go home? I wouldn't blame you if you did." As long as he kept his arm around me, I'd go anywhere.

Another three teenage girls burst out the door and ran past us. One of them held an empty water bottle high in the air. "I got her water bottle!"

The other two let out high-pitched squeals. One of them jumped and clapped her hands together. "You should get it signed. It'll be worth more." The three girls squealed again, turned around, and ran back into the ski shop. Before the door shut, I heard one of them say, "I'll get it on video."

Hank dropped his arms to his side. "See what I mean?"

Now that he wasn't touching me anymore, I brought my focus back to the situation with Jena. "You were right about her fans. They found her even with the disguise."

"It's gonna get worse the longer we stay here."

"It'll get worse for Jena, not for us. I don't think they'll bother us at all." Why should Jena ruin our day? We were together.

Hank shook his head. "They'll bother us when we're ready to get in the car."

"But that would happen if we left now. What difference does it make if it's now or later? We might as well enjoy ourselves." I couldn't let Jena ruin *our* day.

Hank looked back at the door to the ski shop. "I don't know. It's not what I planned for us."

"Unless you think Jena wants us to leave." I walked over to look into the ski shop. "Do you think she's okay? Is it stressing her out?"

Hank frowned. "It's the price she pays for fame. You're right. It shouldn't affect us."

A few more teenage girls came out of the shop, all of them with Jena's signature on the back of their jackets. Hank rolled his eyes. "Come on. I'll help you figure out the black diamonds. The ones here are pretty tame."

I was okay with the idea of the black diamond slope until I stood at the top and looked down. Steep didn't seem like a strong enough word for it. If that slope were a road, I wouldn't drive down it *without* the snow. And bumpy. The moguls were huge. I swallowed. "Do you think they'd let me go back down the ski lift?"

Hank pulled his goggles over his eyes. "You can do this, Emma. You're a better skier than you think. When have you ever done something great without being scared?"

I pushed my poles deeper into the snow. "And this would be great because?"

"Because you're accomplishing what you've always feared. It'll be a great adrenaline rush. When you hit the moguls, keep your skis parallel, put your weight on the outside ski, then turn your body in the direction you want to go. What's the worst that can happen?"

"Death."

He put his hand on my shoulder. "Stop listening to your fears and start believing in your abilities." Then he plunged down the slope. I watched him turning effortlessly through the moguls, then skidding sideways to a stop. "Come on, Emma!" he called. "You can do it."

Hank was counting on me. I had to prove I was the woman he thought I was. "I can do this," I told myself as I slipped down the slope with the tips of my skis angled inward. If I was going to do this, I was going to do it snowplow style.

"Keep your skis parallel!" Hank yelled.

So much for my snowplow skill. I straightened my skis. I went faster. I shifted my weight to my left leg. I turned left. I shifted my weight right. I turned right. Shift. Turn. Shift. Turn. Mogul. Shift. Turn. Mogul. Shift. Turn. Mogul. I shifted my weight, but before I knew it, I was lying on my side and heading downhill. My body slid against another mogul before I came to a stop.

Hank skied over to me. "Not bad. That was a great crash."

I reached my hand up to him. "Thanks."

He pulled me up and kept hold of my hands. "Don't be afraid of falling. That's how you learn. Next time, let your hips guide your skis and stick your pole in at the edge of the mogul. That'll give you more support for your turn."

I scooted around to the side of the mogul. "That wasn't as bad as I thought it would be."

"Isn't that the way it is with everything?" he asked before he plunged down the hill.

I followed him, doing my best to loosen my hips, turn my body, and keep my skis close together. Everything was going according to my plan. I was falling for Hank Weston. And he was falling for me. I imagined driving with him—the two of us—in his Lexus, talking with him for hours on the phone, running my fingers through his curly hair, wearing his jacket when it got too cold.

Before I realized it, I'd gone through thirty or forty moguls. Once I started thinking about how well I was doing, I lost my rhythm and fell. Before Hank noticed, I got up, dusted myself off, and started skiing again. He wasn't waiting for me any more.

By the time we reached the bottom, I'd fallen three times, not three hundred times like I'd anticipated. That called for a celebration, and I couldn't think of a better celebration than a hug from Hank Weston. Only, Hank was too distracted by a crowd of people at the ski lift. "There are more of them now."

I sidestepped closer to Hank. "Does this have something to do with Jena?"

He groaned. "I told you we shouldn't have brought her."

I pointed to the jumble of people. There were probably fifty people all crowded together where the line to the ski lift should have been. "So she's in the middle of all that?" Jena might not have liked me that much, but I wasn't going to stand by while a bunch of tweens trampled her. I clicked out of my skis and handed them to Hank. "I'm going in."

It wasn't as easy as I'd thought to get close to Jena. Those little tweens wielded their ski poles like javelins. I was never so grateful for the blocking skills I'd learned during my three weeks of Tae Kwon Do classes. Everyone stood so close together, it was hard to find places to step—never mind that my feet were the size of Smart cars in those boots. The closer I got, the crazier those kids got. One of them pulled on my hair to keep me from getting any closer to Jena. "Hey," I yelled, "I'm a friend of Jena's."

That was when the girl let go of my hair and asked if I'd introduce her.

"No way," I told her as I grabbed onto my hair and tried to push past another five or six people. They wouldn't budge. Thanks to my height, Jena could see me now, so she made everyone step aside and let me through. All those kids looked at me as if I were a backup singer or a bass guitarist. One held out a pen, asking me to sign her lift pass. I shook my head and did my best impression of a bouncer— I was, after all, about a foot taller than most of those kids. "Okay, everybody!" I bellowed. "If you want to meet Jena, you have to get in a single file line." I held my arms straight out to show where the line should form. "She'll come through and shake hands, but she's done signing. Is that clear? She came here to ski."

There was a moment of stillness, then a scrambling of bodies and clicking of skis as everyone lined up. "Thanks, Emma," I heard Jena whisper. It was the first time she'd ever acknowledged my help.

Pretty soon, Hank and I sat with Jena on the ski lift, safely tucked behind the restraining bar. "Now that we're alone," Hank said, "I'll tell you my plan for getting out of here. I figured out there's a parking lot at the bottom of this run. While you two were dealing with fans, I gave my keys to Harri. She and Justin are bringing my car around there. All we have to do is get away from these people."

I looked at the lift seats in front of us and the seats behind us. They were all filled with Jena's fans. "I don't see how we're going to get away from them."

Hank lifted the safety bar. "The only way to make it work is if we get off in the middle. Most of these kids aren't going to have the guts to jump off after us."

I stared at the ground below. We were at least eight feet up, maybe nine.

"Follow my lead," Hank said, turning his body around in the seat. "This is as close to the ground as we're gonna get, and there's plenty of fresh snow here to cushion the fall. Don't wait too long though. The lift gets higher up ahead." I grabbed onto the back of the seat as he held onto the side arm rest and lowered himself until he hung backwards off the edge of the seat. Then he let go. The seat bounced, making me so glad I'd gripped onto the back with my paper-clip arm. The girls behind us screamed. Once the seat stopped bouncing, Jena lowered herself down and did the exact same thing, followed by more bouncing and screaming.

Chapter 14

Coach's Tip of the Day:
If all else fails, ask to speak to the manager.

*W*as there something wrong with me that I didn't want to jump off that lift? I hung on while the seat bounced up and down like a carnival ride in a tornado. When it stopped, I pried my paper-clip arm from the back of the seat. For Jena's sake (or really for Hank's), I slid over and grabbed the side bar with one hand and the edge of the seat with the other. I lowered myself as if I were getting into the deep end of a swimming pool. That was when I changed my mind. It was way too high to jump. But now that my arms were extended, I didn't have a choice. With my skis on, I was too heavy. My elbows were about to come out of their sockets. So I bent my knees a little, lifted the tips of my skis like a jumper, and let go, screaming.

I couldn't believe I landed on my feet. My ankles burned with pain, but I was skiing downhill, as if I were some sort of stunt double. Hank was right about the adrenaline rush. I felt invincible . . . until I saw a snowmobile heading toward me. That was one thing about my hair. My ponytail was like a red flag flapping behind me. And the fact that I was six feet tall—I might as well have worn a sign that said "look at me" because people stared at me everywhere I went. I was always the one that got caught. I'd known that since my first experience toilet-papering houses.

As the snowmobile closed in on me, I hit the moguls. With every bump, the pain from my ankles rose through my legs and body. I wanted to keep skiing, knowing Hank and Jena were ahead of me, but the pain was too much. My feet wouldn't turn around another mogul. I hit the next mogul straight on and landed in a snow ditch with one ski still attached. The other accelerated downhill.

I closed my eyes from the pain and heard the ski patrol guy swearing. As I opened my eyes, he reached down and tore off my lift pass. "Dude, you are one sorry skier. Most jumpers at least have some skills. The guys down at the lodge aren't gonna be happy with you. You could have derailed the lift when you jumped." He was a pimply faced teen who seemed happy to have someone to yell at.

I twisted around in the snow like a turtle on its back while he watched me. There was something about getting caught like this that made me feel like a kid who'd wet her pants. Why couldn't I be a rebel like every other young single my age? Was it so bad to break the rules once in a while? As far as I knew, nobody had been hurt. And where were Hank and Jena? Were they going to leave me here? "I didn't know all that about derailing the lift," I told the ski patrol kid. "I wouldn't have done it if I'd known."

He thrust his poles into the snow. "That's why there's a sign. 'Stay in your chair.' You'll have to give me the names of the others too."

Once I had my remaining ski underneath me again, I looked for Hank or Jena. There was no sign of either one, so I followed the patrol guy to the lodge, retrieving my missing ski along the way. After taking away all my rental equipment, the guy took my picture. For the first time in my life, I felt sorry for the women in those police mug shots. It wasn't like a girl could look her best when the person taking her picture thought she was the scum of the earth. Then I had to sit in an office, filling out forms—there was one for me and one for Jena.

I'd finished my form and started on Jena's when I heard Justin's voice outside the office door. "This whole thing wouldn't have happened if you people had done a better job of crowd control for Ms. Farley. You do know this is her favorite ski resort? She comes here all the time." The sound of his voice was like sun shining after a storm. I wasn't alone in this anymore. There was one person to defend me, to tell them I wasn't as bad as they thought.

"Ms. Farley?" the ski patrol guy squeaked.

"Jena Farley, the famous country singer," Justin explained. "You probably saw her crowd of fans earlier."

"Hold on, sir. I think I need to get my manager."

I pushed against the door and peeked through the crack at Justin, standing straight and tall with his chest out. "You okay?" he asked.

I let out my breath. "Yeah." I could relax now that Justin was with me.

He spoke through his teeth. "I told you Hank's an idiot."

I rubbed my ankles, which still hurt from the big jump. "His plan would've worked if I'd jumped sooner."

Justin scratched his head. "You've fallen hard—in more than one way."

"As usual, you don't approve," I said.

He put his hands on his hips. "You jumped off a ski lift because he told you to, Emma."

I swallowed. "It's not as simple as that. We were trying to get away from a bunch of crazy twelve-year-olds." I turned back to the form I was filling out for Jena while Justin went out into the hall. I couldn't remember Jena's house number, so I gave them her top-secret phone number. I also had a picture of her somewhere on my phone.

While I looked for Jena's picture, Justin came in with the manager, the only guy I'd seen all day long who wore dress pants. Justin sat in the plastic chair beside me while the manager sat on the edge of the desk in front of us and folded his arms. He was a middle-aged guy with graying sideburns. "I understand Jena Farley is somehow involved in this incident," the manager said.

I held up the picture of Jena and me on my phone—the one Barbara took of us at the Christmas Eve dinner. "We're her friends."

He took the papers I'd filled out and looked over them. "Please let Ms. Farley know we regret what happened today. It was an oversight on our part. If she'll coordinate with us in the future, we'll be happy to help her with crowd control." He dropped the paper I filled out for Jena into the shredder. I waited for him to put my form through the shredder, but he didn't. "We appreciate Ms. Farley's business, and we hope she'll enjoy Blaze Mountain in the future. In fact, she's welcome to ski for free to make up for her troubles today."

I pointed to the form in his hand. "Are you going to shred my form too?"

He looked at my form as if seeing it for the first time. "It's Blaze Mountain policy to ban jumpers from the mountain. We can't have you putting other skiers in danger."

I slid to the edge of my seat. "But you're not banning Jena. She jumped too. She's the reason I jumped."

The manager dropped my paper into one of the hanging file folders. "Every time a skier jumps off a chair, we risk derailing the lift."

I stood so I towered over the manager. "Are you telling me I'm banned from the mountain, but Jena isn't? She jumped before I did. I was only trying to catch my ride home."

He walked around to the other side of his desk and opened a drawer in the filing cabinet. "That's what I'm saying."

"She needs to fill out another form," Justin interjected, "for her friend, Hank Weston. It was his idea to jump in the first place."

My jaw dropped. Was Justin really going to betray Hank?

Justin stood up. "If you don't mind, I'll go grab a hot cocoa to take to Jena's car while Emma fills that out."

The manager handed me another form, then smiled at Justin. "Wait—I'll get the drink for Ms. Farley. Please let her know that from here on out all her drinks are on the house. We're so sorry for any trouble she had today." He rushed out the door in search of a hot cocoa for Jena.

I gritted my teeth so hard Hank's name came out looking like "Hand Waver." Justin bent over the paper. "Maybe I'd better fill out this one."

I shoved the paper into his hand and wrapped my hands around my ankles—they were still sore. Justin did a thorough job on Hank's form, calling Randall on the phone to make sure he had the correct contact information and referencing pictures Hank had posted online. He finished filling out the form as the manager brought the hot cocoa for Jena.

Then we were out of there. Justin handed me the hot cocoa as we walked out to the parking lot. "This is for you—a peace offering."

I looked at the Styrofoam cup. "I thought it was for your precious Jena."

"I said I was taking it to Jena's car. I didn't say it was *for* Jena. Why didn't you tell me you fainted this morning?"

I took a sip. It was the perfect temperature. "Oh, that. I didn't faint. I just blacked out. It wasn't that big of a deal. It happens sometimes when I don't drink enough water. It's my low blood pressure. You're not going to tell my dad, are you?"

Justin laughed. "About which part?" He looked at me a long time, as if he were my dad, then he said, "I won't tell him. But I wish you'd be more careful."

When we got to Hank's car, I sat in the middle of the back in between Jena and Justin. Hank was in such a hurry to leave that he backed out of his spot before I put on my seat belt. "Sorry you had to take the fall for us, Emma," he said as he rounded the corner out of the parking lot. "I'll make it up to you."

Justin clicked in his seat belt. "You took the fall too, Hank. We had to fill out a form with your name and address. You won't be skiing here anymore. Jena's the only one of you who can come back."

"I guess I owe you one too, Knightley. I'll have to do you a favor sometime."

Justin pulled his iPod out of his coat pocket. "Thanks anyway, but I don't need any favors from you, Hank."

Jena was too busy texting to hear our conversation. Hank laughed that deep laugh of his. "I don't think I'll miss this resort. I've seen better. What do you say about a New Year's Eve party at my house to pay you back?"

"Sounds great," I said. "I love New Year's Eve parties." I nudged Justin in the side with my elbow, trying to get him to accept Hank's invitation, but he didn't say anything.

As we headed down the mountain, I finished off my hot cocoa. Then I went to work taking off my jacket and ski pants. I only bumped Jena once, but, of course, it was the first time she looked at me since I'd gotten in the car. "Sorry," I said. Jena gave a slow nod and turned back to her texting. So much for all the favors I'd done for her. It didn't seem they'd made any difference.

I leaned back into Hank's leather seat and popped one of the ear buds from Justin's iPod into my ear. I didn't know if he'd done it to annoy me, but he was playing one of Jena's songs, something about how everybody needs respect. I stuck my tongue out at him. He laughed as if he did it on purpose, changing the song to "You're So Vain," which made me laugh—until I started to wonder which one Justin thought was vain. Was it Jena or Hank?

Chapter 15

Coach's Tip of the Day:
Proper sleep is the foundation of a well-balanced life.

I believed in the restorative power of sleep. That's why I used a white noise machine and sprayed my sheets with a lavender essential oil infusion. All the experts said to turn off the phone too, but ever since I'd met Harri, I slept better with it on. That night, she called at 3:00 a.m.

"Phil has a new girlfriend," was the first thing she said.

I turned on the lamp beside my bed. "What?"

"He put her picture on Facebook. She's moving down here in a week. She's way prettier than I am," Harri went on. "Have you seen the picture?"

I sat up out of bed. "Give me a minute."

I logged onto my tablet while Harri told me the woman's name was Alexandria and that she had beautiful dark hair. I searched for Phil on my Facebook account, but nothing came up. Even after I put in his full name, I couldn't find him.

"I can't see his pictures." Was it possible Phil was mad enough to unfriend me? "How about I come over and show it to you?" Harri said. "I want to see what you think."

I stumbled around my room, trying to find my purse. "Harri, it's three in the morning. You shouldn't be out walking. This isn't Utah. Around here, you'll get mugged or raped if you walk by yourself at night. I'll come pick you up."

Harri paused for a while before answering, "That stuff happens in Utah too, but I'm not the kind of girl that gets raped or mugged."

"Harri, that is wrong on so many levels. First of all, you're attractive, and second of all, rapists and muggers don't care if you're attractive. They're looking for opportunity, not beauty." Harri may not have wanted a coach, but she sure needed someone to help her rewrite the stories she'd been telling herself.

"You might as well know," Harri said, "I was already walking when I called you. I'm almost to your house now. Can you let me in?"

"Sure, but I wish you wouldn't walk outside alone at night anymore. I care about you too much to let you do that."

By the time I opened the front door, Harri stood there in her coat and pajamas, holding her phone out, waiting for me to look at the picture of Phil's girlfriend. The blast of cold air from the open doorway went right through my double-brushed Portuguese flannel pajama pants.

"Come on in," I told her.

She leaned against the doorframe. "She's thinner than I am. I knew Phil was into skinny girls. That's why he liked you."

I took the phone from her hand. "Come inside already. It's freezing outside."

Dad came out of his bedroom, knotting the belt around his white terry cloth robe. "What's going on?"

I glanced at the picture of Phil cuddling up to a woman with short, brown hair. "Nothing, Dad. Harri just needed to talk."

Dad squinted at the clock on the wall. "A good treatment for insomnia is to keep the lights dim, lie very still, and maybe take melatonin. Would you like a melatonin pill, Harri?"

Harri plopped down on the sofa. "No, thanks. I think you'd have to shoot me with a tranquilizer gun to get me to go to sleep today."

Dad rubbed his chin. "I'll go get some melatonin."

While Dad searched through the medicine cabinet, Harri pointed to the picture on her phone. "I think he's in love with her. How am I going to live without him? He's become a part of me."

I stared at the picture of Phil with his arm around the dark-haired woman. "They look happy. Not that he wouldn't be happier with you. She looks nice, but something's weird about her eyebrows. I think she drew them on in the wrong place."

Harri let out her breath with a groan. "Do you think that's going to make me feel better, Emma, that Phil rejected me for someone with messed-up eyebrows? I think it'd be better if you said she's beautiful."

"I didn't say you weren't beautiful." I sat on the sofa as Dad came back in with a glass of water, a little white pill, and a pillow. "Don't you think Harri's beautiful, Dad?"

Dad handed Harri the items. "Of course, she's beautiful. You're both beautiful. Here, Harri, I sprinkled some lavender oil on the pillowcase. It should help." He switched off the overhead lights. "That's better. Now get some sleep."

I stared at the picture of Phil's girlfriend, trying to find something nice to say about her. "She has nice, full lips."

Harri took her phone back to look at the picture. "Definitely better than my lips. Mine are so thin. Thin lips, fat hips." She made a fishy kiss at me.

"I didn't say they were better than your lips, Harri. You wanted me to find something good to say about her, so I'm saying something good."

Dad kissed me on the cheek. "Emma, I don't think this is helping. Now, if you'll excuse me, I'm going back to bed."

Dad was right. What kind of a coach was I? Harri didn't need to see Phil's girlfriend through my eyes; she needed to see herself. "Harri, first of all, you need to forget about Phil, and, second of all, you need to get over this whole body image hang-up. You've lost fifty pounds. You don't look the same as you think you do."

"I don't think you know how hard this is for me." Her eyes glistened with tears.

"You're right," I said. "I don't know how hard it is, but I still want to help. I'll do something that's hard for me too. It'll help me sympathize." I fished around in my brain for something—anything—that was hard for me. All I could come up with was how I couldn't stop comparing myself to Jena, so I said, "I'll write Jena a letter about how much I admire her." I meant it. If Harri could get over Phil, I could swallow my pride. And after the whole goal-setting fiasco, it was clear that comparing myself to Jena was doing more harm than I'd thought.

Harri threw her head back and laughed. "You would do that?"

"I've compared myself to Jena for as long as I can remember. It's a bad habit. I'll write her a letter and leave it on her doorstep before the sun rises. I'll listen to all her albums too. And we're going to buy some clothes that actually fit you. It'll be my way to pay you back for burning your bum."

Without changing out of our pajamas, we drove to the twenty-four-hour Target in Manassas and headed straight for the clearance racks. I could tell right away that Harri had no idea what size she wore. Even her underwear was too big. I spent a good half hour running back and forth between the dressing room and the racks, trying to determine the right sizes for everything. Harri settled on a bright-colored cardigan, a fitted T-shirt, and a pair of jeans. Because I didn't want to spend another minute wandering around in my pajamas, I also found a pair of workout capris and a top for myself. We paid for the clothes, then headed straight for the restrooms to change.

Harri rustled around in the stall next to mine. "Are you sure these clothes fit me? They feel so tight."

I hung my coat and pajamas on the hook in the handicapped stall. "It's because you're used to wearing clothes that are way too big. Trust me. They fit perfectly."

"Are you sure?" Harri asked. "I hate people to see the shape of my body."

"Clothes are supposed to skim over the shape of your body. They're much more attractive that way. Haven't you ever worn clothes that fit?"

"I mostly wore hand-me-downs from my cousin," Harri said. "It wasn't like I was one of the popular kids or anything. No one paid much attention to my clothes."

I shoved my pajamas into the Target bag. "So your parents never took you shopping?"

"Nope," Harri said. "Mom was too busy, and Dad just wanted me to do my chores and stay out of his way. I was the oldest, so I was in charge a lot. Most of the time, there wasn't anyone watching me. We didn't have money for extra things."

No wonder Harri had let me give her so much advice. No one else ever had.

Two hours later, it was still pitch black outside except for a few streetlights. We were parked in front of the Bateses' home with Jena's latest album playing on my stereo. Jena's music wasn't as bad as I'd thought.

As we listened, Harri talked. "It was a major problem in my high school to be overweight," she said. "I didn't have a lot of friends."

"Do you ever hear from them anymore?" I asked.

Harri looked out her side window. "Not really. One joined the navy. Two got married. And the others got all weird when I started exercising and watching my portion sizes."

"It's normal for our friends to be uncomfortable when we start to make changes," I said.

Harri shrugged. "I guess that should make me feel better. What about you? What happened to your high school friends?"

I flipped down the lighted mirror on my car's visor and looked at my reflection. It was pretty obvious I'd missed five hours of sleep. "My high school friends? They all went off to college. I hardly hear from them anymore. Back in high school, I always planned I'd go away to college too. Then I started getting acceptance letters, and I saw the look on Dad's face. He was pretending to be happy for me. I could tell he couldn't handle being a widower *and* an empty nester. So I stayed home. If I could go back in time, I'd still stay, but I wouldn't give up on my career plans like I did."

"Maybe you should take your own advice," Harri said, "and start designing your future. You can't do anything to change your past." Here I'd been looking for sympathy, and Harri threw my own advice at me instead. Was that how I talked to her? No wonder she'd gotten annoyed at the ski lodge. Harri pointed her finger down the street. "Do you think that's one of Jena's fans?"

I put down my mascara wand and looked at the outline of a bicy-clist approaching in the dim light. "It's a guy, so probably not. Most of her fans are twelve-year-old girls." I pulled the visor back down and worked on my eye makeup. If I was going to write a bunch of compliments to Jena, I was going to look my best before I started writing.

"Then why is he stopping?" Harri asked.

I flipped up the visor to see Hank Weston. As I rolled down my window, he swung a leg off his bike. "I know you two are big fans, but isn't it a little early?" He wasn't wearing one of those weird, span-dex biking outfits. Instead he wore something that looked like black sweatpants along with a yellow bike jacket.

"You should talk," I teased back, my breath steaming up the air between us. "You're here too." Was I ever glad I wasn't wearing my pajamas.

Hank leaned over with one hand on the edge of my window and his other on his bike. "I happened to ride down this street. That's one of the things I like most about Vienna. It's great for biking. What's your excuse?"

"I need to drop something off for Jena." I could have told him more, but I wasn't ready to open up to him about my jealousy issue.

Hank took off his helmet, revealing his mess of short, ruffled curls. "How about the three of us do breakfast together? A nice, slow sit-down breakfast, so we can get to know each other better."

Harri looked at the time on her phone and bit her lip. "Avery wakes up in less than an hour, but you two can go ahead without me if you want."

Hank whipped out his phone and started texting. I guessed his mom was keeping tabs on him. That was no excuse, though. Texting during a face-to-face was rude. If he was going to be a CEO, he'd have to behave better than that. Later on, when things became more serious between the two of us, I'd talk with him about it. For now, though, I'd be patient. When he finished, he looked at Harri. "How about I bike over and get muffins or something? We can eat before Harri has to be back."

I opened my purse. "That sounds good. Here, I'll give you some money."

Hank climbed on his bike. "It's my treat. I'll be back fast."

Harri kneeled backward on her seat to watch him ride away. "He is so into you. I wish I could get guys to buy me breakfast and invite me to their New Year's Eve parties."

She was right. Everything *was* going well with Hank. The next step was a one-on-one date between the two of us. "In case you didn't notice, Hank's buying you breakfast too."

Harri picked up her phone. "He's buying me breakfast because I'm your friend. You should have let me take a pass when I gave you the opening." She stared at that stupid picture of Phil with his new girlfriend again.

"Harri, you have to stop looking at that picture. It's like you're poisoning yourself."

She turned off the phone and stuck it in her coat pocket. "You think you can write a letter to Jena before Hank gets back?"

I opened the package of stationery I'd gotten at Target, then found an old ballpoint pen in the car. At first, my letters looked big and crooked. As I wrote Jena's name, the pen left only an impression—no ink. Wouldn't it figure that even the pen didn't want me to write her?

I retraced the letters with the pen:

> *Dear Jena,*
> *Ever since I was a little girl, I've felt jealous of you.*

No—too undignified. I wasn't going to grovel. I grabbed another note card and started over:

> *Dear Jena,*
> *I've always admired you and wished we could be better friends.*

That sounded too bitter. I grabbed another note card to write:

> *Dear Jena,*
> *I've admired you for a long time, and I wanted to let you know I'm proud of all you've accomplished. You and I are so different. It seems like all my life, people have compared the two of us.*

That one wasn't going to work either. I crumpled it up.

Harri sat still beside me. "Emma, you don't have to write her if you don't want to. You've already helped me a ton."

"If I'm going to get over my problems and become a life coach, I have to stop comparing myself to Jena. If I don't do it now, I'll never do it. On this one, I'm going to forget all about the past and focus on the present."

I picked up another note card and wrote:

> *Dear Jena,*
> *I've listened to your albums, and I wanted to tell you I'm so impressed by your talent. I don't usually listen to country music, but I like some of your songs enough to keep listening to them. My favorite is the one about nosy people, but I liked a lot of the others too. The one about 100 things that make you happy is great. I can tell you've worked hard to accomplish your goals. You're a great example for me.*

I was about to start over and leave out that part about Jena being a good example, but I saw Jena walking toward my car. I signed my name and shoved the card in an envelope while Harri rolled down her window. "Morning, Jena," I chirped. "I bet you're wondering what we're doing here so early."

Jena wore gray yoga pants with a lavender top. She looked up and down the street—probably scanning for paparazzi. "When we noticed you were out here, Mom and I decided to invite you in for breakfast." She looked at the note card in my hand. Since she had no idea it was for her, I could still throw it out if I wanted to.

Harri smoothed on some tinted lip gloss. "Hank went to get us something at the grocery store. We were going to eat out here in the car. You don't have to bother."

Jena smoothed her hair out of her face. "It's no bother. Hank can come too, if he likes." It almost felt like Jena was trying to be my friend. Maybe it wasn't wrong to hope I could heal our relationship.

Chapter 16

Coach's Tip of the Day:
You can never have too many
positive people in your life.

Besides the fact that my stomach revolted at the thought of handing Jena that note, it was way too early for breakfast. I twisted off part of the outside of the croissant that Hank brought me and ate it like I would a piece of cardboard, only it tasted nothing like cardboard. It was buttery and soft, the cotton candy version of bread.

Hank and Jena were both texting. Barbara poured orange juice into glasses. "We always get these croissants for Christmas morning. They're Jena's favorites. It was so nice of you to bring them, Hank. I can't believe you can go biking at this hour of the morning. It's so cold." She handed me a glass. "What about you two? What are you doing up so early?"

I wasn't about to let Barbara in on the whole story. But it didn't make sense for Harri and me to be driving around at 6:00 a.m., even if I was dropping off a note for Jena. "Harri and I went shopping."

Barbara stared at me. "Isn't it a little early for shopping?"

I smoothed the napkin on my lap. "After Black Friday, I got hooked on shopping in the middle of the night."

Barbara took another sip. "Hmm. Well."

The conversation stopped short as Barbara—yes, Barbara— searched for something to say. The silence jolted Hank away from his texting. "I love how the sun rises through the trees here. Vienna is a beautiful town."

Barbara sighed. "When I was your age, I never got up before the sun. Now that you can get flannel sheets for $9.99 a pop, I don't see how you all get out of bed. I *can* understand Jena getting up early. She likes to get out before her fans get here."

Harri reached for a second croissant. "I never went to bed last night."

I pressed Harri's foot under the table, trying to warn her not to spill her guts to Barbara, but she went on ahead, telling Barbara all about Phil Elton's new girlfriend and her midnight crisis. Thankfully, she left off the part about my note to Jena. Barbara's eyes were wide and her hands still as she listened. Hank and Jena went on texting through all of it. Jena could have been conducting business, but Hank? He was a college student on Christmas break. If he was texting his mom, what could she have to say this early in the morning? When Jena got up to make a smoothie, I whispered to Hank, "Don't you know it's rude to text at the table?"

Hank slid the phone into his pocket. "That's what I like about you, Emma. You're never afraid to speak your mind."

I bumped shoulders with him. "And that's what I like about you, Hank. You're so cooperative. I'm looking forward to your party."

Hank spoke loud enough for everyone to hear. "Oh yeah, Dad and I have big plans for the New Year's Eve party. We have the basement all set up for karaoke. Tanya's planning the games. We're serving wings, pizza, the whole works. I hope you can all make it."

I took out my phone to enter the date on my calendar. I'd never sung karaoke before, and, if I ever did, it wouldn't be in front of Hank. "Does Randall sing karaoke?" I asked.

Hank chuckled. "Yeah. He's pretty good." Hank wasn't looking at me. He stared at Jena, who was loading the blender with frozen fruit.

"Looking forward to a smoothie?" I asked.

He laughed again, leaning in so I could hear him over the sound of the blender. "Dare me to ask her what Reggie Van Camp likes in his smoothie? She thinks I'm a big fan of Reggie."

I shrugged. "If you really want to know, go ahead. I doubt she'll tell you." How many people paid attention to their friends' taste in smoothies anyway?

Hank stood up. "Watch how she reacts."

It turned out I couldn't see how she reacted because Hank stood in front of her. I couldn't hear either because the blender ran during their conversation. When Hank came back, he whispered, "Mango and pineapple with coconut milk."

Before Jena could pour us whatever smoothie she'd made, Harri announced she had to get going. I forced myself to hand that note to Jena.

Jena set down her smoothie to take the note. "Is this for me?"

I stuck my hands in my coat pockets. "Yeah."

I was hoping she'd open it right away to read it, gush about how I'd listened to all her albums, and give me a hug. Instead, she tossed it onto a big pile of unopened mail on a corner of the kitchen counter. "Thanks."

"Aren't you going to read it?" I asked.

Jena picked her smoothie up again. "Oh, is it time-sensitive?"

Harri looked at her watch, reminding me we didn't have time to spare. "No," I said, trying not to sound disappointed. "It's just a friendly note. Thanks for breakfast."

Hank scooted in his chair. "I guess I'd better be going too."

On our way out, we passed Barbara's stack of tabloids, and there on top was a picture of Justin standing with Jena on her front porch. The title read "Renovations or Rendezvous?" All my good feelings about Jena rushed out of me like air out of a popped balloon. I shouldn't have worried about it because what Justin did was his own business. And it wasn't like he was actually dating her—as the article claimed. But there was something about the possibility of Justin dating Jena that I hated. It wasn't like I could go on being friends with Justin if they started dating—or if he married her.

The minute we left the house, I noticed Danny, Jena's tabloid photographer, looking at us through his camera. Behind me, Hank groaned. "Does that guy ever give up? Here, let me take you to your car." He grabbed my hand.

I squeezed his hand. "Thanks for breakfast."

Hank led me down the front steps. "My pleasure."

A teenage boy and girl called out to us from the sidewalk. "Is it true Jena Farley lives here?"

Before I could answer, Hank yelled back. "I'm afraid you have the wrong address. This house belongs to Barbara Bates."

I giggled as we walked down the driveway to the street.

Hank stopped in front of my car and drew me closer. "Do you have a busy day planned?" It was the perfect opening for a date invitation.

I stepped closer to him. "It depends who's asking."

"Maybe I'll call you later on."

I turned to see Harri was already in the car. "That'd be great. I better get going. Harri has to get to work."

When I turned back, his face was in front of mine, then he kissed me—on the lips. It wasn't a long kiss, but it was definitely a kiss.

After dropping Harri off, I drove straight home, where I expected to head straight for the bathroom and waste at least twenty-five gallons of hot water in the shower, pondering the meaning of Hank's kiss. Instead I found Justin building a playdough Jurassic Park in the kitchen with our nieces. Though I usually enjoyed it when Justin showed up early in the morning, today was different. I needed my space. "Don't you have to work today?" I asked.

Justin set his Elasmosaurus in a lake of blue playdough. "A little. I'm helping Jena with some remodeling this morning. I have to check in on my other projects this afternoon. John and Isabella didn't get much sleep last night, so I brought the kids over here."

"John and Isabella aren't the only ones who didn't sleep."

He looked at me. "You too?"

I pointed to the circles under my eyes. "I've been up since 3:00 a.m. Can't you tell?"

He shrugged. "There's no point in saying you look fine because you won't believe me."

I plopped down on a chair beside Kyra and rolled a snake out of red dough. "No, I wouldn't."

"How about a criticism sandwich?" he said. "You're grumpy but you look great, even though you have a smudge on your eyelid. Do you believe me now?"

"I guess." I rubbed my eyelids. "Have you ever wondered what it feels like to be in love?"

"Is this about Hank Weston?" Justin lifted Zoey up to smell her diaper.

I slid to the edge of my seat, promising myself not to mention this morning's kiss. "It's more of a hypothetical question. Don't you ever wonder what it's like to be in love?"

Justin grimaced at the smell of the diaper. "Sure I've wondered. Do you have any diapers around here?"

I walked to the hall closet. "I guess to know what it feels like, you have to be in love." I grabbed the little diaper bag Tanya made for Isabella's kids.

I gave the bag to Justin, but he shook his head. "It's your turn this time. I did the last one." He put a changing pad down on the floor and laid the baby on it with her legs facing me. "If you want to know what I think, I think being in love must be a lot like being friends, only you feel a stronger affection for that one person than you do for anyone else."

I peeked inside the diaper, which didn't look good. "I saw the article about you and Jena, by the way. Care to fill me in?"

"There's an article about me and Jena?"

"Barbara has it on her paper stack. Maybe you haven't seen it yet. It has a picture of you standing together on the front porch. It shows the back of your head."

The corners of his mouth pulled up a little, then they went down. "What's it to you?" Did I detect a hint of Southern accent?

"Nothing."

"If you're not going to change her, I will." He swiveled the baby around and reached for the diaper. "Jena and I aren't dating, if that's what you want to know."

That didn't tell me anything. What I really needed to know was whether he *wanted* to date her. I swiveled Zoey back around and opened up her diaper, which made me regret turning her back around. "Well, keep me in the loop, okay?"

"Don't go playing matchmaker with me and Jena." His accent was in full force now.

"I wasn't going to."

"Good," he said. "Because I don't need any help in that area."

Chapter 17

I wasn't going to sit around the house all day waiting for Hank to call me, so I told Justin I'd help him with his projects. That way, at least I wouldn't look like I was desperate. A woman perusing the aisles of the home improvement store never thought about love—plumbing or painting maybe, but not love.

What did a kiss from Hank mean? Was it a friendly, Southern gesture? If it were, he would have kissed Harri too. But he didn't kiss Harri. He only kissed me. It had to be a romantic kiss. The next logical step was dating. I could see him spending a lot of money on restaurant meals and concert tickets. We'd go biking and scuba diving and all the other things you could do if you were dating a guy with a lot of money. And the New Year's Eve party—I'd have someone to kiss at midnight. This was what I thought about while Justin found the supplies to finish Jena's bathroom.

Hank called while Justin was picking out grout. By the time I answered, I was ready to ask about the kiss. I was also ready to say yes to the restaurants, concerts, and scuba diving.

Too bad he'd called for another reason. "My grandpa passed away this morning, so I'm on my way to Huntsville now. Sorry I didn't have time to say good-bye in person."

This explained why Hank had been texting so much—it had to do with his grandpa's health. I took a few steps toward the doorknob aisle, prepping myself for a private conversation. "I'm so sorry about your grandpa, Hank. Don't worry about me. You need to focus on your family's needs."

"I told my boss I'd probably be gone a few weeks. I have to help Mom settle all of Grandpa's affairs."

I forced myself to smile, so I wouldn't sound disappointed. "I understand."

"Try not to miss me too much," he teased.

Considering his grandpa had just passed away, it wasn't the best time, but I liked to define my relationships early on. "Hank, what did you mean by that kiss?"

He chuckled. "You're on to me, huh? I knew you were starting to suspect something. Listen, I'll back off, okay? That guy with the camera makes me do stupid things."

Whatever Hank's hang-up with the paparazzi was, it was beside the point. I whispered into the phone, "I usually don't kiss guys I'm not dating."

"I know, Emma. I'm sorry. I should have thought it through a little better. It was a spur of the moment idea."

"I understand, Hank. I get a little too spontaneous sometimes."

"I'll have to postpone the party. Do you think it'd be okay to have a New Year's Eve party on January fifteenth?"

The fifteenth? I'd have to wait more than two weeks to see him again. Knowing Hank's mom and her penchant for delaying his departures, it might be longer than that. I let out my breath and tried to seem optimistic. "It'll be great whenever we have it. Just try to be back before Valentine's Day, okay?"

"Sounds like a plan." He paused. "Now that you know my secret, can you imagine how disappointed I am to have to leave?"

My heart raced at Hank's confession. "It's very disappointing." I wanted to say something equally as tender to him, but Justin was walking toward me. I had to think of something that wasn't too mushy. "I've enjoyed our time together. I hope you have a safe trip. Sorry about your grandpa."

We said our good-byes and hung up as Justin came to a stop beside me. "Did you see any doorknobs you liked over here? Jena wants me to replace hers."

How could I think of Jena's doors when Hank was leaving? There would be no party, no dates, and no kissing for at least three weeks. I couldn't disguise my disappointment, so I told Justin, "That was Hank. His grandpa died, so he's headed back to Alabama."

Justin picked a package of doorknobs off the shelf. "That's too bad. You were looking forward to his party." He held the package for me to see. "What do you think of these?"

I looked at the copper-colored knobs and groaned. Is this what my life had come to? Picking out doorknobs? "I'm sure I'm the last person in the world qualified to choose Jena Farley's doorknobs."

Justin put the package back on the shelf. "Come on, Scarlett. Pick some out for my house, then."

I pointed to some brushed silver levers. "If you're going to call me Scarlett, you'll have to pick out your own doorknobs. I don't think I'm much like Scarlett O'Hara."

Justin blew out his breath, causing his lips to flap. "I call you Scarlett because it means red, and you have red—or auburn—hair. It doesn't have anything to do with your temper." He grabbed the silver lever handles off the shelf.

I folded my arms. "My temper?" The words came out louder than I'd intended.

Justin tried not to crack a smile as he loaded door handles into his cart. "What I meant to say was it had nothing to do with your personality." Justin pushed the cart past me. "Why don't we go grab something to eat?"

All I wanted was bacon dipped in maple syrup, but I convinced myself to order food that would improve my overall health and well-being. I got a spinach omelet made with flaxseed oil, hoping it would cheer me up. It didn't. I still had this dread inside me, a sort of boredom with my life—all because Hank was leaving.

While Justin applied the grout on Jena's bathroom floor, I sat cross-legged in the hallway. The new bathroom was bigger—Justin's crew had knocked out a wall and included what used to be a closet as part of the bathroom. It now had a shower and a jetted tub. The walls were tiled with sandy-colored natural stone, and the floor was a grayer stone tile.

"I think I'm falling in love with Hank," I told Justin. I faced his back, which made it easier to talk to him about love.

Justin concentrated on applying the grout against the edge of the bathtub. "What makes you say that?"

"I feel so bummed he's leaving. It's like everything is going to be completely lifeless without him. I've never felt that way about anyone before."

Justin removed his hoodie, revealing his blue Starfleet Academy T-shirt, along with a good look at his biceps. That was the thing about men who lifted heavy things for their jobs—they had great muscles. "Maybe you need to get out a little more—plan a vacation or something," he told me.

A vacation? I'd confessed my love for Hank, and Justin suggested I take a vacation. "You don't think Hank and I are a good match, do you?"

He tossed me his hoodie. "You want the truth?"

"Yeah."

"You're not a good match."

I folded his hoodie, which carried a hint of his signature laundry detergent scent. "Is it because I'm a community college dropout?"

Justin moved a squeegee over the tiles. "You're not a community college dropout. If he were a decent guy—a guy like Rob Martinez—that wouldn't matter to him anyway."

"I really am sorry about Rob."

"You broke his heart."

"You mean Harri broke his heart."

"I meant what I said, Emma, but that's beside the point. You know I don't like Hank, so why would I think he's a good match for you?"

That made sense. Justin didn't like Hank, but he did like me—at least he liked me the way a guy liked his pesky little sister. "You think he's not good enough for me." Justin didn't say anything. I noticed the way he wore his belt tight enough so his pants wouldn't slide down in back. Believe me; I'd seen enough of the plumber effect to appreciate that kind of modesty in a man. "Where's Jena, anyway?" It made sense that I should weigh in on his relationships too.

Justin nodded in the direction of the hallway. "In her room. She told me earlier she had a migraine. That's why I let myself in. I usually knock."

I wondered if Jena might be jealous of the time I spent with Justin. I lowered my voice in case she could hear us. "Does she usually spend a lot of time with you when you come here?"

Justin wiped excess grout off the tiles with a sponge. "Are you working for the tabloids, Emma?"

I shrugged. "I was just curious."

Justin rinsed his sponge in a bucket of water. "I spend most of my time on the bigger projects, so it's not like I'm here all that much. I'm only doing this grout job because all the guys are on vacation, which reminds me—you never said what you thought about my vacation idea."

A vacation *was* a good idea. "Where would we go? Disney World? I've never been to Florida."

Justin chuckled. "I was thinking more of a day trip to somewhere close by. Got any places you've always wanted to see?"

With my Dad being so afraid of car accidents, I hadn't been to many places at all. "It's not too hard to think of places I'd like to see—I've never seen New York City or visited the Amish. I've never sailed on Chesapeake Bay. I've never been to Williamsburg or Gettysburg or Kings Dominion."

Justin raised his eyebrows. "Kings Dominion? You didn't miss much—other than a couple of good roller coaster rides. What about Sugarloaf Mountain? Harri told me once she'd like to see it. Have you ever gone there? And we ought to take her to see the bluebells at Bull Run when they bloom."

I remembered a picture I'd seen of blue blossoms carpeting the floor of the woods around Bull Run. "Yeah, we ought to do that, and I've always wanted to go on one of those Potomac River cruises, but that's more of a romantic thing."

"You know what my mom would say? 'There's no use putting life on hold waiting for a romantic relationship,' " Justin said.

I rolled my eyes. "You're one to talk, Mister I-don't-have-any-furniture."

"Get a group together, and we'll all go."

While Justin worked, we had two hours to chat about all the places we'd go and the people we'd invite to come along. It was a good project to keep me distracted while Hank was away. First on the list was Sugarloaf Mountain. We'd go there in early April.

When Justin had almost finished, I carried a pile of leftover tiles to his truck. I was passing back through the kitchen, when I noticed a new addition to Barbara's stack of tabloid pictures, an article printed off the Internet. It read, "Jena Farley Engaged." I picked up the article to examine a picture of Jena opening her sliding glass door. Wasn't it illegal for the paparazzi to take pictures from Jena's backyard? There was also a smaller picture, showing a detail of Jena's left hand. It looked like she was wearing a ring—a *ginormous* ring, as Harri would say.

Justin had said he wasn't dating Jena, and I was pretty sure he would never buy anyone a ring that large, but I wasn't absolutely sure. I *had* to know about the ring. There couldn't be any harm in asking Jena about a ring, could there? Walking downstairs, I knocked on Jena's bedroom door. "Hey, Jena. It's Emma."

I'd never seen Jena look so terrible as she did when she opened her door. Her face was red and splotchy. Her hair was a lopsided tangle of knots as if she'd gone to bed with it wet. It must have been a terrible migraine if it could transform her so much from the way she'd looked that morning. She shielded her eyes from the light in the hallway. "Hi, Emma."

I stepped into her room. She'd installed a new hardwood floor since the last time I'd visited the place, and she'd gotten new furniture. "Barbara probably already showed you this, but I wanted to make sure." I held out the article. "It looks like someone's been taking pictures of you from your backyard. Isn't that illegal?"

Jena took the article from my hand, rubbing the back of her neck while she examined it. "They probably used a telephoto lens from the street out back."

I waited for Jena to invite me to take a seat on one of her armchairs. "You should get a taller fence. It looks like a nice ring, though."

Jena looked at the article again. "Ring?"

I pointed to the detail showing her left hand. "The paparazzi must think you're secretly engaged to Justin." I laughed, but Jena didn't. My laughs around Jena were always lonely. Maybe if I learned more coaching conversation techniques, I could connect with her. She always seemed so distant.

Jena walked to her dresser. She pulled open a drawer, popped open a velvet box, and showed me a huge diamond ring. "What do you think?"

In a second, I was standing beside her, gawking at the ring. "Wow. That's . . . nice." It looked bigger in real life—definitely over a carat. Could Justin afford a ring like that? Maybe if it were cubic zirconium.

Jena snapped the ring box shut and tossed it back in the drawer. "I got it for a video. I wanted to see if I could stand to wear it for ten hours at a time." She opened her door. "It's for a new song called 'Separation Anxiety.' " Clearly, she couldn't wait for me to leave.

I stepped out into the hallway. "I just wanted to make sure you knew people were taking pictures from the backyard."

Jena had already closed the door part of the way. "Thanks, Emma, but you don't have to worry about me. I can take care of myself."

Chapter 18

Coach's Tip of the Day:
A messy house can be therapeutic.

The next day, when Hank hadn't called me, I wrote it off—he was busy with the funeral. After three days, I began to wonder if I'd said something to offend him. I checked with Randall and Tanya to see what they'd heard. All they knew was the funeral was that morning. I checked for messages every hour and made sure I stayed within my cell phone range. But the only call I got was Isabella inviting me to go to a movie.

Hank didn't call on Sunday, which was New Year's Eve, either. I did, however, get to meet Alexandria Amethyst Hawkins, otherwise known as Phil Elton's girlfriend. When the Sunday School teacher asked if there were any visitors, Alexandria stood in her hot pink dress, smoothed her short brown hair, and said, "I'm Alexandria, and I'm from New York City. My close friends call me Ali, but I'd rather everyone here call me Alexandria. Lots of people get confused and call me Alexandra or Lexy or Alex. So remember I'm named for Alexandria, Greece, not for the one in Virginia."

I told myself that once I got to know Alexandria, I'd probably like her. Before church was over, I'd invited her and Phil to our family home evening group. We'd scheduled that week's activity for

Tuesday because Harri had to watch Avery all day on Monday so the Coles could attend some New Year's Day charity event. "Did you have to invite them?" Harri asked as we grabbed our coats off the jangling metal hangers on the church's coat rack.

"I did it for your benefit, Harri," I whispered as I slipped into my coat. "The sooner you get to know that woman, the sooner you'll get over Phil."

When I got home, I called Hank. He didn't answer. He didn't call back either. By Sunday night, I was angry. What kind of guy doesn't call a woman he just kissed to wish her a Happy New Year?

I spent Monday morning in a frenzy of cleaning. I started by dumping out all the leftovers from Christmas Eve dinner. How stupid was I to try to impress a guy like Hank anyway? He was used to four-star restaurants and top-of-the-line caterers. I vacuumed the living room, hoping to suck up any dead skin cells Hank may have left laying around. I shredded my map of Blaze Mountain, the last remaining evidence of our ski trip. After that, I tore through my dresser and closet, ending up with two trash bags of charity donations.

I was in the laundry room cleaning behind the dryer when I realized I'd allowed Hank Weston to derail my life plan. If I wasn't ready for marriage, why was I obsessing over Hank? Why was I letting him influence what I ate, what I wore, and what I thought about all day? I had two choices. I could try harder to get Hank to love me. Or I could decide he was a temporary diversion. Once I thought about it that way, I knew I had to pick the second choice—Hank was a fling. Eventually, I would dump him. Considering his behavior for the last few days, I didn't think he'd be too devastated. We were both the strong, independent types. Yes, I was his favorite, and he was mine. But Hank was nothing to distract me from my pledge to stay out of the whole marriage meat market.

The next day, it was a relief to go back to work at the dentist's office, where I was separated from the rest of humanity by a long black counter that I wiped down twice a day with Lysol. As much as I hated being a receptionist, there was a certain simplicity in handing people the same forms to fill out, in calling the same insurance companies, in filling in little grids on the calendar with appointments, and in having a lunch break. Numbers and insurance companies were so much more predictable than people. I liked looking out over a half-empty waiting room and listening to the sound of the serenity fountain on the opposite wall, where water fell across a tarnished rectangle of copper colored metal. I was getting back to life as normal, and I was going to stick to my life plan—becoming a coach. I'd written my New Year's resolution on a yellow sticky note that was right there on my computer monitor, reminding me: *Study Life Coaching.* Since I'd met Harri during the snowstorm, I'd barely cracked open my books.

Justin called me at 11:00 a.m. "I'm working on a house near your office. When's your break? I thought we could do lunch together."

I twisted my mom's Black Hills Gold ring around on my finger. Feeling the need for a mother's encouragement, I'd dug it out from the bottom of my jewelry box that morning. "Sorry, I can't. I have to study my life coaching stuff, unless . . ."

"Unless what?"

"One of my assignments is to do a free coaching session. You wouldn't be interested, would you?" I traced the multicolored leaves on Mom's ring, hoping he'd agree to it. Now that Harri'd refused to be my project, I needed a new practice client.

I could hear Justin exhale on the other end—a long, drawn-out breath.

"It has nothing to do with matchmaking," I added. "I need to do a practice session so I can pass on to the next level."

"Okay," he said, "as long as we don't talk about relationships."

We met at a deli across the street from my office. It was a little shop with an abundance of white tile and red countertops. I only realized after we'd ordered that it wasn't the best choice. My jaws were sore because I'd clenched them so much thinking about Hank

Weston the day before. I couldn't chew, so Justin ate both halves of our foot-long meatball sub. I settled for a bowl of cream soup.

Justin rubbed the side of his face. "I should tell you Harri called me last night at 3:00 a.m."

I didn't ask whether it was because of Phil. I knew it was. "What'd you do?"

"I talked with her a little, and we prayed together over the phone."

"That's all?"

Justin shrugged. "What did you expect me to do? I wasn't going to go to her house at 3:00 a.m."

"Why not? It's only Harri."

Justin folded his arms. "If you were a man, Emma, you wouldn't say that."

I pointed to a drop of red sauce beside his lip. "But you're just friends."

Justin rubbed the side of his lip. "There's no such thing as being 'just friends' with a woman. You never know when a complication might come up."

He hadn't gotten all the sauce off, so I reached out with a napkin to wipe it off. "But you and I are friends, and I wouldn't call it complicated." I didn't get all the sauce on the first try, so I had to wipe his face a little more.

Justin batted my hand away. "I guess that's because you're not like most women."

I couldn't tell whether that was an insult or a compliment. "Thank you. Next time Harri calls in the middle of the night, you should call me instead of only saying a prayer with her. She needs real help."

Justin scoffed. "Like you could have done more than God." His words jolted me as if I'd licked an electric socket. The whole time I'd been helping Harri, I'd never prayed about any of the decisions we made. For all I knew, Harri hadn't either.

I let a few spoonfuls of soup slide down my throat as I opened up *Introduction to Life Coaching* and tried to think of a power question to begin our session. "So what are you working on in your life right now?"

Justin chewed on his sub. "Nothing much." He wasn't going to make this easy for me. That was no surprise. Men were usually more difficult to coach than women.

"Well, let's pick a category where you'd like to see changes—health, fitness, physical appearance—not that you need to work on any of those—work, home environment, spirituality, finances." I let my words hang there while Justin chewed some more.

"I've got some changes to make at work." He explained how he had a long list of customers who hadn't paid their bills. Since he always required customers to put down a seventy-percent deposit on the materials and labor before he started the job, he figured the final thirty percent was nothing much to worry about. He could still cover all his expenses if they didn't pay up. The problem was, more and more customers were defaulting on the final thirty percent. It was making a huge dent in his profits.

"Sounds like this problem's really draining your energy. What do you think you should do?" I asked.

Justin punched a fist into the palm of his other hand. "I guess I'll have to turn them over to a collection agency."

Realizing this was going to be easier than I thought, I closed the book. "That's what Dr. Metzdorf does, only he sends out a warning letter first, giving the customers fourteen days to pay up before he hands it over to the collection agency."

Justin took another bite while he thought. "That's a good idea. In the letter, I could tell them to contact me if they're having any sort of financial hardship, so we could work out a payment plan."

"It sounds like you have a goal," I said. "All you need is a deadline."

"I'll send the letters out by the end of the week." He gulped down some soda. "Thanks, Emma. That was . . . helpful."

I laughed. "Why do you sound so surprised? I'll follow up with you next week to see how it went. What else is on your mind?"

Justin shrugged. "Nothing much. I need a new shirt—something I can wear when I'm doing estimates. My old one's wearing out." Leave it to Justin to have only one casual shirt.

As far as I knew, fashion consulting wasn't part of the coaching process, but it fell within my skill set. After we finished eating, we had forty minutes—enough time to run to the mall and have Justin try on a few shirts. We settled on a striped polo that was slightly fitted through the chest and shoulders. "This is the perfect casual shirt for work," I said. It also would have been a great choice for a date, but I didn't tell him that.

Harri met me after I got home from work to help set up for family home evening. She wore the outfit we'd bought her at Target, and she'd done her hair for the first time in weeks. After laying out the refreshments with steady hands, she sat on the couch talking to Justin, as calm as a Saturday morning. Then Phil and Alexandria came to the door. You'd have thought we were counting down for a game of hide-and-seek. Harri disappeared into the kitchen before I noticed she'd moved.

"Nice neighborhood," Alexandria crooned as I swung the door open. "The house next door reminds me of my sister's place—only I think her house is a little bigger." She stood in the entryway while Phil helped her out of her coat and then removed his own. He handed me both their coats and ascended the stairs without a word. It was like I was the butler.

Phil introduced Alexandria to everyone—everyone except Harri, who stood in the kitchen doorway. When he got to Jena, Alexandria interrupted. "You don't need to introduce me to Jena Farley. I already know who she is." She reached her hand out to shake Jena's. "You can call me Ali. I studied music dance theater in college, so we have a lot in common."

It didn't get any better from there. My lesson on judging others turned into a debate between Alexandria and me. When I read a scripture about how the Savior doesn't want us to judge other people, Alexandria rebutted: "In my opinion, there's such a thing as good judging. Like when you're dating someone, you need to be judgmental. I personally prefer to know every single flaw. For instance, I'd want to know if someone had a tattoo." Phil smiled at her and nodded.

"I see your point," I answered, trying to stay calm, "but even in dating, I think sometimes there's too much emphasis on judging. I think if we're not careful, we'll start rating other people the way we rate movies or the way teachers give grades in school."

Alexandria shook her head. "If a society doesn't strive for

perfection, what kind of society is it? No one wants to go to a doctor who got bad grades. And I wouldn't want to watch a movie with a bad rating either."

I looked at Justin, who was standing beside Harri on the other end of the room. "What do you think, Justin?"

Justin laughed and cleared his throat at the same time. "I think you and Alexandria are raising two different arguments. It's a commandment not to judge others but it's also good to have high standards—as long as you only impose them on yourself. You shouldn't expect your friends to have higher standards than you do."

Jena raised her hand. "As a performer, I see a lot of what Emma's talking about. It's so easy to criticize and pick someone apart. Anyone can do that. People judge me all the time because I'm famous. I chose to go into the music industry because I wanted to help people, not because I thought I could ever have a perfect performance. If you want to make a difference in the world, you have to stop judging and start doing." I wanted to skip across the room and hug Jena for this little speech. It was exactly what I wanted to get across.

Alexandria flapped her hand at Jena. "I know how you feel, Jena. You're burned out. You need to take a break, get away, and focus on something else."

Jena tilted her head to the side. "I've been taking a break for the past month, but it seems like my job follows me wherever I go."

Alexandria slapped her hands on her lap. "You could serve a mission. I know it'd be hard, but it'd be so good for you. I served in Italy. The best decision I ever made."

Jena smiled without parting her lips. "I always wanted to serve a mission, but now isn't the right time for me."

I thought Alexandria would let it go at that, but she didn't. "Have you prayed about it?" I froze in my seat, shocked that Alexandria had asked such a judgmental question. It was hard for me not to judge her for that.

Jena's lips tightened. "Yes."

Leaning back, Justin folded his arms. "Maybe Jena's mission is to be a good role model for teens. She already does that."

I could tell Alexandria was preparing another rebuttal in her mind, but I was done. I returned to my place on the sofa. "Why don't we go on with the activity? Jena planned a 'Name That Tune' game for us."

Sitting there, watching Jena pluck out familiar tunes on her guitar, I imagined how lonely it would be to have fans trying to worm their way into my private life, snapping photos every time I stuck my head out the door. What would it be like to have every song critiqued, every outfit scrutinized, and every relationship documented? For a celebrity, Jena wasn't a snob. If she were, she wouldn't have sat there in my living room, playing "It's a Small World" on her guitar.

After the activity, Alexandria scanned my chocolate chip cookies, said something about them being overdone, and then dispensed her good-byes. "Thanks for inviting us," is what she said to me. "I'm dying to get to know you better," is what she said to Jena. She didn't say anything to Harri. As for Justin, I couldn't hear what she said to him because she whispered it. As she and Phil left the house, I shook my head. "I'll never understand men."

Harri fiddled with the edge of her blouse. "He's in love. I can tell. He feels the same way about her as I felt about him."

I dragged Harri into the kitchen. "If you cared about yourself the way I care about you, you'd realize he doesn't deserve you."

Harri slammed her fist on the counter. "I can't help it, Emma."

Justin wandered into the kitchen, his mouth full of chocolate chip cookie. "What's going on?"

I grabbed my purse off the counter. "I'm going to drive Harri home. Can you take care of things until I get back?"

Harri and I sat in my car outside her house for a half hour while she cried. It was dark enough that the people she worked for couldn't see us. After she'd used all the tissues, I asked, "Do you want to talk about it?"

Harri sniffed. "I guess I should be all happy because he's happy, but I'm not. I still wish he'd picked me. I guess I'm selfish that way."

"I think you're being *un*selfish to still like Phil. Did you notice he didn't say a word to either one of us the whole time? Not even to introduce you."

Harri looked out her window. "How could I not notice?"

"We should focus on the positive. Look at all the progress you've made since we met. You've made new friends, learned to ski, pumped up your style, and improved your child-care skills."

Harri hugged her knees to her chest. "I don't think I'll ever be good enough for someone like Phil. I'm not like you. I don't come from a nice family. I used to think it didn't matter that much, that I could be different from my parents. But I'm not that different. I'll never go to college. I'll never have money like other people. I don't want to be like my parents, but how can I help it? I don't know any other way to be."

I rested my head against the steering wheel. "Harri, you're better than you think you are, and you can accomplish anything you want. You deserve someone better than Phil, someone who'll appreciate you."

Harri opened her door. "It's nice of you to say that, Emma, but I can't trust you anymore. You've given me too much bad advice." She stepped out of my car before I could think up a reply.

Had I really given Harri bad advice? Sure, I'd messed up with her and Phil, but how was I to know he wanted someone like Alexandria instead? It's not like I could know everything about people. I'd given Phil exactly what he'd asked for in that personal ad: someone to be in his videos and rock out to country music. Harri was all of that and more. Life coaching was much harder than I'd realized.

I drove home with a plan in my mind. I would eat chocolate chip cookies until my mind went numb, until I'd forgotten all about Phil, Alexandria, and Hank. All I wanted was cookies. They'd make it all better. When I walked into the kitchen, the cookies were gone.

I called Justin on the phone. "I want my cookies back."

He laughed like a cartoon villain. "Cookies? What cookies?"

"I'm coming to get them," I said as I walked out the door.

Justin's house was close enough to walk to, but I drove. He met me in the driveway, a Ziploc bag full of cookies in his hand. "Why don't you come in? I've got chocolate milk."

"Give me the cookies."

He held the cookies out of my reach. "After you tell me what's wrong."

I pulled on his arm. "They're *my* cookies. I made them."

He pulled away and ran for the front door. I followed, grabbing his T-shirt and pulling his arm down with both hands. As soon as I let go to reach for the cookies, he pulled his arm back up, so the cookies were out of reach again. Buttercup was doing her best to help, climbing up on Justin with her front paws. "Has anyone ever told you your eyes are iridescent?" he asked me.

I let go of his arm and jumped for the cookies. "No." I wasn't even sure what *iridescent* meant.

He ran toward the kitchen. "They're different every time I look at them. Sometimes they're brown. Sometimes they're blue."

I ran after him, being careful not to trip over Buttercup. "They're hazel. Stop trying to distract me."

He hugged the cookies to his chest as he opened the refrigerator and got the milk. "The inner part, near the pupil, is the color of apple juice."

I held out my arms to block him in. "Hand them over."

He pivoted through my block. "The outer rim is blue. The middle part's a brownish green. That's the part that changes the most." He set the milk on his card table. "I'll give you a cookie if you'll sit down."

"Okay." I sat down on the floor and held onto his shin. It was a silly, immature thing to do, but it felt so much better than acting like an adult. Buttercup came to lick my face.

Justin laughed, dragging me across the floor to grab a couple of glasses. He threw some dog biscuits into the living room. That was all it took to distract Buttercup. "And you have these little rays of color going through the iris," Justin said. "Sometimes they're brown. Sometimes they're gold. Are you going to eat at the table or on the floor?"

"The floor."

He sat on the floor beside me, hugging the cookies to his chest. "Tell me what's wrong." He set the glasses on the linoleum and poured chocolate milk into them.

I reached for the bag of cookies. "I'm giving up on life coaching, so it's back to square one on the career plan." I dunked the cookie in chocolate milk and bit.

"You shouldn't give up. You'd be a good life coach."

"If you knew how much I've messed up Harri's life, you wouldn't say that."

"I know how much you've messed up Harri's life." He spoke with half a cookie still in his mouth.

I dunked the other half of my cookie. "These cookies *are* overdone."

Justin laughed. "I'll take your cookies over Alexandria's any day."

"Now who's being judgmental? You haven't tasted hers."

"You want to know what I think? I think you've been so busy solving Harri's problems, you've ignored your own. It's not selfish to take care of yourself. Isn't that part of being a life coach—teaching people how to take care of themselves?"

I reached for another cookie. "But isn't there a scripture that says we should lose ourselves in service to others."

"Yes, but we're also supposed to improve ourselves. Wouldn't you rather give Harri your new-and-improved self, instead of last year's model?"

"That makes sense." I picked up a cookie crumb off the floor. "Speaking of Harri, did you notice that Alexandria refused to say anything to her?"

"We're talking about you, not Harri. Why don't you let me worry about Harri for a while? Take a break and work on your life coaching course."

I took a sip of chocolate milk. "You haven't bought Jena any jewelry lately, have you?"

"Why would I buy Jena jewelry? Stop trying to change the subject. Can you listen to me for a minute?"

I grabbed the bag of cookies and stood up. "I have to get going. Thanks for the milk."

Justin followed me to the door. "Promise me you won't give up on life coaching. There are a lot of people who need your help. Oh, and I forgot to tell you—I already sent out those letters we talked about this morning."

I looked at the bag of cookies in my hand. As much as I hated it when Justin was right, he was right. I couldn't give up because of one failure with Harri. "I'll give it one more try," I muttered. Removing two more chocolate chip cookies for myself, I handed him the bag. "You keep the rest."

Chapter 19

Coach's Tip of the Day:
Reduce your goals, don't recycle them.

*W*e had a new patient coming into the dentist's office on the first Tuesday of February—Philip Elton. When I saw his name on the schedule, I thought he was taking me up on that offer for a free teeth-whitening treatment. Then he walked into the office. There was no mistaking the way his face fell as he caught sight of me sitting there at the reception desk. He must have forgotten I worked for Dr. Metzdorf. Instead of coming up to put his name on the list, he found a seat at the far corner of the waiting room beside the serenity fountain. I gave him a little wave. He stared at his *People* magazine, holding it a little higher than he had before.

That was fine. I'd be extra friendly to make up for any lingering awkwardness between us. Assembling the required paperwork, I came out from behind the desk, walked through the door to the waiting room, and handed Phil the papers. He took them without looking at me. "I'm not interested in getting my teeth bleached."

"Okay." I went back to my desk, wondering why these sorts of things happened to me. I'd never meant to offend Phil, and I wished we could still be friends like we were before the whole fiasco with Harri.

When my phone vibrated, I thought it was Harri. Slipping into the back room, I saw the number was Hank's. He'd been gone for over a month, and he hadn't called since the day he left, giving me plenty of time to fall out of love. I waited another four rings before answering. "It's about time you called."

"I hope you didn't miss me too much."

I sighed. "I missed you, but not too much." Now would've been a good time for him to apologize for never calling.

"I guess you heard I'm back."

"Nope." I hoped he could sense some of the irritation in my voice.

"I had to bring my mom with me. She's had so many health problems, I couldn't leave her."

I caught my breath. "You mean you brought your mom to stay with Tanya and Randall?"

Hank laughed. "No. We're at the extended-stay hotel."

With all I'd heard about Hank's mom, I couldn't help suspecting she was sick on purpose. "Sorry. I mean, I'm sorry about her health."

"Losing Grandpa was hard on her. Now she's had to move and change doctors. Do you think your dad could recommend some doctors for her?" That's why he called me—because my dad was a doctor. It wasn't the first time someone had contacted me for that reason. I just wasn't expecting it from Hank. When I didn't answer, Hank added. "I've told Mom all about you. She wants to meet you. And I haven't forgotten I owe you a party."

I heard the hygienist calling my name. "Listen, I've got to run. Send me an email about your mom's medical needs. I'll have Dad look it over."

After locating a patient record the hygienist wanted, I sat back down at my desk, feeling empty. Phil was ignoring me. Hank was using me as a physician's referral service. So much for my social life.

I remembered how I'd promised Justin that I'd try to focus more on my own needs. After I recorded Phil's information in the computer, I read through my latest set of goals, assessing how I was doing on each one. I was supposed to make life-coaching brochures, define my niche, ask acquaintances for referrals, set up a website, order business cards, decide on my fees, and start an email newsletter. On top of that, I needed to prepare my Sunday School lesson. I hadn't done any of it. In fact, I'd done nothing other than write down my goals.

What if Harri was right? I had so many goals, I couldn't even remember what they were. If I'd had a life coach, she would've told me to pick one goal I could complete within a few weeks. I needed to feel the satisfaction of finishing.

I left work determined to rededicate myself to one goal—finishing my life coach certification. That evening, as I sat in the lobby of the hair salon waiting for Harri to get her roots colored, I spread out all my life-coaching course materials on the little table where they kept magazines in the waiting room. Leafing through *Introduction to Life Coaching*, I cringed as if I were looking at one of my worst credit card bills. My mistakes were so obvious. The more I read, the more I saw what I'd done wrong. Life coaches didn't give advice. They didn't make decisions for their clients. They didn't shoot down their clients' opinions. They encouraged people to make their own decisions. I'd acted more like a palm reader than a life coach.

Speaking of palms, mine were sweating. I fanned through the pages of the book. It was 556 pages long. That didn't include all the assignments. And tests. Finishing the course would mean sacrificing lunch hours, weeknights, and Saturdays to study. I'd also have to find more practice clients. Even if I put the time in, could I change enough to become a good life coach?

I took a deep breath, trying to ignore the smell of permanents and nail polish. Desperate enough to pray, I closed my eyes and whispered my question: "Can I really do this?" I waited, breathing in and out.

A chair squeaked beside me, and I opened my eyes to see the guy who followed Jena around taking pictures—not at all the answer I'd expected. He grinned, showing his yellow teeth. "Did I scare you?"

I choked on the salon's chemical-filled air. "No. Where's Jena?"

He grabbed a magazine off the table. "At home, last I saw."

He didn't have any hair to cut, and I was pretty sure he wasn't there to get his head shaved. How hard could it be to shave a head? Glancing around, I didn't see anyone I thought he'd know except for Harri and me. But how would he have known we were there? I walked to the back of the salon, where Harri was all tricked out in aluminum foil. "You know what's weird? Jena's photographer is here."

Harri bopped her forehead with the butt of her hand. "I forgot I told Danny I'd go to ice cream with him tonight. He's not all ghetto like you think, Emma. He served in Iraq twice. The only reason he works for the tabloids is because he couldn't find a better job when he left the army. He's the type of guy who wants to change the world. He reminds me of my dad."

I'd tried hard the last few weeks to be Harri's friend, not her coach. I wasn't going to give advice. "I don't trust him."

"He wants to interview me about being a nanny."

I shook my head. "I don't know if that's a good idea."

Harri bit her bottom lip. "I think he gets depressed sitting out there in his car all day. What can it hurt to talk to him a little?"

As the hairstylist lowered Harri's head into the sink, I turned to leave. "I guess there's no reason for me to wait, then."

I left the salon, wondering how Harri could choose to associate with a paparazzo instead of me. Remembering my mistakes with Harri sent an avalanche of bad memories crashing through my brain. I remembered how many times I'd quit, how often I'd disappointed my father, and how often I'd given up on my goals. Why couldn't I be more like my mom or Jena? Sitting in my car, I knew it was time to pray, but I didn't want to. I wanted to sink into my negativity and maybe go eat a quart of ice cream. But I closed my eyes again. "Is my dream hopeless? Can I become a life coach?"

I waited, trying to think of something hopeful. What I needed was springtime. I imagined little green leaf buds growing on trees and crocuses popping up from the mud. I thought of myself cart-wheeling on the green grass in my backyard. Then I put myself in a canoe, floating on a lake in the summertime. "Can I become a life coach?" I asked again. "Do I have what it takes to help other people?"

A feeling as delicate as a dragonfly came flitting into my mind. It was love—my love for Harri, Heavenly Father's love for Harri, but also Heavenly Father's love for me. That's when I knew that not only would I be a life coach, I would get a new client—someone much more challenging than Harri or any of my other friends or family members. My new client would be *me*—because if I was going to accomplish my goal, I needed a coach more than anyone. I needed all the encouragement I could give myself. And this time, I would be the right kind of coach.

Chapter 20

Coach's Tip of the Day:
Life is not a competition.

After six weeks of waiting, we were going to Hank's party, which ended up being right in time for Valentine's Day. Harri and I arrived to see Justin emerge from a brand-new shiny black pickup truck. I rolled down my window. "Nice truck. It makes you look successful."

Justin gave me a half-smile. "Thanks . . . I think." That's when I noticed Barbara and Jena coming out of the passenger side. Why was he driving Barbara and Jena around? Justin waited for us while Barbara and Jena walked down the driveway. "Randall's worried about Jena. He asked me to give her a ride."

"Why's he worried?" I asked.

Justin lowered his voice to a whisper. "He saw Jena out riding her bike in the dark a few nights ago. She didn't even have reflectors."

First Harri, now Jena—what was it about women going out alone at night? It didn't make sense for Jena to ride her bicycle when she had a car and a treadmill. I stopped before we entered the house, considering the situation. "Jena must feel like a prisoner, living in that house with Barbara and having her fans follow her around whenever she leaves. I don't understand why she doesn't go back to Nashville or buy her own place."

Justin leaned against the stair rail leading to the front door. "This is her home. She wants to live a normal life for a while."

"I like walking at night," Harri said. "People can't stare at you." She held her hand up as if to stop me. "But don't have a spaz attack, Emma. I haven't walked in the dark since that night we went to Target."

Tanya let us in, took our coats, and pointed me straight toward the front room, where Alexandria sat by herself on the black leather couch. "Emma, can you sit with Alexandria while I get things set up?" Tanya asked. "I need Harri's help in the kitchen."

Alexandria patted the sofa cushion beside her. She wore a red sequined top with black jeans, much fancier than my rust-colored sweater. "I'm so excited about this party. I've been looking forward to it all week."

I sat down. "Me too."

She pointed to the top of her left eyebrow. "I hope you don't mind, but I should tell you while we're alone. Did you know you have a zit here?"

I touched the tiny bump. "No." Never in my life had anyone told me I had a zit. It didn't even feel very big. Did this have something to do with the teeth-whitening treatment I'd offered Phil?

"I have a friend with terrible skin, but you'd never know it. She uses hemorrhoid cream every night . . . on her face, not on—you know." She laughed with a snort. "It reduces swelling, so it works for acne *and* wrinkles. You should try it."

I gave a courtesy laugh. "I'll have to remember that."

Alexandria gazed around at the furniture in the room before settling on something else to say. "I can't wait to meet Hank. The way Phil describes him, he sounds a lot like my friends in New York. Before I moved down here, I was afraid I wouldn't meet anyone who was my type in Virginia. If Phil had told me about Hank Weston, he could've spared me all my worries."

"Maybe Phil was afraid Hank would steal you away."

She shook her hair back. "There's no danger of that. Phil is the only man for me. I shouldn't say I wasn't at all excited to move here. I was excited to meet Jena Farley. I feel a connection to her."

That's when Hank walked in. "Emma, I'm so glad you could make it." He extended his arms, and I rose to give him a hug. After I introduced him to Alexandria, he turned all his attention back to me. "The karaoke's all set up downstairs. You and I could kick things off. I already picked out a few songs we could sing together."

I raised my eyebrows. A coach would've said, *It'll boost your creativity to try something new. It'll empower you.* "As long as it's only for fun," I said. "Karaoke isn't part of my skill set."

Hank hooked his thumbs into his jeans pocket. "Why else would anyone sing karaoke if not for fun?"

Alexandria picked a piece of lint off her sweater. "I like to listen to some people a lot more than others."

Hank grabbed my hand, pulling me out of the room and into the kitchen. "I agree. The worst singers are always the most entertaining."

We headed downstairs while Hank listed my song choices. Since he wanted us to start off singing two songs together, I chose "Don't Go Breakin' My Heart" and "Black Horse and the Cherry Tree."

Hank's karaoke machine sat on an old table in the basement. The machine was a black box hooked up to a TV and some stereo speakers. Hank handed me one of the two wireless microphones and pointed to the TV screen. My insides jittered as blue words on the screen let us know we'd be singing in the key of A—not that I knew enough to adjust my voice to that key—and that there'd be twenty-four bars of instrumental music at the beginning of "Don't Go Breakin' My Heart." Because I'd watched *Ella Enchanted* about sixty times as a teenager, I knew the song well. My voice was much weaker than Anne Hathaway's, but singing with Hank made me feel like I'd done okay. I kept singing as loud as I could, even though I was slightly off key. When we were done, Hank gave me a high five.

"Black Horse and the Cherry Tree," had no melody in the accompaniment. I started off belting out all the *Woo Hoos* and *No Nos* fine. The other lines went faster than I remembered, and my timing was off. At first, Hank sang an octave lower, but for some reason, he sang the second verse in falsetto, which sent me laughing. Then he was late on all his lines because I made him laugh. Finally, he signaled a time-out and handed his microphone to Jena, who got up off one of the metal folding chairs to sing a few lines. That got Hank back on track. He started singing again, and I joined him with Jena singing beside me. My voice didn't reach the notes the way Jena's did, but I reminded myself that if Hank thought the worst singers were the most entertaining, I was doing great.

After our stint, I was still a little shaky. I sat in a folding chair, trying to keep from jiggling my legs, while Jena challenged us to find a song she couldn't sing. The only rule was that it had to be written for a female vocalist. Alexandria rushed to the machine. "I know one. Have her sing 'At Last' by Etta James." Hank pulled it up, and Jena nailed the entire song—every husky note of it.

When that was over, Hank had another song lined up for her. "See if you can sing this one: 'And I Am Telling You I'm Not Going' from *Dreamgirls*."

Jena held her stomach. "You got me with that one."

Hank pushed the play button. "You asked for it."

I'd never heard the song before, but Jena's take on it sounded impressive to me. It was a big, soulful song with long, loud notes that didn't give her much chance to catch her breath. She struggled through the longer notes, bending over to force her breath out. Justin, Harri, Phil, Barbara, Randall, and Tanya all came downstairs halfway through the song. Tanya's mouth hung open. Justin clapped his hands.

As for me, I decided it was time to end the competition with Jena. How could I be jealous when she had such an amazing talent? We needed to heal our relationship once and for all. When Jena finished singing, I grabbed onto her arm. "That was amazing, Jena!" But all the other compliments drowned out my words.

Hank raised his voice to get everyone's attention. "How about we take a break from karaoke and play a game?"

"But I have all my songs picked out," Alexandria protested.

"You'll be first on the list after the game," Hank assured her. "For this game, we'll need to divide into two teams. Each team gets five rolls of duct tape. The object is to tape one of your team members onto the wall over here." He touched an unfinished, concrete wall a few steps behind the karaoke machine. "One player stands on a chair while you tape them. When the time's up, we take away the chair. Whoever stays on the wall the longest wins."

Phil took a roll of duct tape. "I say we have Alexandria on one team and Jena on the other. They're the smallest ones here."

Hank handed out rolls of duct tape to the others. "No, Harri's smaller. Harri should be on one team and Jena on the other—as long as they're okay with it." He looked around at Harri and Jena.

Harri fiddled with a tie on her blue peasant blouse. "I'm pretty sure Alexandria's smaller."

"No," I whispered. "That's just your inner critic." I'd used coaching lingo without even thinking. Hopefully Harri wouldn't catch on. "You really are smaller."

Phil stepped forward. "Alexandria and I will be on Jena's team."

Justin glared at Phil. "I'll be on Harri's team."

Hank placed two folding chairs against the wall. "The rest of you, pick sides." We scrambled into two groups as Hank found the stopwatch app on his phone. "Ready, set, go."

The sound of ripping duct tape filled the room. In between rips, I overheard Tanya's conversation with Phil. "You're the ward mission leader, aren't you, Phil?"

"I am," Phil answered.

Tanya smoothed tape across Jena's stomach. "I have a question for you. If you've gone to church all your life, but you were never baptized, do you still need to talk to the missionaries before you get baptized?"

Phil wrapped a piece of duct tape around Jena's arm. "If you're nine or older, you talk to the missionaries before you're baptized."

Tanya secured Jena's rib cage to the wall with another piece of tape. "I have a new investigator for you, then."

"Great!" Phil said. "We're always looking for people to teach."

Tanya taped across Jena's hips. "Don't you have the elders teach at your house when they're teaching a woman?"

"Sure. We can start tomorrow if our schedules mesh. Who is it?"

Tanya ripped off another piece of tape. "Harri."

I looked at Harri. "You're not a member?"

She bit her lip. "I never got baptized."

Phil dropped his roll of duct tape. "On second thought . . . I might not be able to have them teach at my house. I'm in the middle of remodeling." As I listened, the roll of duct tape in my hand transformed itself into a weapon, one I wanted to hurl at Phil's head. Justin must have seen the look in my eye. He took the tape from my hand and replaced it with a duct-tape harness he'd made.

Harri stared straight ahead and pressed her lips into a tight line while I held the harness down where she could step into it. She slid her foot into one of the holes. "Are you sure that's going to fit me? It looks too small."

"I'm sure," I said, trying to ignore Tanya's conversation with Phil. "Why didn't you tell me you were never baptized?"

Harri put her other foot into the harness. "I always went to church with my grandma. My parents wanted me to wait until I turned eighteen to decide about getting baptized. When I came out here, I thought I'd get baptized right away, but everyone treated me like another member of the ward. I didn't want to admit I wasn't a member. I wish I'd told you before Randall figured out I don't have membership records."

"We don't mind if you're not a member," I said. "You don't have to get baptized just to please us."

"No, I want to get baptized. I've always wanted to."

Justin rolled duct tape into a rope. "The missionaries can teach you at my house if you want, Harri."

Harri pulled the harness up. "Really?" The smile was back on her face, and I had Justin to thank for it. I would've hugged him if we hadn't been in such a hurry to stick Harri to the wall.

Justin shrugged. "Sure. It's not that big of a deal. I'll give them a call later."

"Speaking of missionary work," Alexandria said as she taped Jena's upper arm to the wall. "Have you thought any more about serving a mission?"

Jena looked like a scarecrow with her arms stiff against the wall. "Not really."

"If Phil and I weren't engaged," Alexandria said. "I'd want to go on another mission." She slapped her hand over her mouth. "Oops. I wasn't supposed to say anything about our engagement yet. I guess I'm too excited."

There was a moment of shocked silence until Tanya offered her congratulations. Soon the guys were slapping Phil high fives while

Jena spewed out compliments about what a great couple they made. I kept my mouth shut. While our team secured Harri to the wall with duct tape ropes, Alexandria and Phil were so busy explaining their engagement story that they forgot all about Jena. She didn't stick to the wall for five seconds after we took the chairs away. Harri, on the other hand, hung suspended for an entire 36 seconds, reaffirming the fact that she was smaller than she realized.

After we won the game, Alexandria rushed to the karaoke machine. I followed Justin upstairs to the kitchen. "It *was* a big deal," I shouted over the music. "Saying you'd help teach Harri." I was already planning how I could thank him—a big dinner, a plate of his favorite brownies, a new T-shirt, or maybe all three.

Justin looked around to make sure no one could overhear him. "I don't know what's wrong with Phil. It's not like him to be so rude."

I shook my head, pretending I had no idea how to interpret Phil's mysterious personality changes.

Hank wandered in, motioning for us to follow him into the living room. "Ali's going to sing three songs, all by Celine Dion." He stuck his tongue out the side of his mouth. "It's no fun to listen to bad singers when they think they're great."

I followed Hank into the living room. Harri came in, holding her phone. "I suddenly have this urge to erase all the pictures clogging up my memory." Using sign language, she spelled out P-H-I-L and held the L to her forehead, signaling loser.

I hugged her. "It's about time."

Harri took her phone out of her pocket. "Remember how you said those pictures are like poison for me? That made me think. I've been poisoning myself, and not just with the pictures—with negative thoughts about my body. I need to be a better friend to myself." I watched her erase a picture of Phil's hand, one of the back of his head, and another of his shoe. Maybe my coaching *was* getting through.

Justin came into the room, holding his phone to his chest. "How's next Saturday? The missionaries are free around three o'clock."

Harri checked the calendar on her phone. "That sounds great."

Justin got back on the phone to confirm everything with the missionaries. After he hung up, Hank asked, "Is it all right if I come?"

"Sure," Justin said. "Everyone's welcome. We'll do something fun afterward, maybe laser tag or something."

I sat on the sofa. "But only four people can fit around your card table."

Justin sat next to me, crossing his legs. "Looks like I'm going to have to break down and buy some living room furniture. I've been meaning to tell you—I made so much money after I sent out those letters, I could furnish a couple of living rooms. Want to help me pick something out?"

I bumped shoulders with him. "Like I haven't been offering for the past four years. When do you want to go shopping?"

Chapter 21

Coach's Tip of the Day:
Don't fight your battles alone.

The beige slipcovered sofa and love seat looked at home in Justin's living room. They made the honey-colored hardwood floors seem shinier and the bay window classier. Plus, they were roomy. Jena, Hank, the missionaries, and Justin were all seated with room to spare. Buttercup sat on the floor beside Justin, her head resting on his knee. The only one missing was Harri. I looked at my watch. She should have been there fifteen minutes ago. "It's not like Harri to be this late."

Hank walked to the door. "I saw her talking to that paparazzi guy when I came in."

As he opened the door, we could hear Harri yelling, "There's no way I'm going to do that!" I'd never heard Harri yell before.

Hank stepped outside. "I'll be back in a second." Buttercup raised her head off Justin's leg, listening.

I scooted over on the couch to see what was going on. There was Harri standing on the sidewalk, facing Jena's photographer. Hank walked out and stood between them with his hands on his hips. He seemed to be playing referee, trying to keep things civil.

"Do you think we should go help?" I asked. I remembered the

time a few weeks ago that Danny interviewed Harri. Maybe he'd started following her around, trying to get a date.

Justin shut the door. "Hank seems to be doing fine." Buttercup followed at his heels.

Jena asked the missionaries about their families at home, but I didn't listen to their answers. The scene outside the window was much more interesting. The way Hank dashed in to save Harri showed he had stronger feelings for her than I'd realized. Hank stood in front of Harri while Harri inched closer to him, holding onto his arm. Maybe he wasn't the right guy for me, but he could be right for Harri. The thought rushed through me, firing up all my romantic instincts. Harri's prospects weren't as dismal as I'd thought.

When Harri and Hank came inside five minutes later, Harri's face was red, and she was still yelling. Only now she was yelling at Hank instead of Danny. "Are you insane? I can't bug a congress-woman's computer. Why did you tell him I'd do it?"

Hank drew the curtains closed. "Relax, Harri. I have a plan. Have you forgotten I'm a programmer?"

"What's going on?" I asked.

Harri sank into the sofa and buried her face in her hands. "Emma, you will not believe the ginormous problem I've caused. When Danny interviewed me about being a nanny, I said some things I shouldn't have about Karen, some things that made it sound like she might be having an affair—not that I think she is. It wouldn't matter, except she's a congresswoman. Now Danny wants me to put a program on Karen's computer. If I don't, he's going to publish the interview."

Hank held up a flash drive. "I think it's a key logger."

"What's a key logger?" I asked.

Hank walked to Justin's computer in the corner. "It's a program that records keystrokes. It'll let Danny read whatever's typed into her computer, so he can learn passwords, read emails, and snoop around on her online accounts. Can I borrow your computer, Justin?"

Justin typed in his password. "Go ahead."

Harri tightened her hands into fists. "If the Coles find out about this, I'll never be a nanny again."

Hank stuck the flash drive into Justin's computer and waited. "The Coles aren't going to find out about it."

"Why can't you tell the Coles about the interview?" I asked Harri. "It's not like you said anything wrong. Danny's the one who's accusing the congresswoman of having an affair, not you."

Harri shook her head. "You don't know the Coles, Emma. They would totally freak. Their last nanny got fired just for posting a picture of Avery online."

I stood behind Hank, watching the computer screen as he paged through the code. "What are you going to do?" I'd taken a programming class at the community college, but this program was much bigger than anything I could handle.

"It's probably set up to send Danny the data through an email," Hank said. "I'll change the program so it sends Danny a virus instead of the information he wants. We won't even install it on the congresswoman's computer. I'll send it to him from here."

Jena stood to peek through the curtains. "I don't know. Danny's a pretty smart guy."

Hank typed into Justin's computer. "Relax, Jena. You remember how I won that hacking contest last year?"

Jena froze. "How would I remember that? I hardly knew you back then."

Hank scratched his neck. "Give me another hour to work on this. You all go ahead with the discussion. Afterward, Harri can pretend to install the key logger on the congresswoman's laptop."

While Hank typed away in the corner, the rest of us participated in a lesson on the restoration of the gospel. Since there wasn't much for Harri to learn, the lesson became an exchange of testimonies. It was cozy, the way I'd felt as a little girl when I cuddled up on Dad's lap. The elders asked Harri a few questions, she answered them, the elders bore their testimonies, and Harri bore hers. I'd never considered serving a mission, but I could see now why other people would. Hearing Harri's testimony gave me that Christmas movie thrill.

Harri told the missionaries prayer had helped her get over feeling worthless. Now she wanted to pay Heavenly Father back and make a bigger commitment to living the gospel. I peeked at Justin, expecting to see an I-told-you-so nod—after all, it'd been his idea to pray with Harri—but the crease in the middle of his forehead convinced me he was thinking of something else entirely.

Harri, on the other hand, looked much more peaceful than she had before the lesson started. She'd changed, and it had nothing to do with me. Her eyes were no longer bloodshot like they'd been a month before. Her skin was clear with a healthy shine. Hank would have to be blind not to notice how beautiful she looked.

The discussion ended before Hank finished programming, so Harri and I went to her house to start our part of the plan. Since the Coles were watching a movie upstairs, we hung around on the main floor. In the time it would've taken Harri to find Karen Cole's laptop, we sat in the Coles' spacious kitchen, eating soft pretzels. "I think I'm over Phil," Harri said as she dusted a few specks of salt off the white marble countertop.

"I can't believe I ever thought he was good enough for you. I hope you find someone better."

Harri swiveled on her barstool. "I think I have."

"Who is it? Wait." I held up my hand, remembering all I'd learned about coaching lately. "I don't want to know. If I've learned anything, it's that I shouldn't get involved in your love life."

Harri giggled and leaned toward me. "I'll give you a hint: it's someone who rescued me." It hadn't been an hour since Hank rescued her from Danny, and she thought I wouldn't figure out the guy she was talking about. At least her taste had improved, even if Hank was the third one she'd fallen for in three months.

I wanted to encourage her, but I wanted to do it the right way. In my last week of study, I'd learned that a good coach helps clients through goal setting, learning, feedback, and reflection. Reflection seemed like a good place for me to start our conversation: "I keep thinking about how you said you're learning to be a better friend to yourself. Now that you're heading into another relationship—"

"That's what's different about him," Harri interrupted. "He treats me the way I deserve to be treated. He cares about me, you know? When we talk, he's only thinking of me. He isn't like Phil was. He's so good. He might be too good for me."

"Don't let your negative thinking take over. He sounds perfect for you."

"You're right. He *is* perfect for me."

I guessed it was time for goal setting. "I say you go for it."

Harri ate a few more bites of her pretzel before she spoke again. "The problem is he's way older than me."

"Why is that a problem?" I asked.

"I don't care about it, but he might."

"If it's a problem for him, you'll find out soon enough. I'll be here to give you feedback when you need it. Meanwhile, I think you should picture yourself as his girlfriend. If you can see it in your mind, it's more likely to happen."

When Hank and Justin picked us up, Jena was complaining in the back seat. "How can we sit through a discussion with the missionaries one minute and install a virus on someone's computer the next? It's not right. It's probably not going to work anyway. After we send him the virus, Danny will get his computer fixed and keep bothering Harri, only he'll bother her even more."

I had to agree with Jena. It *was* dishonest to give someone a computer virus. Why did Jena always have to be right? And why did I hate it so much that she was right?

We spent the twenty-minute drive talking about other strategies. By the time we arrived at the laser tag place, everyone was sure that if things went as planned, we'd solve all of Harri's problems. And we could do it without hurting Danny.

I hadn't played laser tag since my thirteenth birthday party. The technology had advanced a little bit since then. The vests and headbands were fancier—with flashing green lights. Like the last time I'd gone, we played in a dark room; but this time the room was bigger, with mirrors all over. Before I figured out about the mirrors, I shot myself twice. After that, I retreated to the middle of the room and hid along a row of foam pillars. I waited there while my eyes adjusted, trying to figure out what was a mirror and what wasn't.

Once I got used to the layout, I snuck around to the edge of the room and hid behind a zigzagging foam wall. From there, I shot Justin and Harri. Harri got me back once her gun recharged, but Justin climbed some wooden stairs to a platform, where he shot me sniper style. Laughing, I followed him up there. Together we shot Harri a few times. "Where are Hank and Jena?" I asked. "I haven't shot either one of them yet."

Justin pointed to the other side of the room, where we saw the dim glow of flashing lights. "They must be on the other side." He motioned for me to follow him.

I held onto the back of his vest as we made our way through the dry ice–induced fog. He turned and shot me once. When my gun started working again, I shot him back. As we snuck to the wall where Hank and Jena hid, Justin placed a finger over his mouth. I could hear Hank whispering. "I know it's hard, but it'll be over soon."

"You don't understand what you're getting yourself into," Jena responded. "I'm sick of the dishonesty."

Justin jumped past the wall and shot them both. I waited on the other side. When they chased after Justin, I shot the two of them in their backs. That's when Hank grabbed me, holding me as a hostage so no one could shoot him from the front. While that was going on, Justin, Harri, and Jena all shot me over and over again. I finally broke free, raced across the room, and ran up the stairs. I stopped on the platform to talk to Justin. Rather than shoot me when I approached, he looked off at the other side of the room. "What's the matter?" I asked.

"I'm starting to wonder about Hank and Jena."

I shot Justin in the chest. "Why?"

He pointed to the other side of the room. "They keep sneaking off together."

"That's because Jena's worried about Hank's scheme. She thinks it's her fault Harri's having so much trouble."

He leaned in closer to whisper. "Did you notice how Jena reacted when Hank mentioned the contest he won at school? And now she's talking with him about dishonesty. I think they're hiding something."

I liked sharing secrets with Justin, but this one didn't make any sense at all. "No way. Jena's being a drama queen about all this. I don't see why she's worried." Why was Justin so interested in Jena? I paused, gathering my courage. Harri had said I should ask him about her. Now seemed like as good a time as any. "Speaking of hiding something, some people think you and Jena have something to hide."

Justin laughed. "Not again, Emma. Tanya and I had this conversation last month. I thought she would have told you by now. I like Jena, but not in that way. She's a little too uptight for me."

Now I had something to hide—my relief. I shot Justin in the chest and ran back down the stairs, pretending to search for targets.

Chapter 22

Coach's Tip of the Day:
When someone lets you win, it's your victory.

As part of the plan to defeat Danny, Barbara agreed to host a potluck after church. When Harri, Dad, and I arrived with our fruit and vegetable plate, parked cars filled both sides of Barbara's street. Justin stood on the front steps, waving in people he recognized and shooing away Jena's teenage fans. Harri stayed to help him. In the tiny living room, people were already sitting on the sofa, the two armchairs, and on the floor, holding paper plates on their laps. Others were standing in the hallway. After surveying the kitchen, Dad backed up into the living room. "I'll stay here with the vegetable plate."

I squeezed my way into the kitchen, looking for Jena or Hank. Danny sat at the kitchen table, his plate piled high with chips, dips, and desserts. His camera hung around his neck. Jena sat beside him.

I grabbed a paper plate and helped myself to the mysterious casseroles lying out on the kitchen counter while I strained to hear Danny's conversation with Jena.

Alexandria came up behind me. "Watch out for the crab dip. I hear it's full of calories. Best to leave it for the guys."

I scooped out a heaping spoonful of crab dip. "Thanks for letting me know."

Alexandria made little circles in the air with her fork. "I love the way Jena Farley operates, don't you? She has this aura of simplicity. I'd never dream of having this kind of crowd in such a small house. She would make a perfect sister missionary, don't you think?"

"She would, but I don't think it's what she wants." I turned to walk past Alexandria.

Alexandria stepped into my path. "Randall told me you're thinking of going to Sugarloaf Mountain."

"Yeah, we talked about going there when the weather warms up."

Alexandria raised her eyebrows. "You know what the best thing about Sugarloaf is? It's privately owned. That means no paparazzi taking pictures! Jena will love it. Tanya thought we should go the first Saturday in April. What do you think? We also need to figure out the food. Would you rather do a picnic or eat out?"

Bringing Alexandria and Phil on our day trips was never part of my plan. Harri wouldn't feel comfortable with them along, and I wanted the trip to be fun for her. The only way around it would be for Harri and me to drive separately. Once we were hiking the mountain, we could maintain some distance if we wanted. It wouldn't be so bad. I stepped past Alexandria to grab a napkin. "Whatever you plan will be fine with me."

I scooted around to the other side of the kitchen and stood beside Danny while I munched on my high calorie crab dip. He was complaining to Jena about his computer crash and how he had an article due in the morning.

Jena took a sip from her plastic cup. "I can get your computer fixed."

Danny widened his eyes. "Today?"

Jena lowered her voice. "Today, but you'll have to agree to my terms. I want you to permanently erase every copy of your interview with Harri. And you have to forget about spying on the congresswoman. Got that?"

Danny put his elbows on the table. "The public has a right to know about the conduct of its leaders. My buddies are in the military, out risking their lives for this country. They don't get a congressman's pay or a congressman's respect."

Jena took her phone out of her pocket. "Do you want your computer fixed or not?"

Danny ate three forkfuls of food before he answered. "I want it back the way it was—the sooner the better. Like I said, I have to get this article out."

Jena pushed buttons on her phone. "And what about Harri?"

Danny rolled his eyes. "I'll leave her alone and erase her interview. That's no great loss."

Jena drummed her fingers on the table, waiting for Hank to answer his phone. "Hi, Hank. This is Jena Farley. I wondered if you could come fix a computer for me." She paused, listening. "What do you mean, you can't come?" Jena cast a worried glance at me. "You can't leave your mom for an hour?"

"I could take the computer to Hank's hotel," I offered.

Danny spoke through his teeth. "That laptop is not leaving my sight."

We couldn't give up after we'd come so far. Maybe we couldn't count on Hank, but there was at least one other person we could always count on. I leaned toward Jena. "I'll go get Justin." Pushing open the sliding glass door, I made my way around to the front porch where Justin and Harri chatted with Rob Martinez. There was no time to wait for a pause in the conversation. "Jena needs help."

Justin looked at me. "Where is she?"

"The kitchen."

Justin turned to Rob as he descended the steps. "Do you mind playing bouncer for me while I take care of this?"

Rob sat on the top step. "No problem."

I explained the situation as best I could to Justin before we walked back through the sliding glass door. Once we were inside the kitchen, Justin didn't waste any time. "Get your computer, Danny. I'll drive you to Hank's place."

Danny wadded up his napkin and threw it on top of his plate. "Give me the address. I'll drive myself."

Jena spoke into her phone, telling Hank that Justin would bring Danny over. She paused, listening. "Okay, whatever." She put the phone down, rubbing her forehead. "Hank wants Emma to come along too. His mom wants to meet her."

Justin sat down at the table and reached for a bag of chips. "Go ahead and eat first, Emma. I'm in no hurry."

As it turned out, Hank's mom was asleep when we arrived at the hotel. Hank met us in the lobby and took us around to the lounge where they served the continental breakfast. As Hank sat at one of the granite-topped tables, Danny stood, clenching his teeth. "Why do I get the feeling you're the one who caused this problem in the first place?"

Hank folded his arms. "Listen, I'm only doing this as a favor, so if you don't want my help, you can leave."

Danny put his laptop on the table in front of Hank. "If that computer isn't exactly the way it was before it crashed—"

"It'll be exactly the way it was before it crashed." Hank turned on the laptop and set to work while Danny watched, questioning Hank's actions.

Justin and I chose a booth at the other end of the room, close to the complimentary soft drinks and hot water. We split the only hot cocoa mix while I told him how I'd printed out my coaching brochures and passed three online coaching tests that week. We talked about the houses he was remodeling. Then we played a game on Justin's phone for about an hour. In an effort to resist the free cookies on the counter, I held my arm out to Justin, offering to play our version of arm wrestling.

Justin looked at Hank. "If I asked a girl over to meet my mother, I wouldn't want her arm wrestling another guy while she waited. Not that I care about Hank's feelings, but you might."

Justin didn't know what I knew about Hank's interest in Harri, so I offered another excuse. "Trust me. It won't bother him. He knows you and I are practically brother and sister."

Justin leaned back from the table. "Since when are we practically brother and sister?"

I put my elbow on the table, ready for wrestling. "Since your brother married my sister. Haven't you always thought of me as your little sister?"

Justin rolled up his sleeve and grabbed my hand. "You're not my sister."

I bit back a smile as I grabbed his hand with both of mine. Could it be that Justin thought of me as a woman? An available woman?

He looked into my eyes. "Ready, set, go."

The rules for our arm wrestling game were invented long ago on a rainy Memorial Day at Isabella's house. They were that I could break any rules I wanted; Justin couldn't. So I lifted my elbows off the table and knelt on my seat. We kept eye contact, him smiling, me grimacing with effort. Even with the height advantage, it was a struggle to move his hand. After a lot of pushing, with all my weight against Justin's hand, his arm touched the table. I squealed. "I won." Jumping up to do my victory dance, I bumped into someone standing behind me.

I turned to see Danny holding his laptop case. "It's fixed." He didn't look happy about it. "I deleted the pictures of Harri."

I completed my victory dance while Justin thanked Danny. Once he left, I invited everyone over to my house for a celebration party, but I guess I was the only one who felt like celebrating. Hank headed back to his hotel room. Jena didn't answer her phone. Justin had to do something for church. And Harri wanted to watch a show on TV. It was almost like no one wanted to be around me.

Chapter 23

Coach's Tip of the Day:
Your comfort zone has an exit.

*I*t was only natural to feel jealous when I wasn't invited to Alexandria's parties, not that I wanted to go to any of her parties. But I would've at least liked to be invited. From what I understood, Jena Farley and Rob Martinez were regulars. "I wouldn't worry about it," Tanya said as we set up chairs for Harri's baptismal service. There was room for four chairs on each side of the aisle in the narrow room. Behind accordion doors at the front of the room, warm water ran into the baptismal font. "You don't have time to be everyone's social director. No one expects you to invite Jena and Rob over all the time."

"But I invited them to family home evening, which reminds me—Jena's missed two weeks in a row." Why did I feel like I was back in seventh grade? Maybe I was blowing this out of proportion. Nobody was rejecting me. They were just busy.

"I don't think you ever invited Rob," Tanya said.

"I never invited him because I always thought he'd want to have family home evening with his parents, but all the singles are invited. I'm sure he knows that."

Tanya shut the door that led to the hallway. "This isn't the best time to have this conversation, Emma. What if someone hears us?"

Dad stopped sanitizing a doorknob. "Don't worry about me."

I walked to the front of the room to arrange the bouquet of daffodils I'd brought. "I'll bet anything Alexandria's having her own family home evening group at Phil's house. That's why Jena hasn't been coming to ours."

Tanya lifted the lid on the piano. "I didn't want to say anything, Emma, because I knew it would upset you. She invited us a few weeks ago. Justin too."

I sank down into a chair near the piano. "I've tried to be Jena's friend. Why would she choose Alexandria over me? Am I that bad?"

Tanya placed a hand on my shoulder. "You're wonderful, Emma. I think Jena knows that. But you're busy. Alexandria has more time for her. Maybe that's what Jena needs—quantity time instead of quality time."

Tanya sat down to play the piano as I considered whether I could've balanced my life to spend more time with Jena. Since I'd listened to the missionaries teaching Harri, I'd thought more and more of the Savior. I wondered if He ever felt overwhelmed. He had a huge responsibility, numberless followers, trials of his own, and his own physical needs. Would He have had time for Jena? I'd spent every free minute of the last few weeks working toward my coaching certification and trying to pass out brochures to anyone who could give me a referral. I still had so much to do. There was no time to coordinate another social event.

The door opened as Justin and Harri entered. Justin was performing the baptism, so he and Harri both wore white. Harri came straight over to sit by me. I put my arm around her. "How's it feel?"

Harri smiled. "I've looked forward to this day for forever. You know how you hear in Primary that all your sins will be washed away? I always thought it'd be so awesome."

I thought of my own baptism day and how I'd felt so sure I could lead a sin-free life from that point on. It'd only taken a few days before I'd failed. Perfection was so elusive. And the older I got, the worse it got. I made more and more mistakes every year.

Harri took a deep breath. "Isn't it great to know that because of Jesus, we don't have to be perfect?"

I wasn't sure I knew that. At least I didn't act like I knew it. "I wish I were more like you, Harri."

Justin sat on the other side of Harri. Soon guests wearing their Sunday best came in, exchanging greetings and hugs with Harri as they passed. She shook hands with Rob Martinez, Phil, Alexandria, Barbara, and Jena. The way Harri smiled reminded me of a bride on her wedding day. It was like she'd broken through the barrier to peace and joy. I couldn't take credit for the change. Despite me, Heavenly Father had blessed Harri with a better life. How would it be to have my sins washed away again?

Justin, tired of having people lean over him, traded seats with Harri, giving her the aisle. He held his hand out to shake mine. It wasn't his normal handshake. He held onto my hand longer. "You okay?"

"I know the Savior can take away Harri's burdens and your burdens," I said. "Why can't I believe He'll take away mine?"

"Have you tried to give them to Him?"

"Not lately."

His voice was deep and gentle. "Maybe that's the problem."

The bishop came to ask Harri whether all the guests had arrived. She glanced around at the crowded room. "I think everyone's here."

I saw the empty space beside Randall and Tanya. "Hank's not here yet." Harri would never say she wanted to wait for Hank; I had to look out for her interests.

Justin handed me his watch. "We'll give him five more minutes."

Five minutes later, Harri was so focused on her baptism, she didn't seem fazed by Hank's absence. During the talks, she never once glanced back to see if Hank had filled the empty seat.

When the time came for the baptism, Justin helped Harri into the font. Watching my two friends standing in the water, I was happy for Harri and happy for Justin, but I also felt something I hadn't expected: jealousy. A coach has to be hopeful—and I was. I was hopeful about Harri and all the other people in the room, but not about me. It wasn't that I wanted to take Harri's place. I didn't want to take anything away from Harri. I just wanted to share the peace I saw on her face.

After the service, when everyone ate punch and cake in the cultural hall, I was in the women's restroom, trying to repair the damage to my face. That's right. I'd cried. It wasn't like me at all, and, what was worse, it hadn't even been for all the right reasons. Paper towels did nothing to erase the mascara streaks, so I lathered up the hand soap and washed my face the regular way. While I worked on the smudges, I heard rustling sounds coming from the handicapped stall. "Is that you, Tanya?" I asked.

Looking through the mirror, I could see a pair of sneakers peeking out under the stall. I was finishing up with a swipe of lip gloss when the stall's occupant emerged. It was Jena, decked out in running gear. "Can you do me a huge favor, Emma?"

"Sure."

Jena placed a duffel bag on the counter. "I'm going on a training run, but I want to get a head start before anyone finds out I've left. When they start looking for me, can you tell them I've gone running and I'll be home in a couple hours? And can you give this bag to my mom to take home for me?"

My conversation with Tanya was still fresh in my mind. I was determined to do more for Jena. "You're leaving from here? There isn't a sidewalk for a half a mile, and the road's narrow."

She placed a pair of sunglasses on top of her head. "I'll run on the shoulder. It's better for my joints."

"But everything's muddy," I said. "I could drive you to the bike trail if you want."

Jena pushed open the bathroom door. "Thanks, Emma. But I like running on the back roads. I don't care about the mud."

"I understand." I'd learned enough about paparazzi and fans in the last few months to sympathize with Jena's craving for privacy. And I'd always understood how hard it was to be around Barbara. This was my chance to prove myself to Jena, to show I could be a true friend. "I'll help you sneak out."

I thought I'd need to distract a fan or a photographer while Jena ran out the other side of the church, so I grabbed a plate of cake to take with me. When I got to the parking lot, there was nobody but Hank Weston. He took the cake I offered him, scraping the frosting off the top as we walked into the church cultural hall. He looked around the room. "I don't know why I bothered to come so late. Half the guests have already gone."

I looked around to see Barbara sweeping, Phil stacking chairs, and Alexandria snapping pictures. Others chatted in small groups. "Most people are still here, especially the most important one. Harri will be so happy to see you." I pointed out where she stood with Rob and Justin in the kitchen.

"You mean this is all that came? I thought there'd be more people."

"The only one who's left is Jena. She went on a training run. Don't say anything, though. She didn't want me to tell the others until they noticed she's gone."

"Oh." He looked at the ceiling of the cultural hall. "She picked a bad day to run. It's supposed to rain."

"How's your mom?" I asked.

Hank smashed the side of his cake with the plastic fork. "What?"

"I said, 'How's your mom?'"

He looked at the ceiling. "As good as can be expected . . . This church is a heap. They should tear it down and build a new one. How old is it?"

I looked up, trying to figure out what he was scrutinizing. "I don't know—maybe fifty or sixty years old. A lot of people are attached to it. I've gone to church here all my life."

Hank put his plate of cake down on the table. "You have my sympathy."

I stood in front of Hank, glad I'd already given up any ideas of the two of us getting together. I wasn't as patient as Harri when it came to people's moods. In my mind, a negative person would bring me down, especially today. It was simple math: adding two negatives together could never make a positive. Still, if I was going to be a life coach, I'd have to learn how to cheer people up.

Hank dug his hands into his pockets and leaned against the wall. "I'm sick of commuting every day on the metro, living in a hotel with my mother, getting stuck in traffic, and smelling mold everywhere. You don't notice it because you've lived here all your life, but everything around here smells like mold or mildew."

I lifted his plate of cake off the table. "Maybe you'd feel better if you ate something. And why are you complaining about your commute? It's the weekend." I scooped up a forkful of cake and held it to his mouth. "It's good cake. Tanya made it. You're lucky there was a piece left." He opened his mouth, and I slid the fork in. "Now be a good boy and have another bite." It was my way of getting him to shut up. "You have everything going for you—looks, personality, grades, and a good internship. You have nothing to complain about."

He took the plate from my hands. "I'm going to feed some of it to you."

I shook my head. "No thanks." I handed him a napkin and pointed to the side of my lip. "You got some frosting here."

He wiped his mouth. "I hope you're not afraid of my germs." He stepped closer to me, holding the fork to my mouth.

"Don't get all flirtatious with me, Hank. I know I'm not the one you're really interested in."

"You're perceptive." He turned the fork around and ate the cake himself, then he handed the plate back to me. "It tastes better when you feed it to me."

"You don't deserve her." I fed him another three bites before the cake was gone. When I went to throw away the plate, I noticed Alexandria and Phil staring in our direction. Dad, Randall, Tanya, and Barbara gawked from across the room. Rob grinned and Harri giggled behind her hand while Justin kept his back to us.

Hank laughed. "Looks like we have an audience."

I rolled my eyes. They probably thought we were flirting. "I was only trying to cheer you up."

He pulled out his phone. "It worked. We should get out of here. I'm in the mood for an adrenaline rush."

"I don't know where you'll get one around here. You, of all people, should know how boring it is to live here."

Ignoring my sarcasm, he pushed the keys on his phone. "How about rock climbing? There's bound to be a climbing wall somewhere close by."

"I know where we can go," I told him, remembering a wall where I'd climbed one time with Justin.

Once I convinced Hank that our climbing wall was good enough, we invited everyone to come along. Most of the guests didn't want to change clothes or had already decided to go to a movie. Dad, Justin, and Harri were the only ones who came. Rock climbing was one of Justin's things. He liked the unusual sports, the kind you couldn't get a letter for in high school. I'm pretty sure Dad wouldn't have gotten past signing the release form if Justin hadn't convinced him it was safe.

The wall was thirty feet high and forty feet wide, allowing room for eight or nine climbers at a time. It was pieced together out of something that looked like drywall with plastic, multicolored holds dotting the surface. For beginning climbers, the wall went straight up. For the more advanced, the wall jutted out at an angle. Climbing ropes hung from pulleys attached to the ceiling. Justin and Hank were the only experienced climbers, so Hank climbed first while Justin belayed. Hank went fast, reaching the top of the hardest part of the wall in a couple of minutes. "Who wants to go next?" he called as he rappelled down the wall.

Once Hank was on the ground, Justin helped Harri attach herself to a rope on one of the easier parts of the wall. Since she'd never climbed before, she had to experiment a little as she went. Her climb was slow.

Hank clicked a belay device onto his harness. "You ready to go, Emma? I'll belay you."

"No," Dad said, tightening his harness. "I'll go next." After carefully attaching himself to the rope, Dad slowly climbed up the wall, watching Harri's progress as he went. By the time Harri got to the top, Dad was only eight feet up. It was almost as if Dad didn't trust Hank, as if someone had told him what happened at the ski resort. He only began his descent when Harri reached the floor.

I tied the rope Harri had used to my harness. When Justin stood in front of me to check my figure-eight knot, I forgot for a moment that we were just friends. Excitement skipped through me, the thrill of being close to a man. I wanted to step closer and nestle my head under his chin, inches away from his lips.

The attraction must've been all on my side. He tightened my harness with the efficiency of an expert, as if he were fastening a saddle on a horse. "Looks good."

His words roused me from my fantasy. I remembered what I'd meant to ask him. "Did you tell my dad about the ski lift?"

Justin pushed his eyebrows down, looking offended. "No."

"He wouldn't let Hank belay me," I said. "I wonder why he doesn't trust him."

Justin stepped back from the wall, pulling the rope taut. "Because he's a good dad . . . Are you gonna go all the way to the top this time?"

I looked up at the thirty-foot wall. "I never have before."

"You should. I won't let you fall. Just don't look down."

Once I was on the wall, I couldn't keep from looking down. I had to see where my feet were supposed to go. Before, I'd always assumed that meant I had to look at the floor too. This time I didn't look farther down than my feet. I took the wall one hand and foot at a time. My goal was to keep moving. After a few minutes, I saw the top a few feet away. Was I actually going to make it? That's when I looked down—all the way down, and my grip started slipping. My arms burned. "Finish it, Emma!" Justin called. "You're almost there."

Refocusing on my goal to keep moving, I reached for the next handhold, one more foothold, another handhold, and a foothold until the next place to reach was the top of the wall. I pulled myself up to the top and looked all the way down at Justin cheering for me. I'd done it. I'd finished. I'd conquered my fear. Funny how it wasn't any scarier than almost finishing.

Chapter 24

Coach's Tip of the Day:
Don't talk when your mouth is full of your foot.

From a distance, Sugarloaf Mountain looked like a series of soft bumpy hills, the same shape you'd get by pouring a bag of sugar into a loaf pan. It was a warm day for April, even at the higher altitude. Harri and I drove up the narrow winding road with the windows rolled down and summery music blaring from my stereo. I expected the best from Sugarloaf, hoping for the kind of spiritual renewal that came from nature.

It'd been a week of achievement for me. I had two new coaching clients—both referred to me by one of Dad's doctor friends. They were sisters who'd recently lost their mother, and I was coaching them for free to fulfill some of my requirements for certification. I knew what they needed because I'd been there. I knew how it was to lose my most important role model in life. I was someone who understood, someone to tell them they were capable, one more person to counter the poisonous culture of high school. So far, we'd talked about what they wanted out of life and I'd helped them set goals to achieve that. They did the work, and I cheered them on. The side benefit was I'd stuck to my own goals better than I ever had before.

Harri and I admired the well-groomed woods as we drove. When we arrived at the parking lot, the others were waiting beside a wooden pavilion. Alexandria chose the hike based on Barbara's fitness level, so it was nothing rigorous. We followed a dirt path through the tall trees and undergrowth.

Spring came later on the mountain than it did lower down, so I was glad for warm patches of sunlight sifting through the branches. The woods smelled muddy. Yellow-green leaves were emerging, and green moss grew on the sides of the trees.

Alexandria seemed to think this was a great time to convince Jena to serve a mission. "Justin, what was your mission like?"

Justin stepped off the path to avoid a mud puddle. "It was hard. I loved it, but it was hard."

Alexandria peeked back at Jena. "Going on a mission was the best decision I ever made."

Hank paused on a boulder growing thick with lichens. "I have no regrets about my mission either, which is something I can't say for most of the other decisions I've made."

Jena must have had enough of the mission talk. She took off running ahead of us on the path. "I'll see you guys at the top!" she called back.

It was obvious all the mission talk was for Jena. As soon as she left, Alexandria changed the subject to her wedding plans. I hung back a little, trying to focus on the beauty of the woods. As we approached the summit, the dirt path changed to stone steps leading up to a rocky cliff. We'd gone up at least fifty or sixty steps, and I wasn't sure if we were halfway up yet. We were breathless by the time we reached a small landing, where we rested before ascending more steps to the top. Once we started climbing again, the summit appeared around a corner. We'd reached the top.

The view was worth the climb. I stood on a gray boulder and looked out on a view that rivaled the background of the Mona Lisa. Different layers of green faded away into the blue horizon. I traced the outline of a river, a distant town, and pastures—all framed by the foreground of green-leafed trees and rolling hills.

Our little group sat together on some boulders that looked over the view. The conversation had turned to Alexandria's wedding plans again. "I think a Chinese New Year theme would be fantastic," Alexandria said, "but I can't get Phil to agree to it."

Phil took a sandwich out of his backpack. "First of all, August is the wrong time for Chinese New Year. Second of all, fortune cookies aren't really Chinese." He still did that thing where he didn't open his mouth enough, but I'd learned my lesson—I wasn't going to keep looking. "You could do a Chinatown theme," I suggested. "Then you wouldn't have to worry so much about authenticity."

Alexandria nodded. "As long as we can have fortune cookies. I want to have each fortune personalized with our names on them. Don't you think that'd be cute, Justin?"

"I wouldn't know," Justin responded.

I couldn't help smiling when Alexandria asked Justin whether he preferred roses or gardenias. He answered respectfully. "No matter what kind of flower you get, they'll die within a few days. You might as well save your money and go with the roses."

Alexandria recorded Justin's answer in a little notebook. "What about you, Hank? Roses or gardenias?"

Hank pulled a leaf through his fingers. "You should be asking these questions to someone with real style. Ask Emma."

"Emma has a talent for decorating," Tanya said. "I've always thought so anyway."

"But Emma has such different tastes than I do," Alexandria said. "I'm sure we'd never agree."

Randall grinned. "It's like I told you, Hank, Emma is practically perfect in every way."

I laughed. "Don't compare me to Mary Poppins, Randall. I'm not perfect in any way at all."

Hank took a swig from his water bottle. "He's saying that because you helped him snag a perfect wife."

"Emma also has a talent for matchmaking," Tanya said, "but I wouldn't say I'm a perfect wife."

Alexandria stood up from her rock. "I think I'm ready to head down. Aren't you, Phil?" Phil grabbed his backpack and followed Alexandria to the path that led down the mountain.

Hank waited until they were out of hearing range. "Now there's someone you could've helped, Emma. Why couldn't you have picked a better woman for Phil? Something tells me he's beginning to regret his decision. Why do men get married anyway? It's much easier to be single."

I cast a sideways glance at Harri, who picked a little bit of nature out of Justin's hair and pretended to eat it like a monkey. It reminded me of the way she'd been when I first met her.

"I don't think Phil regrets his decision," Jena said. "He told me this morning how much he admires Ali. He's not afraid to let anyone know."

Hank threw a rock into the woods. "He'll regret his decision soon enough. Ali's one of those women who pretends to be someone she's not. By the time Phil realizes what she's really like, he'll already be trapped. I speak from experience."

Jena threw a rock too. "I speak from experience when I say that men can be the same way."

Barbara looked at the trees above us. "I think Alexandria's wonderful. She's a good friend to Jena. And you should see what she's done with Phil's flower beds. They're lovely. She must have planted a hundred pansies. Pansies always remind me of that song, you know: 'Little purple pansies touched with yellow gold.'" Barbara recited both verses of the song, ending with, "'Dark the day or sunny, we must try, try, try, Just one spot to gladden, you and I.' I've always wanted to be like those little purple pansies."

"That's a perfect description for you, Barbara," Tanya said. "You're like a little purple pansy."

"Only the little purple pansies don't talk so much," I joked. It got so quiet, I realized I must have sounded meaner than I'd meant. I backtracked, "I mean, you're cheerful, and it's always fun to be around you. It just always takes longer than I plan."

Barbara laughed nervously. "I see what you mean. I should try not to talk so much."

"Oh no, Barbara," I said. "You don't have to change. The rest of us need to be more patient. That's all." I felt Tanya's foot pressing against my shin.

Jena stood up. "I think I'll try to catch up with Ali and Phil. Do you want to come, Mom?"

Justin stood to help Barbara up. "I'll walk with you if you don't mind."

We watched Jena, Barbara, Harri, Tanya, Randall, and Justin walk off. I caught myself examining Justin's physique as he sauntered along behind Barbara. Lately, I'd been enjoying the way he looked more than a friend should.

That left Hank and me sitting on the boulders. Hank stretched his arms above his head. "I think I'll take a power nap. Will you wait with me, Emma? I need someone to protect me from the wild animals." He leaned back on his sun-drenched boulder, resting his head on his hands.

"Sure." I stared at where water had collected in a hollow place on the boulder. Dead bugs were floating in it. I still hadn't felt the spiritual renewal I'd expected to find here. It was so easy to focus on the bad stuff even with all the beauty surrounding us.

While Hank napped, I had a silent conversation with Heavenly Father. I thanked Him for the scene around me. I thanked Him that Harri was in a good place. Then I listed some of my other blessings. I didn't say all the things I could've said because I wanted to get on to my question. It was a question I'd thought about since Harri's baptism. I wanted to know if Heavenly Father really would forgive me, not that I'd done anything all that bad, but there were plenty of little things I'd messed up—a lot of it having to do with Harri. I asked Him about forgiving me and waited for an answer while I watched the wind blowing through the trees. By the time Hank woke up—his nap took all of fifteen minutes—I was still waiting.

When Hank decided to run downhill to catch up with the others, I had no choice but to run after him. I wasn't about to walk by myself on some isolated mountain trail. At Hank's speed, it was impossible to admire the trees budding or to look for any of the birds I heard singing around us. I had to watch the path so I wouldn't trip over roots and rocks or step in the mud. By the time we reached the others, I was breathless.

"I have an announcement," Hank called out to them as we approached. "I've decided what I'm going to do with my life. After I graduate, I'll spend a year backpacking through Europe. When I come back, I'll find a job, and Emma will find me a wife. Will you do that for me, Emma?"

I knew Hank wasn't serious, but I couldn't help thinking of Harri. "I'd love to."

"There *are* online dating services for that type of thing," Alexandria said. "That's how Phil and I met." She seemed so serious, I was sure she didn't know Hank was joking.

Hank shook his head. "No, I think Emma could do a better job. Who wants to mess with an online profile?"

I laughed. "You're too good looking for online dating." I paused to breathe. "You'd be flooded with requests."

Alexandria stopped with her hands on her hips. "Phil is good looking, and he wasn't flooded with requests." I guessed that meant Phil hadn't used a picture of Rapunzel's boyfriend for his profile picture on the dating website.

"But Hank has such a great personality too," I countered. "It's a deadly combination."

Jena looked at her watch. "I think there's still time for me to run the loop before we leave." She took off running ahead of us.

Alexandria nudged Phil. "I dropped something along the trail. We'd better go look for it." They both turned to walk in the opposite direction.

"I'd be happy to help," Randall offered.

"No need," Alexandria called back. "It's not that important. It's a cheap little bracelet."

Tanya and Randall turned to follow. "No, we'd love to help."

Hank whispered to me. "How much you wanna bet there isn't a bracelet?"

I laughed. Justin glared at us. "What's so funny?"

Hank shrugged. "Nothing's funny. I was just wondering if anyone had seen Ali's bracelet earlier."

Barbara shook her head. "I didn't see a bracelet, but I noticed her earrings—gold hoops. Ali's very fashionable. I always like to see what she's wearing. Yesterday, she had on the prettiest turquoise bib necklace. I asked her where she got it. I think she said—oh wait, I'm doing it again, talking too much."

Justin glared at me again. "You're not talking too much, Sister Bates."

We walked the rest of the way in silence. When we got back to the parking lot, I went in search of a bathroom. Justin followed me. As soon as we got far enough away that the others couldn't hear, he stopped. "Emma, do you remember that time we burned our bad habits?"

"Yeah."

His nostrils flared. "I made a promise not to criticize you any more. Until today, it hasn't been that hard to keep my promise."

I looked at the path ahead of us. "If you mean what I said about Barbara talking too much, I was just kidding."

Justin folded his arms. "Maybe you could've passed if off as 'just kidding' if you hadn't gone on about how the rest of us need to be more patient with her. That was rude. You made her sad. If any of us had to be patient, it wasn't because of Barbara. It was because of you."

I looked at his left shoulder, anywhere but his face. "I didn't mean to hurt her feelings."

"Well, you did, and what was that you said about Hank having a better personality than Phil? Were you trying to hurt Phil's feelings too?" His voice was angry.

I twisted Mom's ring around on my finger. "Phil and Alexandria take everything too seriously. Hank and I were joking. They—"

"I thought you were better than that. I thought you'd left behind the whole catty high school attitude. But now that Hank Weston comes to town, you're willing to insult your best friends . . . I've lost a lot of respect for you today."

I kept my eyes on the ground. "I'll never be good enough for you, will I?" Why was it so important for me to please him? Why did it matter to me so much?

Justin kicked a rock out of the path. "Not as long as you keep acting like you're better than everyone else. I know you're not a snob, but you sure come across that way."

I turned toward the parking lot. "I guess I'd better go home before I disappoint you any more." My effort to cover the hurt made my words come out sounding angry.

"I think that's a good idea," he said.

I walked down the log steps in the direction of my car.

"Didn't you drive with Harri?" Justin called.

"If you're such a great influence, why don't you drive her home?"

Already certain he had enough room in his truck for Harri, I didn't wait for his answer. I hopped in my Civic and sped down the winding lane, vastly exceeding the speed limit of fifteen miles per hour.

Chapter 25

Coach's Tip of the Day:
"I'm sorry" is easy enough to say; it's just awkward.

I spent most of Saturday night writing out apologies to Barbara, Alexandria, and Phil. Three little notes didn't seem like enough to control the damage I'd caused, so I woke up early on Sunday morning to make muffins. I made apple streusel for Phil, low-fat pumpkin chocolate chip for Alexandria, and lemon poppy seed for Barbara. I hoped they'd taste my remorse. By 10:00 a.m., I had three cellophane-wrapped baskets of muffins ready to go. By 10:30 I'd sent off text messages to everyone that I'd be stopping by soon.

Alexandria answered the door in her bathrobe while she was on the phone. Her eyebrows were a smudge, but considering my own flaws, I was willing to overlook hers. I handed her the basket. "I hope you weren't offended by what I said about online dating yesterday. I didn't mean anything by it. I think you and Phil are a great couple."

Alexandria spoke into the phone. "I'm sure you can get an appointment with the bishop today. Can you hold on a second?" She held the phone to her chest. "Emma, how sweet. I was just talking to Jena. Did you hear she's decided to go on a mission?"

I shook my head. "No."

"After you and Hank left," Alexandria said, "we went out to

dinner at the cutest little country place. That's when we finally convinced her. Now she can't wait to go. She wants to leave as soon as possible. I think she needs a break from being a celebrity. She wants to do something that'll really change people's lives. We had so much fun after you left."

"Oh." I hadn't expected Jena to cave in to Alexandria's advice on serving a mission. Even so, it was like Jena to make such a bold decision.

"I'd invite you in, but I have to run and get ready. Thanks for the muffins."

She closed the door before I had a chance to say, "You're welcome."

Phil's house was less than a mile from Alexandria's apartment. After I rang the bell, he opened the door a crack. "Ali's not here."

I held out the basket. "I know. I just dropped by her apartment. I came to apologize for the things I said yesterday. I didn't mean to imply that you weren't—"

Phil opened the door wider to reach for the basket, allowing Alexandria's cat to dart past. "Come back here, Mittens." Phil went running after her.

"I'll leave this on the doorstep," I yelled to Phil, who was already halfway down the street. I considered helping him chase down his cat, but knowing my track record with him, it was better to leave before things got any worse.

From there, I drove straight to Barbara's. I'd saved her house for last, hoping to squeeze in a little visit with her and Jena. Pushing past a crowd of fans on the sidewalk, I walked to the door. "Don't bother," a preteen girl called. "She won't answer. We already tried." The steps were littered with flower bouquets and paper cards.

"I'm a friend of the family," I explained before ringing the doorbell. I heard footsteps as someone came to the door to check the peephole. Then the footsteps walked away. I waited, thinking Barbara had to get her bathrobe or something, but no one came back.

"See!" the girl called. "I told you she wouldn't answer."

Maybe I *wasn't* a friend of the family anymore. I took the basket back to the car with me, determined to catch Barbara later on at church, which meant I'd have to go early. Dad and Barbara attended the ward right before the singles ward.

I got to church a few minutes before Barbara was supposed to get out of sacrament meeting. After the closing prayer, I made my way to the back of the chapel, where Barbara and Jena sat. Thanks to the buzz about Jena deciding to serve a mission, people were lined up at Barbara and Jena's pew as if it were an all-you-can-eat buffet. Everyone was saying how Jena's example would help other young women want to serve missions. I couldn't get within speaking distance of Barbara until she rushed through a gap in the crowd, wearing one of her signature jean jumpers and dabbing her eyes with a tissue.

I followed her out into the foyer. "Could I talk to you for a minute?"

She walked down the hallway. "I'd love to talk, but I don't have time. I'm late for nursery. Have you heard Jena's going to serve a mission? I know I shouldn't cry about it. It's supposed to be a happy thing. It's just that I'm going to miss her so much."

"That's okay," I said. "I understand how it would be hard for you. Listen, I'm sorry about the things I said yesterday. My words came out all wrong." Barbara opened the door to the nursery, allowing the cries of children to drown out my words. "I hope you don't think I meant any of it."

Barbara reached down to pick up a toddler. "It's okay, Emma. No need to worry."

I held out the basket of muffins. "I made these for you. They're lemon poppy seed."

Holding the toddler, Barbara reached for the basket with one hand. "Oh, my favorite! Thank you. They look delicious."

Jena rushed past me as I walked out of the nursery. "Hi, Jena," I called. She didn't say anything, and she walked so fast, I didn't have a chance to congratulate her on the whole mission thing. She couldn't still be angry at me for having one tactless moment, could she? I took a deep, calming breath and told myself she'd feel better about me when she saw the note I wrote to Barbara.

Satisfied that I'd patched things up the best I could, I headed off to the back row of pews in the chapel to look over the lesson I was supposed to teach in Sunday School. I hadn't cracked the manual open for at least a month—that was how long it'd been since I last taught. The lesson was on spiritual gifts. At the moment, I didn't feel spiritual or gifted—much less spiritually gifted—but I forced myself to open the lesson manual anyway. By the time our sacrament meeting started, I'd read through all the material and felt satisfied that I could pull it off. If it was like every other lesson, people would make so many comments, all I'd have to do was moderate the discussion.

Justin was still mad at me. I could tell by the way he and Harri walked right past me in sacrament meeting to sit near the front. Harri waved; he didn't. Then, in Sunday School, he kept his eyes on his scriptures. Normally, he pulled faces when I taught, trying to get me to laugh. Whatever he was reading must have been really interesting; he read the same page for the entire lesson. I hoped it said something about forgiveness.

Tanya came to sit beside Harri and me during Relief Society. "I guess you've heard about Hank?"

"What about him?"

"He had to take his mom to Alabama—something about an emergency visit with her doctors."

"That's too bad," I said. "I hope she's okay." I wasn't as disappointed as I'd been the last time Hank had to leave. In fact, my feeling could better be described as relief. It'd be nice to put a little more distance between us. My only disappointment was for Harri's sake. I kept an eye on her during the Relief Society lesson, watching for signs of a breakdown. Nothing. She focused on the lesson the entire time, smiling at some of the comments and even making one herself. During the closing hymn, she swiped on some lip gloss.

Justin caught up to me in the parking lot when church was over. "Hey, Emma, I'm headed off to Richmond this afternoon. I thought I'd better say good-bye before I left." He held Barbara's basket of muffins.

"You're leaving? Today?"

His Adam's apple bobbed up and down as he swallowed. "It's a last-minute thing. John's needed my help for a while. The work's piling up down there." He pulled me in for a hug, pressing the basket of muffins against my back.

My heart raced at his touch, but I stepped back from his embrace. "How long will you be gone?"

"As long as it takes."

"Do you want me to watch Buttercup?"

"No, thanks. I'm taking her with me." It sounded like he was going to be gone a long time.

I pointed to the basket. "Where'd you get those muffins?"

"From Jena. Someone gave them to her. She didn't want them."

I could see the note I'd written to Barbara still inside the cellophane. Watching him walk to his truck with Harri, I hoped he would read the note. Then, at least if I hadn't healed any other relationships, I could heal the one that meant the most to me.

Chapter 26

*Y*ou can't help running into someone when you both live in the same town. On Friday night, Dad and I were slurping wonton soup at our favorite Chinese restaurant when the door swung open and Jena walked in with Barbara. While she waited for a table, her eyes drifted in the direction of our little booth in the corner. I waved. She whispered something to her mother. Then she turned and walked back out the door. Barbara followed her.

"They must have decided to eat somewhere else," Dad said. "Barbara tells me Jena's been sick lately. Maybe she didn't feel up to Chinese."

I adjusted the napkin on my lap. "I'm sure that's what it was." All my life Dad and Tanya had told me not to worry about what other people thought, that most of the time they weren't thinking of me at all. I'd always believed them. This time, though, I was sure it was all about me.

I looked across the restaurant to see myself reflected in the gigantic mirror on the opposite wall. Why did restaurants have to have mirrors? How could seeing your reflection in a mirror help you

201

feel comfortable about eating? My hair looked like a mess of frizz. My face seemed pale and splotchy. I looked back down at my soup, never lifting my eyes again to the mirror.

When we got back home, I wanted to call Justin and vent to him about Jena. How could she be so unforgiving? But I was too ashamed to talk to Justin or anyone else who'd been at Sugarloaf Mountain with us. I was sure they'd all take Jena's side. It was one of those days I wished Mom were still alive; maybe I could've talked to her. Instead, I called Isabella.

After I'd told her everything, Isabella groaned. "Emma, you'll never know what real stress is until you have a husband and children and a business to run. John's had so many new contracts, I've had to take over the paperwork. So I'm busier, and he's busier. There's no one to watch the kids while I'm working. It wasn't so bad until Zoey learned how to open doors and Kyra decided she's scared of the dark. I'm hardly getting any sleep. It's insane, Emma."

"I thought Justin went down to help you."

"He helps John during the day, but at night, it's like he's in his own little world. He hasn't helped me at all."

I wasn't sure I believed her. "He's usually such a good uncle," I said, sure she'd put a negative spin on reality.

"Not this week. Hold on a second." I could hear her tell Zoey not to pull on the cat's tail.

When she got back on the phone, I said, "I wish I could help."

"Quit trying to save the world, Emma. Enjoy your life while you still can."

The only thing I was enjoying right at the moment was my life-coaching course, so that night, I shut myself in my room and finished another online chapter test. The next day, I held two practice coaching sessions and passed another test. That weekend, I set up the *Coach Emma Woodhouse* website, decided on my hourly rates, and ordered business cards. After passing another test during my lunch hour on Monday, I discovered I was only four tests and three practice coaching sessions away from earning my certification. I could have earned it by the end of that week, as long as nothing interfered. Wasn't that the way it always was? As soon as I got close to accomplishing my goals, something interfered. And that week, it happened on Wednesday—two days before I would have finished.

Chapter 27

Coach's Tip of the Day:
Your moment of fame may
come sooner than you think.

Two preteen girls came in for check-ups right before closing time on Wednesday at Dr. Metzdorf's office. They sat in the corner, whispering and giggling. It seemed normal enough, except they kept looking at me. Most people were content to ignore the receptionist. Figuring it must have something to do with my hair color, I moved to the other side of the desk and bent over my keyboard. My strategy didn't work. The girls came right up to the counter to stare at me. "Can I help you?" I asked.

This sent them into a fit of giggling. Finally, one of them put her phone in front of me. "She wants to know if you're the one who kissed the guy who's gonna marry Jena Farley."

"Excuse me?" I picked up her phone to see a picture of the one time Hank kissed me. Danny had posted it on some country music website. Even as my cheeks burned with guilt, I wanted to lie and say it wasn't me. But I knew better. Everyone always recognized my hair, and there it was in full color for all the world to see. "That's me, but he isn't Jena's boyfriend."

I read the headline, "Jena Farley Announces Engagement."

Scrolling down, I saw a picture of Jena displaying her diamond ring. "Are you kidding me? That ring was for her video. This is all a hoax."

The hygienists came to call both girls back for their appointments, but only one of them left. The other stood there, watching me. Finally, she said, "I'm gonna need my phone back."

"Oh, sorry," I said, handing her back the phone. After that, I should have finished up the reminder calls for the next day's appointments, but instead I did a quick Internet search for "Jena Farley engagement."

A picture of Hank and Jena holding hands came up with the caption: "They've kept their relationship secret for months." Hank and Jena? No way. Hank didn't even like Jena. *And* she was going on a mission. Someone must have Photoshopped the picture. Scrolling down through the article about a supposed engagement, I found the same picture of Hank and me kissing. This time I slammed my fist onto the top of the desk. Danny had no right to post that online, even if no one could see my face. I was a private citizen. He couldn't invent stories about me and get away with it. This was libel.

Finishing up my office duties, I made six reminder calls to six voice mail systems, struggling to keep my voice slow and professional. How could Danny lie about Jena? How dare he post my picture online? What would Justin say when he saw I'd kissed Hank? What would Dad say?

I couldn't go home until I'd hashed this out, so I drove to Tanya's house, gripping the steering wheel as if I could choke it to death. My stomach growled from hunger. Tanya was kneeling in the garden beside her front steps, planting pansies in between her tulips. I got out of the car and walked toward her without saying a word.

Tanya took off her gardening gloves and sucked in her cheeks as if she were preparing for the worst. "So I guess you've heard."

I sat on her front steps. "How could he lie like that? It's not fair."

She sat beside me. "I don't blame you for being upset, but you should see how happy he is."

I knew Tanya was much more charitable than I'd ever be, but I couldn't see how she could sympathize with a paparazzo. "He doesn't deserve to be happy. He shouldn't be able to make money telling lies."

Tanya smoothed her hand across my back. "What he did was

inexcusable. If he hadn't explained everything to us this morning, Randall and I would probably never speak to him again. But he's so in love, and they've had so many obstacles to overcome."

"Are you talking about Danny or—"

"Hank. I'm talking about Hank," Tanya said.

"Hank?" I said. "So the pictures, the articles about Hank and Jena—they're true?" It couldn't be true. They didn't even like each other.

Tanya looked at me as if I were about to break. "It's true. They've been dating—secretly dating—for over a year now. And that's not all. They've been engaged since Christmas, except when Jena broke it off. Believe me, Emma, if I'd known, I wouldn't have tried to set you up with him. Randall and I feel awful about it. I'm not sure we'll ever be able to forgive Hank for the way he's treated you."

I thought about how Hank had treated me—all the flirting, the kiss, and the way he'd always picked me first. Anyone would've thought he was after me, not Jena. "He sent out vibes that he was available—not just available. He acted like he was interested in me. He used me, didn't he? He wanted everyone to think he was dating me. That's why he kissed me—to fool the paparazzi and everyone else. What a jerk!"

Tanya combed through my hair with her fingers. "I told Randall I was sure you'd get over him, and I know you will." She thought I was still hankering for Hank.

I let out half a laugh. "I'm already over him. When he went back to Alabama and didn't call me for a month, I knew he wasn't serious about me."

Tanya pushed my hair away from my face, searching my expression. "So he didn't break your heart?"

"No," I said, "but I'm still mad at him. Why did he think it was okay to fool everyone? It's not like Hank and Jena are the only ones who can keep secrets. Why couldn't they trust us? Did Barbara know about it?"

Tanya shook her head. "Hank and Jena agreed they wouldn't tell anyone, not even their family members. You know how Barbara is; she's not good with secrets, especially if she's excited about something. Hank's mom knew at first, but she made the mistake of telling him not to date Jena. She thought the publicity would hurt the family business. With Hank being the future CEO, everything he does has to be conservative and proper. They couldn't afford to have him in the tabloids—not that Hank would've done anything worth putting in a tabloid, but you never know. Jena wanted to avoid the spotlight too. She'd dated guys who liked the publicity more than they liked her. And others who couldn't take it at all."

I let out my breath, releasing some tension in the process. "I can see her point. All that publicity would be hard on a relationship."

Tanya hugged me sideways across my shoulders. "But the secrecy was just as hard on their relationship. Jena broke up with him a few weeks ago. It was around the time we went to Sugarloaf Mountain. That's when she decided to serve a mission."

My mouth hung open as Jena's behavior started to make sense. "That's why she was in such a bad mood."

Tanya twisted her wedding ring around on her finger. "She had her mission papers all filled out and ready to submit. When Hank found out, he decided he had nothing to lose. Yesterday morning, he told his mom about the relationship. I guess her health problems have softened her a little. She said she wants him to be happy whether or not it's good for her business. He flew out here yesterday afternoon and proposed to Jena all over again, this time in front of Danny. Have you seen the pictures?"

I blew my hair off my face. "Yeah."

"I think Jena really did want to serve a mission," Tanya said. "She loved helping the missionaries teach Harri."

That's when I remembered—if anyone would be heartbroken about Hank marrying Jena, it was Harri. I had to find her and break the news before she found out some other way. For all I knew, this would be just as bad as when I'd told her about Phil. It could be worse.

I found Harri giving herself a mani-pedi in her bedroom. She smiled at me. "Have you heard the news?"

"What news?" I asked. It couldn't be the same news. She was too calm. Her fingers were steady as she brushed blue polish on her fingernails.

"That Hank and Jena are getting married," she said.

"I heard it. That's why I came over here." I searched her face. There was no evidence of tears. "I thought you'd be upset."

Harri blew on her nail polish. "Why would I be upset? You're the one who should be upset. You've been crushing on Hank since Christmas."

I sat on the bed beside her. "I thought *you* were crushing on him. You told me . . . You gave me that hint—you said you liked someone who rescued you?"

Harri held her fingers out, examining her paint job. "Yeah, but it wasn't Hank."

"I could've sworn—it was the same day he helped you with the computer program."

Harri giggled. "If you have to know, I was talking about Justin."

"Justin?" She couldn't be serious.

Harri unscrewed the purple nail polish to start on her toenails. "He's the sweetest guy I've ever known, and he's totally hot. Things are going great between us."

I gnawed on my fingernail. "Are you sure Justin feels the same way about you? I mean, we've been wrong about these kinds of things before."

Harri rolled her eyes. "You don't have to remind me, Emma. I've been ultra-paranoid about everything. But it's so obvious. You remember how I called him a couple times to help me get over Phil? He started calling me every night after that. Then he had me come to his house for the missionary discussions. I know you're going to say it was all him being nice. But did you see how much he talked to me at Barbara's potluck and at the baptism?"

I raced through my memories. What she said made sense, but she couldn't be right. Justin couldn't be interested in her, could he? "Maybe he wanted you to get together with Rob. Wasn't Rob there too?"

Harri stopped painting to look at me. "Yeah, but Justin was the same way at Sugarloaf Mountain, and Rob wasn't with us there."

I drew in my breath. "Does he still call you every day?" He hadn't called me in at least three weeks.

"We talk every night."

All the evidence was there. How could I have ignored the way Justin paired off with Harri? I closed my eyes and pinched the bridge of my nose while I considered how to respond. There was no reason Harri shouldn't have Justin. Didn't I want the best for her? Still I wanted to shout no over and over again as if she were a baby about to crawl into the street.

Harri broke the silence. "What's wrong?"

Borrowing a trick from Jena, I rubbed the back of my neck. "I don't feel so great. I think I'd better go home."

Harri opened a drawer in her bedside table. "Do you want an Excedrin? I have a ton."

"No thanks." I made my way to the door, thinking of all Justin had done for Harri in the last few months. He'd hosted her missionary discussions and performed her baptism. He was invested in her. He'd spent time with her. He'd convinced her that she was beautiful and convinced himself in the process. They'd become a couple, and I hadn't even noticed. How could I not have seen it?

I didn't want to go home, where Dad would ask me what was wrong. He would never understand. So I drove to Giant Grocery store, grabbed a box of cookies-and-cream ice cream from the freezer section, and picked up a spoon at the deli. Why should I bother avoiding ice cream when no one wanted to date me anyway?

I put the ice cream on the conveyor belt for the express lane.

"How are you?" the checker asked.

I couldn't lie to her. "I'm afraid to face my emotions. How are you?"

"I'm good, thanks." She picked up the ice cream but didn't scan it. "Did you find everything you needed?"

I felt the tears coming. I wasn't the type of woman who cried in the express lane. There were two people standing behind me in the line. Why was I buying ice cream? If I dug into that ice cream, I'd eat too much, my blood sugar would spike, and I'd feel guilty. "Actually, I needed something else," I muttered, taking the ice cream back from her and squeezing past the others in line.

Tears slid down my cheeks and into my mouth as I replaced the ice cream in the freezer section. I bought a bowl of Italian wedding soup from the deli, grabbing a handful of saltines and a pile of stiff paper napkins in the process. Harri's words echoed in my brain: *We talk every night.*

I sat in the deli section, trying to hide myself and my unreasonable tears. I was not going to look into any of the mirrors that surrounded the little group of tables. Sitting there, I held a self-coaching session, asking myself: Why should it matter that Harri chose Justin? Was I so scared of losing another friend? Didn't I want them to be happy?

With my eyes closed, I tried to visualize Justin marrying Harri. If I could see it in my mind, maybe it'd be easier to accept. But I couldn't see it. I could see Justin holding out an engagement ring. I could see him coming out of the temple with his bride. I could see him having children. But Harri wasn't there. *I* was always beside him.

I'd spent so much time trying to figure out what I wanted out of life. I wanted to be a coach. I wanted to help people. What I hadn't realized was that coaching was only a step toward my bigger dream. My highest goal was to have someone to share my life with. Justin was more than my best friend. He was the man I wanted to be worthy of.

Who was I kidding? He wasn't going to marry me—someone who disappointed him, someone who constantly failed to live up to his standards. Harri, though—Harri was moldable. She'd proven she could change. She could conform. She could make herself into a perfect wife for Justin, one he deserved.

I'd tried to help Harri, and because of it, I'd ruined my own life forever. If only I could undo the past five months and go back to the way things were before. What would I do without Justin? He understood me more than any other man ever had. It'd been less than two weeks since he'd left, but I already missed his sci-fi T-shirts and the way he rang the doorbell. I'd do anything to hear him tease me again. I could put up with the way he drank milk straight from the carton and collected airsickness bags from airplanes. I'd even listen to country music and keep a cardboard cutout of Yoda in the living room if it meant we could be together. There was just one problem: I was too late. I wanted to scratch my fingernails across Hank Weston's face for lying to me. Why had I let him distract me?

I was sobbing now, wiping my face with cheap napkins and not caring who saw. I had no more control over my life than I did over the weather. As far as I could tell, there was a one hundred percent chance of devastation.

Chapter 28

Coach's Tip of the Day:
You can't change the past, but you can
stop beating yourself up over it.

The next day, when I pulled into the driveway after work, Harri sat on our front steps beside her duffel bag and a few boxes. I'd kept my composure all day at the office. I hadn't cried when Dr. Metzdorf chewed me out for scheduling three root canals at the same time. I hadn't cried when one of the hygienists showed me the pictures from her honeymoon. Seeing Harri, though, I couldn't hold it in any more. I choked out a sob before I knew it was coming. Then I stared straight ahead and felt two tears sliding down my face. This wasn't like me at all. I wished I could pull back out of the driveway. Instead, I blew my nose, wiped my face, and got out. "What's going on?" I asked, my voice shaking.

Harri stood up, hugging her sock monkey to her chest. "This morning I told Karen about the interview."

I stopped. She would have to do this *after* we went through all that trouble to get Danny off her back. "What was that again?" My anger gave extra force to my voice, so it almost sounded normal.

Harri rocked back and forth on the balls of her feet. "I told Karen about my interview with Danny. I couldn't keep it from her anymore.

I made a promise to follow Christ, and I wanted to be honest."

I dug the keys out of my purse. "What did she say?"

Harri looked down at my feet. "She fired me. She said to get my things and leave. I'm never going to see Avery again."

"Did you tell her you refused to put that program on her computer? And that we got Danny to delete everything? It's not like you did anything wrong."

Harri sniffled. "She said it didn't matter. I violated her trust. What am I gonna do without a job?"

I unlocked the door and helped Harri take her stuff to the guest room. As a coach, I should have been happy that Harri was aligning her actions with her core value of honesty, but right then, I couldn't find joy in her progress. I went to my room, locked the door, turned up my music as loud as it went, and screamed into my pillow. After that, there was nothing to do but pray. It's not like prayer and screaming go together. It would've been better if I'd knelt down in my church clothes while I listened to the Mormon Tabernacle Choir. But I needed help fast.

The worst part about praying was that Heavenly Father sometimes told me things I didn't want to hear. In this case, the thought that came to mind was that Isabella needed a sitter. It was the perfect solution. Isabella would've loved to have Harri help with the kids, and Harri would've had an instant job. The problem was I'd be sending Harri straight into Justin's arms.

After another scream into my pillow, I promised Heavenly Father I'd think about sending Harri to Richmond. In the meantime, she and I were going to have a movie marathon. That way, I wouldn't have to talk to her.

I don't know what gave me the idea that watching *Gone with the Wind* was a good choice. I guess I thought of glamorous actors in ball gowns, not the horror of war. I'd also forgotten how boring old movies could be. We fast-forwarded through the war parts and tried to sympathize with Scarlett in the other parts. It wasn't easy. How could anyone sympathize with someone as selfish, stubborn, and racist as she was?

Harri ate leftover pizza and snuggled up with a jacket Justin had left behind. "This smells like him," she told me, offering me a sniff.

I declined. My nose had already memorized Justin's mix of Irish Spring and fresh laundry. I wasn't in the mood for pizza either.

Harri fell asleep a half hour into the movie, which freed me to analyze myself in comparison to Scarlett. I found too many parallels between us. I'd rejected Rob Martinez because he lived in an apartment with his parents. I'd flirted with Hank Weston after I'd lost my attraction to him. I'd bossed Harri around. I'd offended Barbara. I'd gossiped about Reggie Van Camp. I'd obsessed over my clothes. In some ways, Scarlett was better than I was. In most ways, she was worse. But there was one thing we had in common: we weren't good enough for the men we loved.

There was nothing like watching Scarlett's sins to make me regret my own. I paused the movie, grabbed a piece of paper, and listed everything I could ever remember doing wrong. I started with the stuff on Sugarloaf Mountain and went back in time until I'd filled an entire page with my transgressions. There were a lot of them. No wonder Justin was disappointed in me.

Was this what repenting was about? Feeling bad about things in the past? I remembered what Justin had said at Harri's baptism about the Savior taking away my sins: *Have you tried to give them to Him?* I hadn't.

There were some things I couldn't fix anymore. Kneeling down on the floor in my bedroom, I held the list in front of me. I prayed about each mistake on my list. With each one, I explained how I'd tried to make up for my mistake, then I asked for forgiveness. I knew Christ had sacrificed Himself for my sins. He wanted me to accept the gift He'd already given. It made sense. Why wouldn't He forgive me? All I needed to do was *accept* His gift. I scribbled through the first line, then the next, until I'd scribbled through the whole page, shedding the guilt with each stroke of my pen. That's when I felt it—the peace I'd seen in Harri.

With my paper full of cross-hatching, there was one more thing I needed to do. I sent a text message to Hank: "I forgive you." Even if Hank had been more of a jerk and a liar than I'd ever be, he and I weren't that different. We were both humans. We both made mistakes. I couldn't deny him the peace I felt, the peace of knowing I'd been forgiven.

Walking to Dad's office, I passed the mirror in the hall, and there I was with my bright red hair and pale face. I'd been too pre-occupied to do my makeup that morning. My hair was frizzier than usual, further evidence that I'd been neglecting my appearance. As I looked at my reflection, I remembered a painting at the National Gallery of Art, a picture of three boys sailing on the ocean. Dad had told me once that it was Mom's favorite. The artist had originally painted another boat in the background but then changed his mind, scraped it off, and painted over it. Anyone who looked at the painting long enough could see the mistake. Still, even with the flaw, the painting was beautiful.

I looked straight into my mixed-up hazel eyes. If I could love that imperfect painting, I could love myself. Though I wasn't a work of art, I had a marvelous Creator. My imperfections were part of life. They didn't take away from my beauty. They made me human. Underneath, I was still a daughter of God.

I went to Dad's office and plugged in the shredder. As I sent my page full of scribbles through its teeth, my phone buzzed. It was Hank. "Have you figured out about the Gibson?" he asked.

"What?" Hank and I obviously weren't on the same wavelength.

"Remember how you thought it was from Reggie Van Camp?" Hank explained. "It was from me."

I remembered the guitar Jena got for Christmas. "Haven't you embarrassed me enough, Hank? I wish you hadn't told Jena what I said about Reggie."

"I could always count on you for a laugh, Emma." I could hear the grin in his voice.

I sighed. "I hope Jena will forgive me."

"That's a given. She's already forgiven me. How could she not forgive you? You didn't do anything wrong. I'd let you talk to her now, but she's on the phone with our real estate agent down in Nash-ville. We're looking for our first home."

I wondered if Jena had seen the picture of Hank and me kissing. "Tell her I said, 'hi.'"

"Will do. While I have you here, I wanted to ask—when did you figure out about Jena and me? I always had the feeling you knew more than you let on."

"Honestly, Hank, I didn't have a clue."

"I thought you'd caught on that morning when you met me riding my bike to Jena's house. After I kissed you in front of Danny and you called me out for it, I thought you knew I was using you as a decoy." He sounded much more positive than he had the last time we'd spoken. "Remember how I couldn't keep my eyes off Jena that morning? I still can't. She's so perfect. I don't deserve her."

"That's true," I admitted.

"Then I slipped up and said something about how Jena should remember that hacking contest I won." He was acting as if I remembered all these things with amusement instead of remorse. "And you caught the two of us arguing about dishonesty at the laser tag place. You didn't suspect me after that?"

"No," I said, "but Justin did."

"She's the most incredible woman I've ever known. I can't believe she loves me."

I'd had enough. "Hank, I'm happy for you, but if I have to listen to any more of this, I might throw up."

We said our good-byes, and I pushed the play button on *Gone with the Wind*. Within a few minutes, my thoughts of Hank merged with thoughts of Rhett Butler. I'd expected Rhett would remind me of Justin. But Justin wasn't Rhett at all; he was Ashley, the man Scarlett really loved, the man who rejected her.

As much as I wanted to finish *Gone with the Wind*, I couldn't do it. Some things just weren't worth finishing. I turned off the TV and heated up a slice of leftover pizza in the microwave. There was something about forgiving and being forgiven that made me want to feed myself, to take care of my body the way I'd take care of a child. I thought of Mom's favorite painting as I ate, savoring the blend of spicy tomato sauce and mellow cheese. It was okay to be imperfect. I ate the whole slice, feeling in control of my imperfect life. All my choices had led to where I was right then.

Now I had another choice: what to do with Harri. Should I send her back to Utah, where Justin would have to chase her down, or to Richmond, where Isabella needed a nanny and Justin needed someone to love? I remembered what Justin had said when I asked him what he thought it was like to fall in love. He'd said it would be like a friendship. Thanks to me, he and Harri were friends. If I loved him, shouldn't I want him to fall in love? He'd put his life on hold for so long, waiting to find the right woman. He needed Harri.

Chapter 29

Coach's Tip of the Day:
Positive thoughts make good things happen.

I took Harri to the bus station the next day and bought her a ticket to Richmond. It was a selfless decision on my part, but I didn't send her because I was selfless. I sent her because neither one of us had the money for a ticket to Utah. Then again, we could've asked Dad for a loan, so maybe I was just the slightest bit noble.

After I came back home, I wanted to hit something. My pillow had already taken enough abuse, so I grabbed a couple cans of tennis balls and my racket. Though I had no friends left to impress, I dressed in my favorite tangerine workout top and coordinating sneakers. Walking to the tennis courts a block away from my house, I recited every positive statement I could think of: "I am worth it . . . I can do all things through Christ . . . I'm not giving up . . . I'm staying in the game . . . I am a child of God." I said them out loud over and over again as I walked down the sidewalk and through the parking lot. If anyone saw or heard, I didn't notice, and I didn't care. I was alone, and I would take care of my problems by myself.

I was alone at the tennis court too—the only one there at 3:30 p.m. on a Friday afternoon, practicing my serves to no one. It felt good to pelt the ball across the court, better to nail the fence on the other side. I'd counted ninety-seven successful serves when I saw Justin walking through the parking lot with Buttercup in tow. After tying her leash to a nearby bench, he walked onto the court. He carried Isabella's old racket and wore the striped polo I'd helped him pick out. It was different from his other shirts, more fitted through the shoulders and chest area. I tried not to notice the way his biceps peeked out below the sleeves. How was I supposed to resist him in that shirt?

I hit a ball extra hard against the fence. "What are you doing here?" It'd taken all my strength to send Harri down to him. If he'd stayed there, the worst would be over, and I could deal with my grief by myself. I bit the inside of my cheek so hard I tasted blood.

"Nice to see you too." Frowning, he stepped onto the court. "I wanted to talk to you. Your dad said you were playing tennis, so I came over."

"Okay." I served a ball in Justin's direction, wondering if Harri would mind if I helped Justin shop for clothes and furniture after they got married. What was I thinking? Of course she would mind.

Justin hit the ball over the net. "I can understand how you'd be upset."

He thought I was upset that he and Harri—two of my best friends—were dating. What he didn't know was it was so much more than that. I volleyed the ball, trying to act like nothing was wrong as the ball went past Justin. "Why should I be upset? Everything is going great. I'm almost done with my certification." My voice shook as I spoke.

Justin stood on his centerline. He didn't chase after the ball, even though there weren't any balls left on my side of the court. "You don't look like everything's great."

I walked over to his side of the court to retrieve a few balls while Justin stood watching me. I was not going to cry.

Justin scooped up a few balls and handed them to me. "Hank Weston never deserved you. I don't blame you for being upset, but you're better off without him."

That's what this was about. He felt sorry for me because of Hank. I blinked back the tears that were about to come out. "Don't feel too bad for me, Justin. I gave up on Hank a few months ago."

"You did?"

I walked back to my side of the court, hoping he would think I was wiping sweat off my forehead when I rubbed my sleeve across my eyes. I kept my back to him for a few seconds, bouncing the ball, before I felt strong enough to explain. "I haven't been serious about him since New Year's. That doesn't mean I wasn't angry when I found out he lied to us. But I've forgiven him. Now are you gonna play or are you gonna stand there like a target?"

Justin returned to his baseline. I served the ball. We hit it back and forth a few times. I was starting to feel more in control of my emotions. Then he let it pass and walked up to the net. "You can tell me the truth, Emma. I saw the picture of you and him . . . you know."

He meant the kissing picture. I couldn't look at him. It would make it worse. I walked back behind my baseline to find another ball I could serve.

Justin kept on talking. "I remember how you talked about him. He used you. If he were here now, I'd hit him."

I bounced a ball up and down with my racket before letting it bounce away. He wanted to hit Hank Weston. I could hardly focus on the game or the conversation. Why couldn't I have realized how much I loved him before Harri came along? I rubbed a hand across my forehead and left it there, drawing in a jagged breath before I answered. "I like Hank, but he isn't the type of guy I'd want to spend my life with, let alone eternity. You'd really hit him?"

"He deserves some sort of punishment, and it doesn't look like he's going to get one." He sliced his racket through the air, reminding me once again of how good he looked in that shirt.

If I was going to stay friends with him and Harri, I was going to have to overcome this stupid attraction. I looked over at the woods on the other side of the tennis courts. It was late April now. In the distance, a few dogwoods blossomed white against the grays, greens, and browns of the woods. "I think Hank and Jena have already lived through their punishment," I said, still focusing on the trees. "It was torture for both of them to keep so many secrets."

"For some of us, keeping secrets is a way of life." Justin's Southern accent was in full force. What secret did he mean? Did he mean his relationship with Harri?

I looked at Justin, but I couldn't raise my eyes above his collarbone. If I really cared about him, I'd let him tell me about Harri. I forced myself to look into his eyes. "No one should have to keep secrets from their best friend."

Justin clenched his jaw and shook his head. "Telling a secret could be a worse punishment than keeping it." What? Did he think I was going to get angry at him for falling in love with Harri?

"Fine. Keep it." I turned and walked over to pick up another ball. If he wanted to keep thinking of me as some sort of Scarlett O'Hara, then there was no use talking. "Is it my serve or yours?" The truth was, I did feel a little like Scarlett O'Hara. I was completely unbalanced, flipping through feelings of anger, grief, attraction, and regret.

We hit the ball back and forth. Well, not exactly back and forth. I served, and Justin missed. I served again. When he hit it back, I missed. We were both having a terrible game. I didn't care, as long as he never got close enough to see the tears running down my cheeks.

After one of my serves went out of bounds, he dropped his racket. "Emma, I can't do this anymore." He hopped over the net and walked up to me. "I don't think you're gonna like what I'm gonna say, but I have to say it."

I looked down at my shoes, letting my hair fall in front of my face. I couldn't let him know how much this was going to hurt me. He was Isabella's brother-in-law. Even if I moved, we were going to have to see each other at family events for the rest of our lives. "I know what you're gonna say." My voice came out too high and crackly, like a teenage boy in the throes of puberty. "Before you say it, you should know I'm okay being alone." I swallowed. "You know I'm independent." I sniffled. "I'm strong enough to watch my friends get married." Something that sounded like a sob came out of my mouth. "I like being alone."

He stepped toward me, so the tips of his Reebok runners were almost touching my Nikes. "If you like being alone so much, why are you crying?" He smoothed my hair out from in front of my face and lifted my chin with his finger.

I looked into his eyes and saw him studying me. "What?"

He groaned. "Sometimes it's really hard to understand you,

Emma." His face was red. "Since you already seem to know what I'm going to say, I might as well say it." He stepped back, rubbed the back of his neck, and sighed. "I rehearsed all the way from Richmond. I wasn't going to say it today. But here goes. There's a reason I didn't like Hank. I was jealous. He had you, and I didn't. It took me a while to figure it out." He paused, lowering his voice. "It's because I love you. I didn't want to tell you. I didn't want to change the way things are between us. There it is. I can't take it back now. I love you, Emma. I know you like being alone. I know you like being independent, but I can't help the way I feel."

I'd forgotten to breathe while Justin spoke. Now that he'd finished, I sucked in a little air and reached for his clenched fists. Had he just said he loved me? I thought I'd better ask, to make sure I heard right. "You love *me*, not . . . someone else?"

His fingers loosened at my touch, and I slid my fingers in between his, a perfect fit. "I love you," he repeated, this time with more confidence. "Do you usually hold a guy's hands when you're rejecting him?"

"No." I stepped closer to him, much closer, placing my hands on his shoulders. "This is the complete opposite of rejection." He wrapped his arms around me, pulling me close. It wasn't like the songs said. I wasn't losing control at all. I was exactly where I wanted to be. I was at home in his arms.

His cheek pressed warm against my temple. "I wish I'd known you'd react this way."

I was right there in his arms, holding him the way I'd dreamed of holding him. "I only said I wanted to be alone because I didn't think you wanted me."

He buried his face in my hair, brushing his lips along the ridge of my ear. "Who can blame you after the idiotic lecture I gave you at Sugarloaf Mountain? Can you forgive me, Emma?"

I nestled my face into the crook of his neck, smelling Irish Spring and fresh laundry. "I deserved everything you said."

Justin straightened to look me in the eyes. "No, you didn't. If I hadn't cared about you so much, if I hadn't been so jealous of Hank, I wouldn't have been so angry."

It seemed so ridiculous that I'd ever preferred Hank. Justin was better in every way, and now I had him all to myself. "You don't have to be jealous anymore."

"There's still one thing about him that makes me jealous."

"What's that?"

"You kissed him."

I brushed my lips against his jaw line. "I didn't kiss him. We were walking out to my car, and he gave me a little peck. It wasn't like I expected it."

"So he didn't take you on a date?"

"No. Are you gonna take me on a date before you kiss me?" Flirting with him felt natural.

That's when his lips brushed mine. "Would it be okay if our first date is after our first kiss?" One of his hands supported me at my waist, drawing me closer. His other hand cradled my head. In his touch, I felt both passion and restraint, tenderness and strength. Then he kissed me, and my thoughts swirled into a dizzy confusion. I couldn't think of anything but him and me—together. Finally, we were together. It seemed like I'd been waiting for this moment longer than I'd realized, that I'd always known we were meant to be together. There was no doubt he was as attracted to me as I was to him. I could feel it in the desperation of his kiss. All his emotions were right there—everything he'd kept hidden.

Chapter 30

Coach's Tip of the Day:
God can fix your problems better than you can.

I thought I was ready to go on my first date with my best friend until that night when he showed up in a suit, and my heart did a belly flop. He usually wore Dockers to church, so I hadn't seen him in a suit since he was the best man at Isabella's wedding. Yes, he'd already said, "I love you," but something about that suit made it all real.

Justin studied my face as he led me out to his truck. "What's wrong? Is it the tie?"

This was what I wanted, but I'd never had a serious relationship—at least not one where *I* was serious. What if I couldn't do it? I was, after all, pretty good at quitting. What if I quit on Justin the way I'd quit on everything else? This wasn't just another date. This was about forever. Deep down, that was what I really wanted—to be with him forever. "You're really serious about me, aren't you?"

The happiness drained from his face. "I thought you wanted me to be serious about you."

"I did, and I want to be serious about you too, but what if I'm not ready?"

He pulled me into a hug, kissing my forehead. "Can we just enjoy tonight without overanalyzing what's going to happen in the future?"

"Okay."

We drove to the Potomac River during golden hour—that time of day before sunset when all the colors glow. Trees glistened in shades of green and yellow-green on the banks of the river. The sky was a washed-out blue, the river a rippling gray. Driving along, we watched people riding bikes and paddling canoes. The sun was starting to set as Justin pulled into a parking lot beside the docks.

He led me across the first dock to a big white boat with lots of windows and a glass ceiling. I gawked. "Don't tell me we're going on a dinner cruise!"

Justin smiled as he handed over his receipt to a man in a tuxedo. "You said you wanted to go but it was too romantic . . . so I thought I'd take a chance on it."

We stepped on board, greeted the crew, and posed for a picture. As we stood on the deck in the midst of other couples, gazing out on the river, R&B music played in the background. I grabbed Justin's hand. "You even got the music right. I thought I would have to learn to like country."

"We'll play country on the way home to make up for my sacrifice," he teased.

We watched a plane take off from Ronald Reagan airport as the boat launched from the dock. Then a hostess took us inside to a little table set for two, where we ordered appetizers, entrees, and desserts. It was all so formal, but with Justin, it felt natural. The crowded dining room with its steady hum of conversation cloaked us in privacy.

I looked out the window at the Jefferson Memorial, remembering my promise to take care of myself. "Before we eat, there's something I have to ask you."

He leaned forward, focusing on me as if I were the only one in the room. "Ask away."

"Do you still think I'm like Scarlett O'Hara?" My hand nested inside his, warm and secure.

"Scarlett was just another word for red," he said. "It had nothing to do with Scarlett O'Hara. I'm sorry I ever called you that. You're not anything like her. You care about people too much."

"I wish I could actually help the people I want to help. I don't think I can ever make up for what I've done to Harri." I didn't mention the worst of it—how Harri had fallen in love with him and now I would have to tell her we were dating. Thinking about Harri sapped some of my happiness. She was going to be disappointed *again*, and it was still my fault.

The server delivered our appetizers as Justin responded, "God has a way of fixing the problems we create. Why don't you leave things in His hands?"

God had already fixed a lot of things I'd messed up, including my relationship with Justin and Hank's relationship with Jena. Knowing I didn't have to fix everything, I ate the bruschetta I'd ordered for an appetizer, enjoying the taste of fresh basil and tomato. I didn't have to know how or when the solution would come. I only had to trust it would happen.

Justin tilted his head toward the door. "There's more privacy out on the deck."

I followed him to an empty place along the side of the boat. As we passed under a bridge, I looked up to see the bricks that formed the arch. "It's amazing how people build bridges. How do they dig so deep under the river? It seems like that would be hard enough, but they make them beautiful too."

Justin didn't look up at all. "I have something better to look at than the bridge."

I shielded my face from his eyes. "Don't look too close." Then I remembered he already knew my imperfections.

He took my hands away from my face. "I've always thought you were beautiful."

I grasped his hands, leaning toward him. "You're doing pretty well with your bad habit today. You haven't pointed out any of my faults."

He reached inside his suit coat pocket for a scrap of paper and a pen. He wrote on the paper and handed it to me. This time it wasn't in Japanese. It said, "Criticizing Emma."

He took the paper, tore it into little pieces, and threw them out on the river. "I'm renewing my promise. You can remind me if I ever forget."

I watched the tiny bits of paper floating off into the distance. "I'll remind you, especially if you ever say you're disappointed in me."

Justin laced his fingers through mine. "My disappointment had more to do with my feelings than your behavior. After you left me at Sugarloaf Mountain, I took another hike by myself. That's when I faced the fact that I was in love with you. It was killing me to see you with Hank, so I thought maybe if I put some space between us, I could get over you. That's why I went to Richmond. But it only made me miss you more. Did you know Kyra's red-haired doll looks just like you?"

I laughed. "That's what everyone says. It's creepy, huh?" I looked into those light blue eyes of his, so sincere. "When you left, I thought I'd lost you. You know how you said love must be like being friends, only stronger? That's the way I feel about you. I love you."

He pulled me in for another mind-numbing kiss. "So you love me, not someone else?" Leave it to Justin to tease me about something I said earlier.

"I love you, not someone else." It was easier to say the second time around.

He smiled with an exuberance I hadn't seen in him since his parents died. "You want to dance?"

I laughed. "Who am I going to dance with? You don't dance with anyone over the age of five."

He winked. "It's a good excuse for a public display of affection."

Justin led me inside to the dance floor, where I discovered he could dance with a grown woman. Okay, well, he mostly did a two-step, and he was a little off on his rhythm, but he twirled me as if he had some experience. He wasn't forceful about it, though, dragging me around like Phil Elton had. I could get used to being in Justin's arms. He fit me. We danced to three songs, ate dinner, danced a little more, watched the Jefferson Memorial and the Washington Monument as the sky grew dark, and ate our desserts. The boat circled back around to the dock a little before midnight.

Dad's car was in the driveway when Justin brought me home. Justin parked behind it and got my door for me. "This is the part I'm not looking forward to," he said as we approached my house, "telling your dad about us."

We found Dad in bed, reading a medical journal. Justin froze in the doorway, so I tugged on his hand. "We have something to tell you, Dad." I kept Justin's hand in mine.

Dad took off his reading glasses, staring at our clasped hands.

"Justin and I are dating," I said.

Dad folded his arms and blew out his breath. "I've seen this coming for a while." He shook his head. "Don't you think she's a little young for you, Justin?"

I answered for him. "I'm twenty-three. Isabella was twenty-one when she got *married*." I sat on the edge of the bed while Justin remained standing.

Dad pointed at my hand holding Justin's. "How long have you been hiding this from me?" I wasn't surprised that Dad overreacted. He knew Justin was perfect for me, which was why he didn't want us dating. In his mind, dating would lead to marriage, which would lead to me moving out.

I held Justin's hand tighter. "There's six years' difference in our ages," I said. "That isn't all that much."

Dad sat up straighter. "You still haven't answered my question. How long have you been hiding this from me?"

"Less than a day," Justin replied.

Dad put his reading glasses back on and went back to reading his medical journal. "We'll have to set different standards for your conduct in this house, Justin."

Justin swallowed. "Yes, sir."

"See," I told Justin before he kissed me good night, "the worst is over. Things can only get better from here." It was true for Justin, but it wasn't true for me. I still had to talk to Harri.

Chapter 31

Coach's Tip of the Day:
If you want to feel lighter, lose the guilt.

The next morning, I called Isabella long before the acceptable time on a Saturday. After I'd spilled everything to her about Justin and me, she said, "Why don't you let me tell Harri? You shouldn't have to drive all the way down here."

"What kind of friend would I be then?" I asked. "No, I'm coming down as soon as I hang up. It's eight now, so I'll be there around ten-thirty."

I knew telling Harri about Justin would be like opening Pandora's box—unleashing a whole new set of problems. As much as I would've rather spent the day with Justin than deal with Harri's inevitable breakdown, it was only a matter of time before she heard about it, and I wanted her to hear it from me.

I slipped into my favorite jeans and headed out the door, calling out to Dad that I'd be back that evening. Running down the stairs and out the door, I practically tripped over Justin. He was sitting on the front steps, reading the paper. I bent to straighten my flip-flop. "What are you doing out here?"

Justin folded the paper. "New rules, remember? I can't come inside until 9:00 a.m. Otherwise, I might see you in your pajamas."

He couldn't help laughing a little when he mentioned the pajamas. "Why are you up so early?"

"I'm going to Richmond." I tried to act like it was no big deal. "I want to make sure Harri's okay."

"She just got there yesterday," he protested.

I jingled my keys. "So now's a good time to check on her, make sure she feels at home."

Justin studied me. "About yesterday, I didn't scare you, did I?"

I sat on the cold cement step beside him and kissed his cheek. "No. I need to go down to Richmond today for another reason."

He stuffed the newspaper back into the plastic bag. "Would you take a stowaway?"

I shook my head. "I wish I could, but I have to do this alone."

Walking out to my car, I felt a little guilty leaving Justin. He'd probably planned to spend the day with me. I also had to admit I would miss him. I'd already become one of those women who couldn't spend a day without her boyfriend. I paused, reaching for the door handle. I'd never thought of anyone as my boyfriend before. "Here's the thing," I called to Justin, "I have to talk to Harri by myself. You can come, as long as you disappear when we get to Isabella's."

Driving down to Richmond in the spring was like riding a time machine two weeks into the future. The azaleas and lilacs that were starting to bud where we lived were in full bloom farther south. The air grew hotter with each mile and hinted more and more at summer humidity as the minutes ticked by.

Justin never asked what worried me, and I never told him. While he drove, I brainstormed how I could tell Harri about Justin and me. By the time we arrived in Richmond, I hadn't come up with anything better than, "Which do you want to hear first, the good news or the bad news?" This would be one of those conversations where I had to rely on inspiration.

As we drove into Isabella's subdivision, Justin rolled down the windows, letting in the scent of the lilac bushes. With his window all the way down, he rested his arm along the edge of the door. We were almost to Isabella's house when he slammed on the brakes, pulling on his sleeve. "Something flew into my shirt. I think it's a bee." He pulled his T-shirt off. "Ouch! Definitely a bee."

The sting was on the back of his shoulder above his armpit. I scraped the stinger away with a credit card. Then I grabbed the first-aid kit from under my seat. Opening it, I found a Ziploc bag Dad had filled with baking soda. Mixing it with a squirt of water from my water bottle, I rubbed the paste on his skin.

We were two houses away from John and Isabella's. "Isn't this where I'm supposed to disappear?" Justin asked.

"We'd better go in and get you an ice pack. You can disappear after that. Do you think you could put your shirt back on?" The last thing I needed was for Harri to see him without a shirt.

"What?" He pretended to be offended. "Don't tell me I need to wax."

I'd seen his chest at the pool plenty of times. The sight had always impressed me. I squeezed his arm—the one that didn't get stung by the bee. "It's nothing like that. I liked what I saw. I'm just feeling a little possessive. I'd rather not share you with the world."

He put his shirt back on, and we pulled into Isabella's long asphalt driveway. We walked up the steps of the modest brick home and rang the doorbell. Harri answered, wearing the yellow T-shirt and white capris I'd helped her pick out a few weeks before. She was the only one home. "Isabella told me you were coming, Emma, but she didn't tell me about Justin." Skipping past me, she tackled Justin with a hug.

He told her about the bee sting while I filled a bag with ice and brought it to him. "I guess it's time for me to disappear," he said. Before I could object, he planted a kiss on me right in front of Harri. It wasn't the kind of kiss he'd give his sister. When it was over, he touched the end of my nose. "Call me when you're ready to go." He waved to Harri as he headed out the door.

Harri cocked her head as if we were playing a joke on her. "What are you guys doing?"

Not feeling very inspired, I bit my lip. "I need to talk to you about that."

As she processed my words, her smile changed to a scowl. She turned and walked out of the entryway. I heard her stomping through the family room and down the hall before she slammed the door to the guest room. This was going even worse than I'd imagined. I traced her steps, taking a seat on the hardwood floor outside the guest room door. It seemed impossible that Harri could ever trust me after all that had happened, but I had to try. "I'm sorry, Harri. I didn't plan for you to see us like that. I don't blame you for hating me."

There was no response, not even a sniffle. For all I knew, she was wearing her iPod.

"Are you listening? Can you hear me?" I knocked on the door. "Can I come in?"

She didn't answer, so I scrounged around in my purse for a piece of paper and wrote a long note that explained how I felt about everything that'd happened since Harri told me she liked Justin. I folded it schoolgirl-style into a little square—hoping she would think it was funny—and shoved it under her door. It wasn't a technique I'd learned in life coach training, but it felt like the right thing to do.

A few seconds later, Harri opened the door. "As if a note could make up for what you've done." She threw the note at me.

I wedged my foot against the door before she shut it. "If you're not going to read the note, at least let me explain." My foot was starting to hurt from the door pressing against it. "When you told me how you felt about Justin, I wanted him for myself, but I didn't do anything to work against you. I thought you two would get together when you came here. I didn't know he was coming back home."

Harri stopped pushing on the door. "So you thought he liked me?"

I scooted closer to Harri's voice. "I didn't think I had a chance."

She sniffled. "So you stole him from me?"

"Not exactly," I explained, deciding I might as well tell her everything. "He told me how he felt first. He told me he loved me."

Harri opened her door and leaned against the frame. She didn't say anything for a long time. "And you came here to shove it in my face?"

"I came because I wanted you to hear it from me, not someone else. I didn't want to hurt your feelings."

"Well, you did." She closed the door and turned the lock.

I couldn't leave her that way. A good coach always leaves her client better than she found her. In this case, I would have to settle for leaving her better than she was right now. "Harri, I hope you're listening because I'm not done. When I first met you, I saw all these things I wanted to help you change. Now, I look at you and see how much I've learned from you. You're not afraid to try new things or quit old things. You forgive people. You're a great nanny. You're honest.

"You already know I'm proud you chose to be baptized. What you don't know is you changed my life that day. Seeing you so peaceful made me rethink my relationship with Christ. I discovered I was trying to save myself. Last Thursday, after I'd offended every single one of my friends except you and Tanya, I felt like I was hanging off the edge of a cliff. I couldn't see how there was any good in me at all. That's when I turned it all over to the Savior, and you know what? I felt that peace I saw in you.

"I guess that means, in a way, *I* turned into *your* project." I paused, waiting for a reply. When none came, I said, "I feel bad I've hurt your feelings. I was hoping to take you out to lunch, but maybe it'd be better to do that another time."

I waited for her to say something. She didn't, so I went on. "Justin doesn't know how you felt about him, and I'm not going to tell him." I waited a little longer. "I'm leaving now. I hope we can still be friends."

Chapter 32

Coach's Tip of the Day:
It's never too late to mend a friendship.

I'd given up hope of having a satisfying female relationship with anyone outside my family when Jena invited me over for the Fourth of July. That's right: *Jena* invited *me*. She and Hank were on their way back from their European honeymoon and wanted to get together with Justin and me before they returned to Nashville. Since this type of thing would probably never happen again, I had to say yes. There was only one problem—convincing Justin to come along.

I introduced the idea while I drove him home from church. "Do you still feel like punching Hank Weston?"

Justin slid the passenger seat back all the way. "No, but I wouldn't mind if I never saw him again."

"Jena invited us over for the Fourth," I said.

Justin was silent for a while. When he finally spoke, I detected a slight accent. "Are you still attracted to him?"

I swatted his leg with the back of my hand. "No. Are you still attracted to Jena?"

"I never was, even less now that I know her taste in men."

"So you won't mind if we spend the Fourth of July with them?" I prodded.

He blew out his breath, letting his lips flap. "As long as we don't stay more than a few minutes."

Driving to Barbara's house on the Fourth of July, I remembered the last time I'd come here, the day Jena regifted my muffins. So much had changed in the last three months. Hank and I were the lucky ones. He'd married Jena, and I was dating Justin. We'd both gotten more than we'd deserved. On top of that, I'd earned my life coach certification and had gotten my first paying clients—the two sisters I'd coached for free.

Danny's blue Taurus was parked along the front strip, a sure sign that Jena had arrived. "Hold on a second," Justin said, pointing to Danny. "We have to take advantage of this." He parked his truck behind the Taurus.

I kept my seat belt on. "There's no way I'm talking to him."

Justin opened his door. "I didn't say anything about talking. Wait where you are. I want him to take a picture of us." He opened my door, unbuckled my seat belt, and pulled me out to stand beside him, enfolding me in his arms. His kiss made me forget all about Danny—until I heard the camera firing off a round of shots. Our kiss ended with both of us laughing.

It felt like a sauna outside with temperatures in the nineties and humidity that kinked my hair. Barbara's garden overflowed with black-eyed susans, purple coneflowers, pink roses, and orange lilies. While we waited for someone to come to the door, I noticed the delicate purple flowers on the crepe myrtle bushes. We rang the doorbell a second time, which made me worry Jena might be replaying the episode back in April when she'd refused to open the door for me. I didn't want this to get awkward.

We'd given up and were heading down the steps when Jena flung the door open. "Sorry I took so long. I had to finish a phone interview." She ushered us inside. "Hank's out back working on the charcoal. One of these days, we're going to get Mom a gas grill." She led us into the kitchen, where we caught a glimpse of Hank through the sliding glass door, squirting lighter fluid into foot-tall flames. Jena turned to Justin. "Why don't you go on out, Justin? Emma and I have a lot of catching up to do."

Justin kept a grip on my hand. "I don't mind girl talk."

I nudged him in the side. "I'm sure you'll have more fun with Hank."

Justin pointed his thumb toward the front of the house, where he'd parked his truck. "I'll go get my fire extinguisher."

I sat with Jena at the kitchen table, which was full of yarn and round knitting looms. I assumed the supplies were for a service project. It was like Jena to do something charitable. She was always efficient, always working on a goal. I picked at her pile of yarn, wondering why she'd invited me over.

Jena went to work on a pink hat. "Is it true Harri lost her job because of Danny?"

I picked up a loom, trying to figure out how it worked. "That depends on how you look at it. We'd already fixed the problem by the time Harri told Karen Cole about it. So, really she lost her job because she was honest. We found her a better job. She's working for John and Isabella in Richmond." I swallowed, thinking of how I hadn't spoken to Harri since the bee sting incident. All I knew about her was what I'd heard from Isabella—that Harri seemed happy, went out with friends a few times a week, and had taken over a lot of the office duties. When we were on the phone, Isabella mostly talked about her kids.

Jena demonstrated how to weave the yarn around the pegs on my loom. "I'm beyond sorry for all the trouble I've caused. And I'm so ashamed of the way I treated you, Emma. I blamed you for my problems with Hank when I should have blamed myself. I took everything too seriously."

I wove the yarn around like Jena had shown me. "I don't think I would have liked me, either."

"Not if you knew Hank like I know him," Jena said. "For Hank, life is all about having fun. It's like he never grew up. He balances me out."

I decided not to share my opinion about Hank's playful attitude. "It all worked out for the best. Without Hank, Justin and I might not have realized how we felt about each other."

Jena smiled. "It was pretty obvious to me. You and Justin were always together. I can see you getting married. Your kids'll be darling, especially if they get your hair."

"I'm still getting used to being his girlfriend." There was something about knitting hats that made me want to open up to Jena. Maybe it was because I didn't have to look her in the eyes. "Don't get me wrong. I'm in love with him. I just don't know if I'm ready for marriage. I always thought I'd fall in love when I was older, or at least when I felt older."

"I don't know what you're worried about," Jena said. "You're good at everything."

"I am not." Jena, of all people, should've known that.

"I always thought you were. I used to be completely intimidated by you." She sounded like she was telling the truth.

I set down my loom. "I was always intimidated by *you*. You're the one who's good at everything."

Jena kept knitting. "Not everything. I was never good with people like you are. When we were growing up, I would've rather done homework or Personal Progress goals than go to a party."

"Seriously?" I asked. "That explains why you never came to any of my parties. I thought you didn't like me."

"I always liked you," she said. "You were my only friend who understood what it was like to grow up in a single-parent home." In that instant, my image of Jena flip-flopped. She was more like me than I'd thought. Sure, she'd accomplished a lot more than I had, but inside, she was full of insecurities and hang-ups. I'd always thought she was a snob when she was really just shy. She stopped knitting and looked at me. "It's normal to be scared of getting married. You know what Hank always says?" Jena deepened her voice to imitate Hank's. "'When have you ever done anything great without being scared?'"

I reflected that it must've been much scarier for Jena to marry Hank than it ever would be for me to marry Justin. "He told me something like that at Blaze Mountain," I said. "I guess it's good advice for some things . . . but it's bad advice when it comes to jumping off a ski lift."

We both laughed. "My feet hurt for a week after that," Jena admitted. "I'm never jumping off a lift again. It's so much better now that we're not keeping secrets."

On the other side of the sliding glass door, Justin sprayed Hank with the hose. I pointed to them. "What's going on out there?"

Hank grabbed a bucket of water and heaved it at Justin. He missed, and Justin chased him across the yard with the hose. Then Hank grabbed the hose, and the two of them wrestled for control of it, both grinning.

Jena laughed and turned back to her knitting. "There's been a lot of tension between those two. Maybe this'll be cathartic."

I would've rather been outside dumping water on Hank's head than knitting, but Justin was already winning. After another five minutes, they both came in dripping wet and talking about the best way to grill a steak. I was expecting to leave after we ate, but we lingered until the fireflies came out.

Chapter 33

Coach's Tip of the Day:
Sometimes getting what you want
means asking for it.

*A*lexandria got her way about the fortune cookies. They were on every table at her reception. I wasn't invited, so I laid low as Justin's guest. Because it was also my twenty-fourth birthday, we only stayed long enough to go through the line and scope out the decorations. I'd developed a new interest in reception design.

Alexandria rocked the Chinatown theme. Her colors were white and red with splashes of gold and black. Chinese lanterns hung from the ceiling of the cultural hall. The bridesmaids wore traditional red silk dresses. Folding screens lined the walls. The roast duck and dancing dragon were maybe a little much, but everything else was spot on.

As we headed out the door, Harri came in. She wore a lime green tie-front blouse that fit her perfectly and coordinated with her patterned A-line skirt—new clothes she must have bought herself in Richmond. I hadn't talked to her in over four months, and I couldn't imagine why she'd be at Phil Elton's wedding reception. All I knew about her life now was what I'd learned from Isabella—that she'd become an asset to Knightley Remodeling, both as a nanny and as an executive assistant. Without taking time to wonder if she'd forgiven me, I threw my arms around her. She hugged me back. "I've missed you so much, Emma. I keep thinking I should call and thank you for all that stuff you said last time we talked."

"It's okay, as long as we're still friends," I said as I watched Rob Martinez approaching behind her.

Harri turned to smile at Rob, then turned back to me. "Isabella said you got some more people to coach."

I nodded. "I have six paying clients. Once I get a couple more, I'll cut my hours at the dentist's office."

Rob stopped beside Harri and shook Justin's hand.

"John says you found an engineering job. How's it going?" Justin asked.

"Great," Rob answered. "Thanks again for transferring me." He took hold of Harri's hand.

I pointed from Harri to Rob. "So you two are—"

"—together," Harri said, giggling.

I held my hand over my heart. "You don't know how happy that makes me. After you finish with the reception, you two should come out to dinner with us. We have so much catching up to do."

Justin tugged on my arm. "But I planned something special for your birthday."

"I don't mind if Rob and Harri come along. I can't think of anything I'd rather do on my birthday than spend time with them."

Justin fist-bumped Harri, then Rob. "Sorry, guys. We'll have to get together some other time."

"You never told me Rob was working in Richmond," I said as we drove away in Justin's truck.

Justin stared straight ahead at the road. He probably thought he was in trouble. "You never asked."

"I'm asking now. Tell me what you know." To calm his worries, I added. "I should have listened to you when you tried to tell me how great he is. I think they really are perfect for each other."

Justin glanced at me as if to assure himself I told the truth. "I don't know as much as you think. After she moved to Richmond,

Harri quit answering my calls. When I mentioned it to Rob, I found out she'd been calling him instead of me. Would you be mad if I told you that was my plan all along?"

I rubbed my hand along his arm. "No." I looked out the passenger side window, feeling amazed at how well God—and Justin—had fixed my problems.

Justin drove us to the furniture store where we'd bought his sofas. "Are you game for a little shopping?" he asked as we parked in the lot.

"I'm always game for a little shopping."

Justin got out and walked around to get my door. "We'll start with the kitchen."

For years, I'd imagined the table that would work best in Justin's kitchen. I knew what I wanted, and Justin had measured his rooms, so it didn't take us long to find a round oak kitchen table we both liked. My stomach growled. "Where are we going to dinner?" I asked, hoping we'd go there soon.

Justin had other plans. "While we're at it, we should look at dining room tables."

It was the same way with dining tables. I already knew what I wanted. We found a rectangular table that came with eight chairs and two leaves. "This ought to fit the entire family," I said.

Justin squeezed my hand. "For now. I'll get a few extra chairs to go with it. Let's keep looking."

I stopped him before we entered the bedroom section. "Haven't you bought enough for one day?"

He kept on walking. "I'm just getting started."

I followed, looking at my watch. It was eight-thirty, closing time for most furniture stores. A vacuum hummed in the distance. "I thought we were going out to dinner."

Justin stopped in front of a tall mission-style dresser. "What do you think of this one?"

I slid open a drawer, examining the dovetail construction. "It's nice."

"Think you could stand to use it for the rest of your life?"

I pulled out all the other drawers, trying to focus on their depth and construction. Justin lifted it away from the wall so we could look at the back, which looked like solid wood. "I like it," I said. "You should get this one."

"I'll get one for me and one for you. What do you think of the bed that goes with it?"

I swallowed, looking at the bed. It had a simple headboard with square details along the top edge, exactly the kind of design I preferred. "As long as you like it."

He sat on the edge of the bed. "Do you like it? There's no hurry if you don't. We can shop at other stores."

I'd always wanted to help Justin furnish the house. The problem was that in his mind, it was becoming *our* house. I was comfortable with the whole girlfriend thing, so comfortable I wanted to keep it that way. Marriage was in our future, but, to me, it was the *distant* future. "Can we look at something else for a while?"

He hopped off the bed. "How about mattresses? It'll give you a chance to lie still and think about the bedroom furniture."

Justin had slept on a futon for years. I had no right to deny him the privilege of memory foam. That's why I tested mattresses, one in particular, for twenty minutes while he filled out the order forms for the other furniture. The mattress was so comfortable, and so was the idea of sharing it with Justin—*that's* what made me *un*comfortable. Otherwise, I would've fallen asleep by the time Justin came to announce he'd negotiated 30 percent off on everything.

I stretched my arms above my head. "You should get this mattress."

"When I saw how relaxed you were, I ordered it in king size. Come on, it's time for dinner."

Instead of going straight to the exit, we wandered around through kitchen tables until we came to one set with a tablecloth, battery-powered candles, and something that looked like real food. It looked like shrimp panang curry, and I recognized the spicy, garlicky smell. As the lights in the store turned off row by row, Justin pulled out the chair for me. "Happy birthday."

"Wow." It wasn't like Justin to be so creative.

A small wrapped gift sat in the center of the table. Picking it up,

I shook it. "What's this?" Who was I kidding? It had to be a ring box. I put it back in the center of the table.

Justin pushed it toward me. "Go ahead and open it."

I picked it up and pulled on the thin gold ribbon. My hands were shaking. "I don't know if I can do this."

Justin scooted his chair closer to me. "Want me to help?"

I handed him the box, still wrapped in silver paper. "I don't know if I'm ready. I like the way things are now."

He set the box on the table. "I do too, but I'm tired of living by your dad's rules. I like being there when you wake up in the morning, so I can watch you stumble out of your room like the walking dead. It makes my day." He was trying to make me laugh. I didn't.

I stared at the box. It had to be a ring. "You want to get married because you like to see how scary I look in the morning?"

He touched the side of my cheek, turning my face so I looked at him instead of the box. "Yep. There are other reasons too, but I have to warn you, some of them will make you blush. Reason number one: I love you. Number two: you're my best friend. Number three: I want to share the furniture—all of it—with you."

I couldn't say what I was feeling, that I had all the same reasons for wanting to marry him. I still had to get that last idea about sharing a bed with him out of my head. I wanted this to be a logical decision. "What about Dad? Have you asked him about this?"

"We have an agreement."

"What's that?"

"It doesn't matter what the agreement is if you say no."

I took the box again and unpeeled the wrapping. I already knew I would marry him. I knew it as well as I knew how to spell my name. The problem was I wasn't ready to be a wife. That was something my mother did. "I'm not going to say no." I stared at the blue velvet box for a minute before I popped it open. Inside was a classic diamond solitaire set on a gold band with the inscription, *I promise*. "It's beautiful, exactly what I'd choose."

Justin rested his arm across the back of my chair. "You're not going to say no. Let me guess. You're going to say, 'later.'" He knew me too well. I kissed him, but that didn't distract him at all. "How much later?" he asked, his expression so pained that for a moment I wondered if I'd accidentally stepped on his foot. "If you have to know about my agreement with your dad, I promised we'd eat dinner with him four times a week. We also have to call him every day while we're on our honeymoon. I got off easy. You should have heard his other demands. Now will you answer me?"

I handed him the ring box. "What exactly is the question?"

"Will you marry me?"

I pointed to the floor.

He got down on one knee and held the ring out. "Will you marry me, Emma?" His bottom lip stuck out in a way that made me want to push it back in.

I took the ring from his quivering fingers, hoping he was correct in assuming I was ready for marriage. I wanted to be ready. I took a deep breath, praying I could be ready, stop overanalyzing, and enjoy the moment. Looking into Justin's eyes, I knew that marrying him was the best thing I could do for myself. It was probably the best thing I could do for him too. Why was I so scared? If Heavenly Father could help me become a life coach, he could help me become a wife. I slid the ring onto my finger. Hank's words came back to me: *When have you ever done something great without being scared?* That's what it was. I was about to do something great. "Yes," I said. "I will marry you."

Chapter 34

Coach's Tip of the Day:
Make someone happy, and it'll rub off on you.

I woke to the sound of the waves lapping at the shores of our little island getaway in the Florida Keys. There was no sign of Justin, which wasn't a surprise. He always woke up early. I threw off the white duvet, knelt to say my morning prayer, then noticed our only Christmas decoration, one of the little Swedish elves we'd used to decorate the trees at our reception. It was Christmas morning. Digging through my suitcase, I found the gift I'd brought for Justin, a new phone to replace the ancient model he'd carried around for three or four years.

I found Justin, already dressed in board shorts and a T-shirt, relaxing in a hammock outside our bungalow. He held out a gift bag. "Merry Christmas."

I watched the warm breeze rustle the leaves of the palm trees above us. "I thought the honeymoon was my gift."

He hopped out of the hammock. "You still needed something to open on Christmas morning."

Together, we walked barefoot past tall grasses and palms until we came to the shore and sat together on the white sand. The ocean was so clear, you could see right through the blue-green water to the sand below. Dad would have called the sky a buttermilk sky. Tufts of clouds clung to the blue the way buttermilk coats the side of a glass.

"Ladies first," Justin said, handing me the gift bag. Reaching through the tissue paper, I pulled a framed picture out. It was my mother smiling in front of a lake. I'd seen the picture before when I was a child looking through boxes. Now that I was older, I saw myself in my mother. She was beautiful with her red hair and pale skin. I hugged the picture to my chest. "I've never had a framed picture of her before."

He pulled an envelope out of the bag and handed it to me. "This is from your dad."

Inside the envelope was an old note card with violets on the front. It was yellowed and worn around the edges as if someone had opened it many times. It read:

> Dear Barry,
> I know you're nervous about the test. You shouldn't be. You always do so well. I hope you know I'll be proud of you no matter what. It has nothing to do with a test score or a degree. I'm proud because you help people. You treat every patient as a friend. I hope our children will be the same way. If they are, I will be a proud mother.
> Love forever,
> Marian

Justin kissed me on the forehead. "You once said you didn't think your mom was proud of you. Here's proof that she is. Because you help people."

I let his words sink into me with the warmth of the sun. Would my mom be proud of me? I thought of all that had happened since last Christmas. I'd made a lot of mistakes compared to my successes, but I hadn't given up. I was helping people. Harri was in a better place now, working as an office assistant for John and engaged to Rob. My seven coaching clients were meeting their goals. In reality, they'd all helped themselves more than I'd helped them, but I'd been there to encourage them.

Then there was Justin, who'd already achieved success without any help from me. If anything, he was my coach. I watched him tear

the paper off his gift. Making him happy had become a habit with
me. All it took was a compliment to produce a smile. I was addicted
to his grins—the shy ones he tried to hide and the bold ones he didn't
mind if anyone saw. No one had ever taught me in school that it was
one of life's greatest achievements to make a man happy. I couldn't
put it on my résumé. Pleasing Justin was an old and favorite habit. It
was a good one—one I wasn't willing to give up.

Acknowledgments

*I*t hasn't been easy to bring this modern version of *Emma* to life. I needed a lot of help, and thankfully, I got it. Obviously, I owe a debt of gratitude to Jane Austen, my favorite author. She is my hero.

So many people have helped me develop my talents as a writer. Bernis von zur Muehlen, Leslie Norris, Douglas Thayer, Darrell Spencer, and Sally T. Taylor were some of my excellent creative writing teachers. I also want to thank my critique partners and beta readers: Jennifer, Julie, Emily, Cynthia, Valerie, Mary Ann, Andrea, and Cindy. And I couldn't have written about a coach without having such great coaches in my life—Jonathan Roche, Erik Hajer, and Steven Landers have all helped me to live more positively.

A big thank you to everyone at Cedar Fort. I couldn't have dreamed of better editors. Angie Workman helped me shape my manuscript into a book worth reading. Then Melissa Caldwell polished up all the details, including all those en dashes. Thanks also go to Angela D. Olsen for giving me such a fun cover and to Kelly Martinez for his marketing expertise.

My family has been so patient with my writing addiction, especially when I zoned out to pursue my alternate reality in Emma's world. My husband, Eric, helped me brainstorm ideas for the plot and read my early draft. My daughter Emily was my pickiest critique partner. My boys behaved themselves—most of the time—while I wrote. My parents and in-laws provided excellent marketing, making sure everyone—including the bank teller—knew about my books.

Above all, I want to thank my Heavenly Father, who sent me my best ideas.

Discussion Questions

Emma suggests you choose from among the following treats for your book club meeting: s'mores, gingerbread boys, Dove dark chocolates, apples, smoothies, or fortune cookies. If you choose the apples, be sure to eat them with abandon.

1. Justin and Emma both like to give advice. How does this get them in trouble? In your opinion, what's the best way to give advice?

2. Compare this book with Jane Austen's *Emma*. How are the modern characters similar to their counterparts in Regency England? How are they different?

3. Why do you think Emma has a hard time finishing things?

4. Do you think Hank is correct when he says that being scared can be a sign that you're doing something great? How have you benefited from doing things you fear?

5. What role does jealousy play in the book? Who feels jealous of whom? How does each character work through his or her feelings? What are some of the consequences of their jealousy?

6. How does Emma learn to overcome feelings of guilt and perfectionism? Have you had a similar experience in your life?

7. How does Harri change through the course of the book? What helps her to become the person she wants to be? What holds her back?

8. Many times, Emma's friends are not what they seem. When does Emma fail to see things the way they really are? What does she overlook about people?

About the Author

Photo by Rachael Nelson

*L*ooking for love? Rebecca H. Jamison would love to set you up with that special someone, but you're better off reading her books. She has a terrible track record as a matchmaker.

Rebecca grew up in Virginia. She attended Brigham Young University, where she earned a BA and MA in English with an emphasis in creative writing. In between college and graduate school, she served a mission to Portugal and Cape Verde.

Rebecca enjoys running, dancing, reading, and watching detective shows. She and her husband have six children. You can learn more about her at rebeccahjamison.com.